The Story of Bobby O'Malley

Wayne Johnston

HarperCollins*Publishers*Ltd

Published by
HarperCollins Publishers Ltd
Suite 2900, Hazelton Lanes
55 Avenue Road
Toronto, Canada M5R 3L2

First Oberon Library edition
published May, 1991

Published by arrangement with Oberon Press

Canadian Cataloguing in Publication Data

Johnston, Wayne, 1958-
   The story of Bobby O'Malley

ISBN 0-00-617964-9

First Oberon Library edition
I. Title.

PS8569.03918S86 1991   C813'.54   C91-093676-5
PR9199.3.J644S86 1991

91 92 93 94 95 96 OFF 10 9 8 7 6 5 4 3 2 1

This book, though not about my parents,
is dedicated to them

Book One

CHAPTER 1

Strange that our oldest memories are of the days when we were youngest. By the time I was sixteen I had lived in eight houses and I can remember all but the first—my life like strung beads, but convenient, as it makes the telling easier. And yet it was not so much the houses as the world from the window that changed, as if all those years our one house was slowly turning.

Eight houses, but always the same town—we simply moved to different parts of it. We lived in all the neighbourhoods and, in the wars between the neighbourhoods, became a kind of neutral zone. My mother said God kept us moving so that we could share our goodness with as many people as possible.

Actually, the reason we kept moving was that my mother disapproved of borrowing money, so we could never afford to buy a house. We would save, she said, and when we had enough we'd buy a house outright, "none of this mortgage nonsense." My father said this was an excellent idea because by paying cash, we'd get a ten-dollar discount, and that would make the twenty years worth waiting.

I was what, in most parts of the Catholic universe, is considered a rarity—an only child. (I was not, however, as I remember one nun claiming, a living testament to the efficacy of the rhythm method.) I say "in most parts" because we were what my father called "a family of only children." What he meant was that he, too, had been an only child, as had my mother. Indeed, their parents and most of their aunts and uncles were dead by the time I came along, so we had but two relatives, my father's cousin Annie, and my mother's cousin Dola. We called Dola "Aunt Dola," and we called her husband "Uncle Rennie."

I should introduce my father. How deceptive language is. Oxford defines "father" as "male parent" and adds the qualification—"one who deserves filial reverence." The word is not quite adequate. In our house, father meant the man who, having been given a digital clock for Christmas, woke my mother from deep sleep to the dark early morning of Boxing Day, so she could share with him that magic moment when all the digits in the clock window were the same. My father claimed this story was not true; my mother swore it was. For her, the only point of contention was whether the clock said "Two-twenty-two-twenty-two" or "Three-thirty-three-thirty-three."

My father, asked once by someone at work to assess my early years, replied that I was a nightmarish baby. What I think he meant was that, as an infant, I often had bad dreams. At work, however, they took him literally, and would ask him from time to time how "the little nightmare was coming along."

He said he knew early on that I was not the sort of baby that "one normally finds in the basement." I made a bad beginning. I was apparently a rebel of the pot. Naked, I would sit for hours upon it, pouting, hands pressed to my cheeks, elbows on my knees—Rodin's Stinker my father called me. The product of all this cogitation, however, was at best a pool of pee. It was not until my ingenuous keepers had bundled me in clean diapers and overalls that I was seized by inspiration more profound. "A more perverse little beast," my mother said, "could hardly have been imagined." I was almost three before my prolific, if misplaced, output was finally checked. By that time I had routed five maids and very nearly my mother, who admits she was sustained by faith alone.

My father had a theory that babies are born with astronomically high IQs. He believed, such is their profundity at birth, that when confronted with the obtuse silliness of the world, they do one of two things: they scream bloody hell, or else maintain a composed and superior silence. As they grow older, their IQs gradually begin to slide so that, soon, their once-great minds are in free fall. By the time they are three, they are sufficiently stupid to see no reason why, when the world talks, they should not talk back. By this time, they are also walking. The reason they at first seem poorly balanced and frequently fall down is that they are dizzy from their long descent. By the age of three, he believed, there is just sufficient brilliance left to keep the baby bobbing and weaving for a year or so.

He admitted that, being himself "a fallen one," he might have been mistaken about all this. But he pointed out that his theory would account for the passion for self-destruction evident in most babies. He observed that I began by wedging a bar of soap in my mouth. I was discovered, face down beneath my cot, breathing bubbles furiously, with eyes so widely bulging they must already have been focused on the promised land. I was eighteen months old. Next, as if I thought a bath the final indignity, I crawled from my tub and somersaulted gracefully from the kitchen-table—and landed with a providential plop in a hamper of clothes. I was two years old. There were other attempts, including an experiment with a razor-blade when I was three. A photograph of that time survives, taken immediately following the application to my face of 22 band-aids. The band-aids look like some bizarre form of acne, and the picture, my father said, would be a dangerous weapon in the hands of pro-abortionists.

My father said that, when they were teaching me to crawl, he would sit on the chesterfield and put me on the floor at his feet. He would kick my diaper a couple of times to get me started, and then would forget about me. Unknown to him, I would work my finger, sometimes my whole hand, beneath the laces of his shoe, then go to sleep. This, he said, was "very touching," except for the fact that, upon getting up, he either walked on me or, with his first step, sent me sailing across the room. There were even times when my grip was especially good and it took forever to shake me off. He would drag me round the house and, like a cowboy caught in the stirrup, I would scrape across the carpet, or glide along the kitchen floor, my diaper pulling slowly off. When at last my hand came free, he would not stop to pick me up, but would simply leave me there. My mother recalled finding me in all sorts of strange places—under the bathroom sink, on my back beside the stove.

My years of genius behind me, we moved for the first time, from the house I don't remember to Mortrey's. Mortrey's was the name of the family who lived there after us. It was how we referred to all our old houses, by the names of the families who took them away from us. We liked to think that the people who moved out of the houses we moved into did the same. It was nice to imagine families all over town saying, "Remember at O'Malley's."

We were renters, almost always turfed out by people who wanted to buy. The end of our stay in a particular place was usually signalled by the arrival of strangers who would, without warning, begin to paint the house or mow the lawn.

Of Mortrey's I remember little.

A baby died in a house nearby. It smothered in its crib. The babysitter left the house and ran home. Along the way she jumped clean over a fence that was more than a foot taller than she was. She was able to do this because the baby's face was blue.

There was a song on the radio about putting beans in your ears. "My mommy told me not to put beans in my ears, beans in my ears," was how it went. My mother said that, because of the song, children all over were putting beans in their ears. She told me not to do it. I must not do what songs on the radio told me to do.

I remember reaching out, then down into some water. I remember how cold the water was, and how the trout I caught undulated in my hand, seemed to move me back and forth. It might have been, that beating thing, some sliver of life itself.

There were the whirlpools in the pond nearby. The whirlpools could not be seen, but they were there. The proof of their existence was the number of people who had drowned in them—seven—and the fact that one victim was said to have obliged his audience with the declaration, "I'm goin' down in the whirlpool."

There were two theories as to why the whirlpools defied location. One was that they erupted periodically from the lake bottom and rose to the surface, only to disappear hours or days later The other was that the whirlpools were ever-present but somehow moved about, random mobile vortices that, every year or so, coincided with, and promptly swallowed, a swimmer. This last theory was backed up by a piece of hard evidence: some bodies were found in a part of the pond far removed from where they went down.

I favoured the former theory, if only because it was slightly less terrifying than the other. The idea of a dead person going back and forth beneath the surface of the lake, all the while spinning dervishly about, was simply too horrible to believe. Worst of all was the fact that two bodies remained unrecovered. It was left to every decent soul to recoil with a gasp from drawing the obvious conclusion. Such a taboo, however, did not extend to dreams and, one night beneath the waves, I saw them, a veritable swarm of corpses, each within his single cell, some gone back to bones, all doomed to an eternal circuit, never to reach their rest. I had the dream for months and, some nights, people I knew, my father, Aunt Dola, were cocooned in the whirling water, unable to reach out a hand for help. Every night, before I went to sleep, my mother splashed my head with holy water, and every night I dreamed the dream.

I hated it when, at bedtime, my mother turned off the light and closed the door. I was afraid of the dark, not only because of the things I imagined might be in it, but because, when I couldn't see anything, I felt like I was gone. My room had no window so, before my parents went to bed, all I could see was the crack of light beneath the door. I would stare at that and fall asleep, only to wake hours later in total darkness. I'd sit up, horrified, and touch my face and arms and legs, and say my name to see if I could hear it. Then I'd get out of bed and, in a panic, stumble round the room until I found the light-switch. Going to sleep with the light on was like going to sleep with someone watching me.

In the morning, my mother would discover the light on and call me a "sookie." She said only sookies were afraid of the dark. "Sookie calves," my father said. At breakfast, he would moo at me. "Mooooo–ooooo," he'd say, until I started bawling.

Perhaps what I remember most vividly from Mortrey's is Uncle Rennie's re-enactment of the murder of Lee Harvey Oswald. It is a memory that may be corrupted by subsequent retellings of the story on the part of the adults involved. I watched from the doorway of the living-room, beyond which I was forbidden to pass, lest I should see, as I had earlier in the day, the real Oswald being shot down on TV. Uncle Rennie made a good Oswald. He didn't look like him, but he had an enormous belly and, for me at least, no better target for Jack Ruby's bullet could be imagined. Aunt Dola holding one arm, my father the other, Uncle Rennie was led from the chesterfield to the coffee-table—at which point my mother began to cry and said that it didn't matter what that awful man had done to President Kennedy, she just could not bring herself to shoot him. My mother, whose outrage at the death of the first Catholic president had been extreme, was in Uncle Rennie's eyes the mourner most deserving of playing the coveted part of Jack Ruby. She was to have emerged from behind the piano and, at the appropriate moment, lunged forward with a rolled-up copy of the *Vatican Monitor*. But, distraught, in tears, she simply could not do it.

My mother's outburst was my cue. I ran forward and punched Uncle Rennie's belly as hard as I could. His face contorted, his mouth roundly open, Uncle Rennie went down in a heap and, for a while, the only sound was that of a long deflating gasp. Then they started to laugh, Aunt Dola and my father, even my mother, and Uncle Rennie most of all. Rennie grabbed me and, lying flat on his back, lifted me high in the air. I remember his laughing red face looking up at me as I squirmed and kicked to get free. "You showed 'em, hey Bobby," he said, "didn't you show 'em now?" No-one seemed to realize it was my mother I was avenging, not Kennedy.

It was from Little Annie's I started school. Annie, as I've said, was my father's cousin, Little Annie her daughter, to whom Annie gave the house after she kicked us out of it. My father called her, among other things, Little Horphan Hannie. (My father was 200 miles and 25 years from the south coast, but was still willing to drop and/or add an "h," if he could thereby, and with impunity, make a word more interesting. There was a fix-it shop in town called Handy Andy; my father called it Andy Handy. He spoke of Annie's son, whom, he said, was going to be a Hairline Pilot.)

The day Little Annie came to the house to tell us we had a month to move out, my father swore he would never again pay rent to a relative. He would remember Little Annie's, however, not for the shame we suffered there, but as the place where the toilet kept backing up.

There were, as he discovered, two possible causes of our toilet troubles. There might be a blockage in the series of plastic pipes that ran about the basement; or the septic tank itself might be full, causing what my mother called "that awful effluent" to travel back through the pipes and up into the toilet. The procedure when the toilet overflowed was to check the pipes first, and then, if need be, the tank.

My father called the basement "Annie's guts." To unblock the pipes was to "clean the old girl's guts out, make her regular again." He said he was mystified as to why there were so many pipes in the basement, and why, before our "daily deposits" wound up in the septic tank, they had first to be routed halfway round the world; or why, for that matter, the journey involved so many right angles and elbows, or why the slope of the pipes was such that if Niagara Falls itself went down our toilet, "not one solitary turd would make it to the tank."

He would go around the basement, banging the pipes with a wrench until, by the absence of a hollow sound, he found out where the blockage was. If he was lucky, it was close to one of the stoppers, and all he had to do was unscrew the stopper and poke around inside the pipe with a stick. Of course, a good deal of what he called "the stuff that Annie's made of" would come pouring out, and had to be caught in a bucket, but of all the methods of fixing things, this was the quickest.

If the blockage was far removed from any stopper, he had to go to the garage and borrow an "articulator," a long, flexible piece of wire, which we called "the snake," and which could go round corners without getting caught or breaking. Standing on a chair, he would push the snake through the pipes, while an ever-increasing trickle of septic water poured into the bucket below. Whenever he used the snake, the flow of water was especially fast, and he liked to have more than one bucket at hand. It was my mother's job and mine to move the full buckets out of the way and replace them with empty ones. This we did, wearing bandannas like surgical masks, my mother with her eyes closed tightly, her head turned away. "Jesus, Mary and Joseph," she'd say, "how much is there?"

Once, with the pipes making great belching noises, the stuff that Annie was made of started coming out too fast, and my mother and I had to go upstairs and bring down more containers. We brought down boilers, bowls, garbage-bags, everything in the house bigger than a teacup. Soon, the floor was covered with sewage-filled receptacles, and still, as my father said afterwards, still the shit kept coming. "My God, Teddy," my mother said, as the last container, our next-to-new deep-fryer, started filling up, "My God, Teddy what will we do?" "Run for help," my father said, "call the police. Pray. If God could part the Red Sea, he can damn well plug this pipe." At that, my mother blessed herself. She said later she was not asking God to grant "the sordid miracle" my father had requested, but was asking forgiveness for him for even thinking such a thing. In any case, her prayer didn't get to God in time, for, like wrathful retribution, a great gush of water and toilet tissue, preceded by a belch that caused my father to turn and look directly into the pipe, came out and hit him full in the face—and then, just as quickly, stopped. He stood there, on the chair, still holding the snake, still looking into the pipe, a sodden strand of toilet tissue looped like a candy-cane around one ear, every part of him dripping wet.

My mother and I had been lightly splattered and, shrieking, she took me by the hand and dragged me up the stairs, leaving my father to fend for himself. (After a blockage of the pipes, my mother would warn my father and me we had to use less toilet tissue. "I don't know what you do with it all," she'd say. "Every week, I put five rolls in the closet, and when I go back the next week it's all gone." My mother would never admit to using the bathroom. It was one of those things men did to which women referred with affectionate mystification, something for which men, poor brutes, could not be blamed.)

Well, if my mother was embarrassed by blocked pipes, she was altogether mortified by brim-full septic tanks. When it was determined that it was the tank that was the problem, my father had to go out on the front lawn and dig down until he found it—and there was a lot of digging to do. The tank was the size of a coffin, and sunk about as deep. Once he had it uncovered, my father would call Hen, the man who cleaned the tanks. Hen would come and drive up on the lawn with what my father called "the Shit Machine." It was a septic tank on wheels, really, with a great black hose attached, which Hen could barely get his arms around.

As soon as people in the neighbourhood saw my father digging, they would gather on the lawn, so by the time the Shit Machine arrived, there might be 30 or 40 of them, children and adults, come to witness the cleaning of our tank. It was this my mother hated, this, as my father said, having "our poop made public."

"Why would people want to watch?" she said.

But they did. They were fascinated, as if the uncovering and cleaning of a septic tank was the bringing out into the open of a thing that, heretofore, they had never really believed existed.

My mother could not bring herself to watch. She would hide in the house, where no-one could see her. She made me stay indoors, too, but I would watch from the living-room window—the best vantage-point of all, because the tank was directly below it.

Hen would climb down in the hole and stand on the septic tank, with his feet on either side of the hatch. When, with metal hooks and a kind of mini-crane, the hatch had been removed, he would wrap his arms around the hose and lower it into the tank. When the suction started, the hose would buckle and wriggle and he had to hold on tightly, even wrestle with it, to keep it from coming loose. Like someone bringing down a heifer, he would let himself fall backwards, using the weight of his body to control the hose. "Hang on dere, Hen," the crowd would say, "keep hold of 'er now." Hen liked to put on a show, grunting and groaning and screwing up his face, and shaking his head as if to say, "I dunno, she might be too much for me." Sometimes, on purpose I think, he let the hose come loose, and the crowd would draw back quickly as it darted toward their feet. "Watch out now, or it'll suck ye right inside, an' no-one'll know ye ever lived."

When the suction was finished, my father would give me the signal to go in and flush the toilet. If it flushed okay I would come back and nod my head and everyone would cheer and slap Hen and my father on the back. But if it still wasn't working, I would shake my head, and everyone would go quiet and look at Hen who, in turn, would put his hands on his hips and look at the tank; and there would come to his face an expression that said the problem might be any one of a hundred things, and he had, right here and now, in front of all these people, to form a professional opinion about it. But, in the end, all he ever did was put the hose back in the tank and let it suck some more.

It might take several tries, but the Shit Machine always worked. Afterwards, when Hen was headed up the road, my father would shake his head and say, "There goes twenty dollars."

The tank, because it was improperly installed, filled up about once a month. We began to measure time by it. We talked about two tanks ago, and planned two tanks ahead. My father told me to remember that I got older every time I flushed the toilet. I imagined what it was like inside the tank, with the hatch in place, and all that earth piled on it.

"Dark and foul," my father said, "dark and foul."

It was from Little Annie's I started school. The bus that took my mother and father to work arrived long before my schoolbus, so every morning, while they waited outside, I watched from the window. Our house was on the bus-stop side of the road, so most of the time they were facing away from me. Every morning they stood straight and looked straight ahead, and, through the gap between them, I could see the house across the road. They stood, day after day, in exactly the same place. When, after they were gone, I went out, I always expected to see their footprints in the gravel, indelible, side by side. I hope that, if all else fades, I'll remember the two of them there, together, with a wedge of world between. I can see them now. My father is wearing a hat, a cream-coloured raglan and black shoes in toecap rubbers. My mother is wearing a bandanna, a red coat edged with off-white wool, and black shoes with square high heels. I cannot see her hands, but I know that, as always, they are in front, clasping the strap of her purse, tightly, grimly, as if she believes creation but an ongoing conspiracy to snatch that purse away. The space between them opens on memory.

My father was a weatherman, or rather, *the* weatherman, for in all the province back then there were only two television channels available, and, in Kellies, only one—because of a just-too-high hill to the northeast, we could not get the CBC.

My father was a weatherman—not a meteorologist but, as my mother said, "only a weatherman." He often got home from work in time to see himself on TV, from which fact I drew the obvious conclusion: he was magic. It was strange enough that my father should be inside that black box, but that he should, at the same time, be outside it, watching himself inside it—well, I asked a lot of questions.

My father said the man on TV wasn't really him. Who was it, then, I wanted to know. He was "an aggregate of microdots," my father said, "unscrambled by the receiver, having been sent at random wave-lengths, on a fixed frequency, from a transmitter some distance removed." That was his phrase, word for word. He made me memorize it. At gatherings of relatives and friends, he would turn to me and say, "Bobby, what's the name of the man on TV?" Everyone would look at me and smile, expecting me to say something cute, like "it's you, Daddy," or, "the man's name is Ted O'Malley." Instead, I would stand up and, screwing up my face, recite: "the man on the TV is an aggregate of microdots, unscrambled by the receiver, having been sent at random wave-lengths, on a fixed frequency, from a transmitter some distance removed." In some circles this might have gotten a laugh; not in ours. Everyone looked at my mother with puzzled, worried expressions, which, more often than not, caused her to cry and run to her room. My father, whose theory of infant intelligence quotient was well known, would shake his head and ask the others to "forgive Agnes." She was, he said, worried that I was regressing back to genius, and that one morning, when she came to wake me, would find that I had lapsed into the profound and outraged silence that had marked my early years.

When, after a while, the gag became well known, the only point of the exercise was to see if I could get through without mispronouncing any of the words. My father tried to get me to say "aggravated microdots" and "rabid wave-lengths," but I wouldn't do it. I thought the phrase, as an explanation of magic, was itself magic, an incantation, a chant, and I would not profane it. I repeated it over and over in my head, out loud when I was alone. It was so I could say those wonderful words I took to spending a lot of time in the bathroom. My mother would rattle the knob and ask if I was all right, no doubt after fifteen minutes of trying, with her ear to the door, to figure out what I was saying. It got so that I couldn't get the phrase out of my head. It was like something going round and round, at higher and higher speed. It came into my dreams and soon I couldn't sleep. Every night, my father and mother went by in whirlpools, raving like lunatics about frequencies and wave-lengths and microdots.

Finally, I broke down and told my mother what was happening. She consulted our priest, and he advised that we fight fire with fire. From now on, instead of the phrase my father had taught me, I was to say the Hail Mary over and over. Whenever I heard "aggregate of microdots," I was to shout it down with "Hail Mary full of grace," and I was to keep at it until Hail Mary won out. This, as might have been foresen, only compounded the problem, and it wasn't long before Hail Mary and microdots came together in a strange fusion of blasphemous gibberish, such as might be recited by the faithful at a Black Mass.

It was my father who saved me, and why he didn't do it sooner I shall never know. He simply told me that he had made microdots up, that the phrase was only a lot of nonsense that didn't really explain the man on TV at all. That did it. Hail Mary went away, and microdots slowly stopped, like a ferris-wheel winding down.

My mother was still a teacher then. She taught Grades 10 and 11 at an all-girls school in St. John's. Her subjects were English Language and Geography. My father claimed she was one of only a handful of children, in all the history of public education, who had taken with them into adulthood the knowledge of what a gerund was and how to use it; and of that handful, she was, perhaps, the only one who also knew how to make "koumiss," a fermented beverage derived from mare's milk by the nomads of central Asia.

Most of the other teachers at my mother's school were nuns, which suited her because, as she never ceased to point out, she had once thought the convent her calling. She said she discovered, one soul-searching summer, that all women are Sisters of Mercy—it's just that each one wears her habit a different way. "I wore mine," she said, "by marrying your father." The implications of this caused my father no end of trouble. Once, when he was drunk, he asked me what I thought it was like to go to bed with a Sister of Mercy, or to live with someone who thought all women were latent nuns. "You know something," he said, "the closest that woman has ever come to being romantic was when I brought her some flowers one day after work. She pinched my cheek, looked me in the eye and said, 'Teddy, dear Teddy, you are the cross I bear.'"

My mother taught girls because she believed that a child is best controlled by someone of his or her own sex. "You never know," she said, "what boys are going to do next." Her "only begotten son," as she liked to call me, was, God knows, proof of that. She began her teaching career at St. Stephen's—the school in Kellies that, years later, I would attend—but left after a few months for the Heavy Heart of Jesus High School in St. John's. The school was known to its students as Heavy Heart High.

We had maids, one after the other, at Little Annie's. They came in the morning to get me ready for school, as my parents were too busy getting themselves ready to look out for me; and at noon and 3 o'clock they were out on the road to meet the schoolbus. The reason we had them one after the other was that they usually quit in exasperation after a month or so. It was my mother's practice to phone home constantly during the day to, as she put it, "see how they were doing." Where to scrub, where to dust, where to sit, my mother had ideas about everything, ideas which, unfortunately, never seemed to hit her at the same time, but came instead at 50-minute, geography-class intervals. My mother was totally inept as a housekeeper. My father said driving the maids crazy with phone calls was her way of compensating.

I remember the morning my mother fired one of the maids. It was 8.30, and the maid, who was to have arrived at 7 but had only just come through the door, responded to being fired by asking my mother if she had seen her shower-cap. Now my mother had had to miss her bus in order to stay behind and make sure that I was safely on mine. She was not one to make a scene or throw a tantrum, much preferring flight to fight, but on this occasion she was livid, and beyond pretending otherwise. "I'll shower-cap you," she said and, running upstairs, came down seconds later to put what turned out to be her own shower-cap on the maid's head. The young lady—my mother's maids were never more than twenty—was too terrified to move, and simply stood there while my mother performed the absurd courtesy of making sure all her hair was tucked neatly beneath the cap. When she was finished, my mother stood back, as if to judge the effect. "There," she said, "now ye'll have to beat 'em off with sticks." Then she pointed at the door and, with a rare lapse into the vernacular, shrieked, "Now get out, ye saucy ting, before I trows ye out." I remember the maid looked at me, then, as if about to test the reality of what was happening by asking a second opinion. I didn't give her a chance. Standing on my toes and leaning forward, as my mother had, with arms rigid and fists clenched, I screamed, "Get out before I trows ye out." My mother and I began to cry at once, whereupon the maid, still wearing the shower-cap, fled the vestibule and ran down the steps, leaving the door wide open behind her.

When the maid was gone, my mother shut the door and, sitting down on the chesterfield, put her head in her hands and began to cry. I went over, intending to put my arms around her neck and try to stop the shaking of her shoulders, but, her face bursting red round the edges of her fingers, she jerked her whole body away when I touched her. "Go on out and wait for the bus, Bobby," she said. "Go on, I'll be out in a minute." And she did come out later to put me on the bus, but for days afterwards she was either crying or on the verge of tears.

Indeed, from what I remember of that time, my mother seems to have been always crying; and there was often about the house the kind of silence that early darkness can create, winter Sunday silence, when it is easy to believe there are but two kinds of people in the world—those soon to wake, who have slept the afternoon away, and those waiting ones who have not slept, and have not yet turned on the lights. My mother slept, but I did not; nor did my father. We were always waiting in the darkness, he and I, for the world to wake. Each of us, alone, in some separate part of the house, we waited for my mother to come out of her room, eyes blinking back to the light, so that life could start again.

CHAPTER 2

I was eight when we moved from Little Annie's to Duley's. On the settled shore of a small lake, Duley's was the summer home of a St. John's businessman.

We moved into Duley's the first of September, knowing all the while we would have to move out by the middle of June. "Our days are numbered," my mother said. "Our days are always numbered," my father said, "it's just that this time we know what the number is." The number was 289.

But Duley's was a great house, if only *because* our days were numbered. It had wonderful hardwood floors, so waxed and polished you could slide across them on stockinged feet. My father and I had contests to see which of us could slide the farthest. We polished one side of the living-room at least twice a week to keep it in prime condition. In the evenings, my mother would sit and read, or watch television, pretending not to notice as my father and I slid to and fro along the opposite wall, arms outstretched like surfers. Sometimes we slipped. I had sense enough, when slipping, to let myself fall, but my father would fight it until the end. A look of sheer terror on his face, propelling himself backwards with a mad flurry of feet and waving his arms for balance, he sometimes skated halfway across the room before finally encountering the furniture. On these occasions, my mother, as soon as she saw that he was slipping, would get up from the chesterfield and stand safely off to one side. It became a routine inconvenience, one she would perform without in the least interrupting what she was doing; uninterested, as if standing at the movies to let some stranger by, she would not even look up from her book, as my father, like an errant pinball, careered about the room.

There was a chandelier at Duley's, suspended like a great cluster of tear-drops from the ceiling.

There was a bunk-bed, with drawers large enough for an eight-year old to crawl into.

And there was an attic, not the kind in which you had to go round on all fours, taking care you didn't plunge between the support beams, through the ceiling, but the kind you could live in if your mother let you. Of course mine didn't. In fact, after the first day, I was not allowed up there. But it was enough to have seen it once. It was dark and damp and smelled of old wood. At the far end, there was a small round window you could look out of. Except for the big boxes, piled in the blackest corner, it was empty. There was the kind of space that only a mind can fill.

I saw it only once, but I remembered everything: the constant droning whistle of wind; the way the walls were cracked and creased with daylight; that, by sitting to one side of the window, you could look out onto an unsuspecting world. Always, I imagined I was in it, and when we moved, I took it with me. It became the setting for all the books I read, for I read only those with twilit covers, covers that promised cold wind and grey skies, gloomy northern gods and heroes fated for hardship and misery. I loved every minute of it. I was up inside my head, up in the attic where no-one could see me; and what came through that window was dim and dismal, filtered so, through dust and glass, even the sunlight made me cry.

There was the weather. At Duley's, the verandah was enclosed in a lattice-work of wood and glass. It was there I would go on grey or stormy days, and at night. I loved to watch the weather from that verandah. We did not spend a summer at Duley's, so it seems, that year, there was none. There was only fall and winter for me, and me with my face to the glass. Before I was ten, I knew all about weather. I knew how, in winter, with a storm coming, to tell if it would snow or rain, or if the snow would change to rain. I knew the colour of pavement was important; and I saw how, with rain on the way, the hard clean edges of snowdrifts soften, and the texture of old snow changes. I could tell a storm-blue sky, and the difference between cold and the rawness of wind.

My father found my fascination with weather strange. He abhorred my passion for snowstorms. Winter storms have been all things for me. Back then, they brought people together and would not let them go away. They had my mother and father, for a while, live life as I lived it—within walls, safe inside the storm. I loved it when a storm closed in, when the world got smaller and smaller, until it seemed our house was all there was.

My father could not bear to watch the weather, because it was constantly doing things he hadn't predicted. He had me watch it for him. "Snowin' yet, Bobby?" he'd say; or, late at night, pacing the floor: "Jesus Bobby, where *is* that storm?"

In the mornings, my mother was always out of bed before him, and the first thing he would say when she woke him was, "Okay, Agnes, give me the bad news." A synopsis of the weather would follow, punctuated at intervals by my father shouting, "Aha, I told you so," or, more often, "How can that be?"

He was not the "I don't write 'em, I just read 'em" sort of weatherman. He wanted to be, but people would not let him. In our town, my father was both shaman and scapegoat. The first few years, he tried to explain to people that he was not responsible for forecasting the weather: meteorologists did that. Of course this convinced no-one. "Meteorologist" was a word just big enough to be resented, just strange enough to suggest that my father had made it up. In fact, people seemed to believe that my father not only forecast the weather, but somehow controlled it—either consciously, in straightforward witch-doctor style; or unconsciously, in that the weather somehow took on his personality. Whatever way you looked at it, he was an enemy of the people. It got to the point that, when the accusation of rain, drizzle and fog was brought against him, he would, with a shrug and a grimace, goodnaturedly admit his shortcomings—and give promise of better days ahead.

In the telling, a life should open slowly, but it doesn't, because memory accelerates the early years to make sense of them. There is, however, a point where this acceleration stops and real memory begins. This happens at Duley's.

There, my mother and father have faces that I know are not borrowed from later years, so it is a kind of birth for them. Here are my parents, newborn, middle-aged. I find my father in the living-room, with his back to the window. Once I touch him, I will not see him like this again. I will only, through the years, from time to time, almost remember. I will watch him from across a room and almost remember the way he was before he became a part of me. I will not, but almost, remember how to step back and see him, strange and real. Perhaps I should wait. I should walk about him now for as long as it takes and memorize everything. And yet I know that, no matter what I do, the world, when I touch him, will come between us, and I will never see him again. Arms about his neck, I hug him hard and kiss his cheek; and, as I do so, he speaks my name.

I find my mother in her room, at her desk, writing, looking like a woman on the cover of a handwriting primer: feet on the floor and slightly apart; posture perfect; pen-hand, free hand and paper each in its right relation of angle and space. She has stopped, pen poised above the paper. I have caught her in the middle of a sentence already written. There are words on either side, but those to come she cannot see. If I could tell her, now, before I touch her, I would tell her she need not write. I'd say, "put your pen down, please. Stop. Stay here." But I can't. So neither will I remember that, slow as sorrow, I cross the room and, stretching forth my hand, touch my finger to her cheek. There is a fine, tinkling sound, as of sleep falling from her eyes.

They have faces. My mother, 35 years old, whenever she was accused of being beautiful, put on more lipstick, the thick, deep harlot-red kind which, back then, looked unnatural without a wrinkled face behind it. She powdered her face all over, except where there was a redeeming pimple or blackhead—these she would highlight with eyebrow pencil. She wore what my father called a "construction bra," which was, he swore, applied to the body very much like a plaster cast. She also wore a girdle, giving her what he called "that steel-belted look."

More than my mother's body, I remember the things she put on it. What she was like underneath I hardly know. There was her perfume. She always reeked of perfume. She was a woman under siege, behind a fortress of fragrance. She was like a planet, with an atmosphere all her own.

Her hair, which I know from old photographs to have hung, Godiva-like, down her back, she had cut the day before she married my father. According to him, she had, till then, gone all her life without having it cut. Growing up, she was the envy of the other girls. Imagine, to have a mother that would let you grow your hair, they said. But to everyone's horror, the day before her wedding she went to town and had her long brown hair cut, and brought it home in a box. And those who came to her wedding were given cake and a lock of her hair. Afterwards, she kept what was left of her hair short, rolled it with spiked curlers and kept it, all of it, on top of her head. As for the box of hair, not all of it was given away at her wedding. My mother kept more than half, and by "kept" I mean she never did destroy it. She kept the box under her half of the bed, and moved it with us from house to house. She told me once that she cut it so that, in later years, she would have something by which to remember her childhood—a part of life, lopped off, preserved. Talking of her childhood, she would gesture, almost imperceptibly, toward the bedroom.

One day at Duley's, I went into her room without knocking and saw her at the bureau, with the box unopened on her lap. She was absorbed before the mirror, watching herself in the glass. I was in the mirror behind her, but she did not see me. She folded her arms the way the arms of the dead are folded and began, with her hands, to caress the air, as if there was a kitten on each of her breasts. That was the first time I'd seen the box and I didn't know what was in it. Confused and frightened, I backed out slowly and closed the door.

My father was shorter than my mother, though he denied it. He said she was only taller the day after she took her curlers out, because her hair, then, was full and high. He swore that the day before

24

she put them in he and she were exactly the same height—"five foot two and a bit." Had she told him not to, he would probably have worn lifts. My father found it hard to do anything to which my mother did not have at least some objection.

My father did exercises to keep himself fit. He stayed in good shape without, as the book he bought put it, "the benefit of extraneous apparatus."

"For physical fitness," my father read aloud, "all that is required is a body and its environment." Environment in this case was our house and all its contents, including my mother and me. My father did pullups on the door-frames. It was a common thing back then to turn a corner and come suddenly upon him, hanging from his fingertips, his face beet-red, his legs desperately kicking, as he inched upward. "Forty-nine," he would say, his voice a half-heard gasp. Somehow it was always 49. And then, all the while looking at me, as if to say, "for you, Bobby, I'm doing this for you," he would go for 50, eyes bulging, legs pedalling, as if ingenuously, heart-breakingly hoping for footholds in midair. Sometimes he made it. "FIFTY," he would shout, the number given up in agony, extracted, as if it was the secret for which all this torture had been designed. And sometimes, he didn't make it. On such occasions, he would not let go immediately, but would hang for moments in limp despair, arms and legs fully extended, his body swaying and head hung low, resigned to his fate, but not quite ready to meet it. Finally, fingers slowly slipping, he would fall with silent dignity to the floor.

He had me sit on his back while he did pushups.

And he would crouch down, have my mother climb piggy-back upon him and have me climb piggy-back upon her. This done, he would try to stand. "Great for the legs," he'd say, grunting, straining, unable to unlock his haunches, as my mother swayed precariously beneath me. Eventually he would manage it. "Oh, Teddy, I feel so silly," my mother would say, as the three of us slowly began to rise from the floor. "Don't let go, Bobby," she'd say, holding tight to my wrists, "and Joseph this night, Teddy, please don't slip." "SLIP," my father would shout, "SLIP, fat . . . chance . . . of *that*," and with "that" he was standing straight. "TA-DAH." "That's fine, dear," my mother would say, "now please let us down."

"Down?" my father would say, and pause, as if unsure how to go about descending. Then down it was, and down, down to the cracking of his knees, and a moment of panic when the fate of the three of us hung in the balance; then up, up, the three of us up, in some strange calisthenic of family togetherness. My mother could be counted on to panic on the down side of the third or fourth up and down, to let go of my father's shoulders and throw herself, and me, backwards onto the rug, and send my father, arms at his sides, shooting rocket-like into the air.

He did situps, with his feet beneath the chesterfield.

And, clearing a space in the living-room, he did jumping-jacks, wearing hip-waders, and with a seven-pound bag of flour suspended by string from each wrist. Before he was through, he would barely be visible through clouds of floating Five Roses, his weird wings flapping madly like some snowbound bird. He went through two bags of flour a week before my mother finally put a stop to it. "Bobby and I understand, Teddy," she said, "but what if someone else sees you?"

My father was a handsome man, "distinguished," my mother said. "You're a distinguished-looking man, Teddy," she'd say, reproachfully, probably puzzled as to why, if he looked distinguished, he never acted that way. She did her best to convince him, but my father was adamant. "I can't look distinguished," he said, "I'm five foot two."

She was right, though. She said he looked like William Faulkner and he did. My father, at 40, looked like Faulkner at 50—a proud-looking thin man, with blue eyes and a neat little moustache, and hair a reverent shading of brown and black and white. My father was unimpressed, saying that his head looked like a fudge marble-cake. He never did lose his hair. It turned white, but stayed thick and, all his life, he kept it closely cut, fastidiously trimmed at the back and sides and, in front, combed left to right in a modest gallant wave. Pressed by my mother, he conceded handsomeness from the neck up, but wondered what good that was when everyone he met looked down.

Uncle Rennie and Aunt Dola had four daughters, one my age, the rest older. My father was friends with Rennie even before Rennie, by marrying Dola, joined the family. Indeed, it was through my father that Rennie first heard of Dola. As the story went, Aunt Dola was rescued from maiden life by Uncle Rennie, who proposed to her over the telephone without ever having met or even seen her.

Though she was my mother's cousin, Dola lived in town. She was one up on Rennie. She knew just what *he* looked like. My mother had given her a picture of him, which Dola had kept by the phone the six months she waited for Rennie to call. When my mother gave the picture, she asked for one of Dola that she could give Rennie, but Dola swore she didn't have one. "You jus' tell 'm what I'm like, Agnes," she said, knowing, as my father put it, that my mother would be kinder than any camera.

"Dola will you marry me?" Rennie said, at a quarter to seven one May morning, having been up all night drinking with my father, and telling him he would "never Ted, not in a million years, get up de nerve."

Whether Uncle Rennie was at all unhappy with Aunt Dola when he met her a week later, no-one knows, but, as my father said, "we might pardon him for blinking." For when Dola stepped down, fifteen stone, from the bus, she was limping and, despite an orthopaedic shoe and a four-inch-thick steel sole, replied, when Rennie asked her what was wrong, that her foot was asleep from the long ride.

No grownups mentioned Aunt Dola's leg, within or without her range of hearing. It was kept hidden by long dresses and euphemisms. She was unlike other women only in having one more unmentionable.

Uncle Rennie's and Aunt Dola's youngest girl was my age. At Duley's, we made our first holy communion together. I wore an immaculate version of the school uniform: white shirt, red tie, navy-blue blazer, grey flannel pants and black shoes, to which collective indignity my mother added a brushcut, consistent with her belief that, on special occasions, little boys should have as little hair as possible. Bows of light-blue ribbon were tied about my arms; holy

27

medal and ribbon were, like war decorations, pinned to my pocket; and I entered the church arm in arm with Ambrosia, who, as the spitting image of Uncle Rennie, with a fat red face and a way of walking that suggested the existence of some unseen, too-tight garment, was the unkindest cut of all. Ambrosia—that was really her second name, but much better, for certain purposes, than Mary, which was her first—wore a white, lacy sun-dress, a bonnet, white knee-socks and black shoes. She, too, was put upon by ribbon, but hers was red. We were told the ribbon, blue for boys and red for girls, was a symbol of something we were not yet old enough to understand. We were told that, if we must think of it, we must think of it as gift-wrapping—were we not, after all, being given up to God?

We proceeded, 84 of us, up the middle aisle, and parted, boys left and girls right, at the rail. We stayed at the rail throughout the mass, kneeling and standing, kneeling when others were sitting, until the coming of the moment for which, a week before, we made our first confessions. I remember nothing but that, with the host stuck firmly to the roof of my mouth, I could not for the life of me think of the ecumenically approved method of getting it off. I knew that one must not, under any circumstances, touch it with one's finger; on the other hand, my tongue was getting nowhere with it. What to do? It seemed to me not at all unlikely, from what we'd been told, that the body of Christ would very soon begin to burn a hole in the roof of my mouth. I chose to compromise between that agony and the commission of a mortal sin. I chose to begin crying, crying quite loudly, and with a sense of helpless outrage; and, as I cried, so too did a number of the other boys, and the sobbing went down the line and crossed the gap in the altar rail, and soon the girls were started. My face hot with tears, afraid to look up at the priest, afraid to turn round and look for my mother, I danced a spiteful jig for having no place where I could hide.

I expected that, within the moment, some great and awful scene would unfold; something, on such occasions, was always rent asunder. But it was nuns to the rescue. They came forward to the rail, swiftly, silently, and pulled into the folds of their habits those children who were so overcome by this, their first taste of the heavenly host, that they could not—praise God, think of it—could not help but cry. It must have been this, or something like it, they believed, for they did not ask us what was wrong. My nun grabbed me about the head and buried my face in a soft sea of black cloth. I was terrified, especially as my forehead made firm and rubbing contact with the hard, substantial and, heretofore, unsuspected fact of body and bone beneath. The host in my mouth, and her hip on my head, I decided I would come out of that darkness and say nothing, not now, not ever, of what it was that had made me cry.

Afterwards, my father patted me on the back and told me that I was now a man; for a moment, I thought it was wrestling the nun that made me one. My mother was proud, as if my fit was a sign of something, as if, because I had been the first to cry, I had somehow been chosen.

I did not succeed in dislodging the host from the roof of my mouth until suppertime, when it adhered, quite with a will of its own, to a great gob of stewing meat, and went with it down my throat.

I was raised on fire and brimstone, the more subtle, Catholic kind, not hurled from the pulpit, but whispered. The nuns spoke often of hell, their words like sighs. They spoke in my dreams when I was eight. I think I would have preferred an evangelistic onslaught, full of fury and damnation, and apocalyptic final judgment. At least, then, things would have been out in the open. But the nuns and the priest knew where hell was. It was in the mind.

"HELL," the priest would say when, once a month, he came to class, "is whatever scares ye most." He would look around, try to catch an eye. "It's all up here," he'd say, tapping his head with two fingers, "ye can't get away from it, 'coz once the mind turns on ye—" He would grab a handful of air, and hold up a clenched fist. He would never finish the sentence, only smile and look from face to face, as if inviting us to smile with him, in wonder at the greatness of God—for wasn't he wonderful after all, wasn't he, that he could fashion such a fail-safe torture-chamber as the human mind? Each time we sinned, God pushed a button, and our minds, like implanted electrodes, went to work.

This change in tactics, this shifting of the beast from without to within, was someone's idea of humanizing the faith. It was supposed to signal the start of a newer, more healthy approach to religion, like the dropping from the mass of my mother's dear, dead language, Latin, or turning the priest around to face the congregation, or letting women bare their heads in church. It was Vatican II, a time of change in the Church, and so, too, a time of equivocation, of doctrinal fuzziness and confused clergy. I suppose it was the worst time to be a Catholic, if what one wanted was to stay a Catholic. Certainly, it was a bad time to be a little Catholic boy, trying to keep blasphemous doubts at a distance. For, if one thing was changed, why should not everything be changed? It was a time when all things were questioned and, though my every word hung heavy with guilt, I could not help myself—I was one of the great questioners:

How do we know a soul is white if we can't see it? If it is white, why can't we see it? How many venial sins does it take to make one mortal sin? The concept of grace puzzled me. We were supposed to spend our lives getting grace, the more you got, the better, and the more prayers you said, the more you got. The point was to horde it like coupons, and turn it in on the last day, for a discount on your stay in purgatory. As the nuns explained it, it was a kind of pure, luminous ice cream, doled out by God in scoops. Nuns were known to be absolutely dripping with it. They left a little behind on everything they touched.

I was always inventing scenarios whereby I might be damned, or at least have my soul scuffed by the black boot of sin, through no fault of my own. If, for instance, I committed a mortal sin, then hit my head on a rock and got amnesia, and forgot the mortal sin, and so did not confess it, did I go to hell anyway?

The answer to such questions was often silence, but there were some so full of eristic fervour that they could not help themselves.

They answered such questions with limbo. Limbo, that most terrifying of the four afterlives, where those souls went who, on earth, had no will of their own, or who had had it taken away. Those kept from holiness through no fault of their own went to limbo, a place on the border of hell, devoid of suffering and worry, hope and desire. There was nothing in limbo but the souls that were sent there. It was they who gave it place. Distance was the unbridgable gap of soul and soul, and time there was eternal. In that doorless vestibule, in that vault of loneliness, life was to float forever suspended, a limbo of limbos, soul as far from soul as all souls were from God. "They shall live," the priest said, "but they shall not see God." The souls of most of the men who died before the coming of Christ were in limbo, as were the souls of infants who had not lived long enough to be baptized. But also others. People, for instance, who, though born after the birth of Christ, lived in a part of the world to which the news of that birth had not carried by the time of their death, all had their souls consigned to limbo. "Not" as one nun explained it, "people who said No to Jesus, just people he never got round to asking." That this was like blaming an uninvited guest for failing to show up at your party was, on this dear soul, a lost distinction. Bound for limbo were the natives of darkest Africa, almost all of the tribes of the Eskimo and the entire race of the Beothuck Indians — with the exception of Shawnadithit and Mary March who, unlike all their brothers and sisters, had time to convert before the Christians killed them off.

Limbo. What hell could be worse than this dark, dead place? For me, it was the horror of which the priest had spoken: "Whatever scares ye most." Even then, I knew limbo was not a place. It was the mind turning inward upon itself, curling up within walls of itself; it was the mind become self-contained. I was eight and, night after night, dreamed I was a turtle. I pulled my head in and someone stopped up the hole, plugged it with darkness, and I was stuck inside myself, forever.

Not long after my first Holy Communion came what my father

31

would call "the IQ crisis." In March of my Grade 4 year, there was an evening set aside for parent-teacher meetings. (My father, like all the other fathers, never went to these meetings, but still they were called parent-teacher meetings.) My mother never missed a meeting and, most of the time, took me with her, as she did on this occasion.

Outside each classroom, hard to the walls of the corridor, stood a long queue of mothers, waiting their turn. Now, the duration of each mother's stay with the teacher was a kind of status symbol—the shorter the stay the better, for it meant one's child was doing so well, there was really not much to talk about. Waiting in line all those times with my mother, I saw many a mortified woman emerge from behind a door that, for the past ten or fifteen minutes, had been significantly closed. At such times, no-one spoke. Along the line, a damning silence was maintained, until the poor woman made her exit. My mother, by dint of my good marks, usually stole the show. She would have me wait by the door for her, and be in and out so fast it hardly seemed possible that she had spoken to anyone. Then, heads high, hand in hand, we would walk with slow ceremoniousness, queen and homunculus king, down the line of ladies, out the door. So how could something go wrong? It did though.

That night in March, my mother went in, but did not soon after come out. In fact, even by the standards of the problem child, I came close to setting records. And, through it all, I had to stand there, in front of those women, in whose eyes the joy of my come-uppance was brightly shining. I stared at the floor, but I could feel them looking at me. They were transfixed, and who could blame them? I was an ongoing catastrophe, a little icon of perfection flaking slowly away. I looked up and caught one lady's eye; she was standing rigid, with lips pressed primly tight, as if wondering why a boy so obviously delinquent had always seemed so nice. The fact that I knew I had done nothing to displease anyone made no difference; guilt, unlike grace, did not have to be earned.

When, at last, my mother came out, I was afraid to look at her. When I tried to take her hand, she pulled away and grabbed me instead by the wrist. "Come on you," she said, loudly, and in a tone of voice to let the ladies know she took as dim a view of my un-named crime as they did, and, until now, had not known more about it. And then she dragged me down the hall. As we went past, the ladies pretended not to notice, but, before the door was closed behind us, their gleeful chatter had begun.

Outside, on the steps, beneath the red porch light, my mother let me go and turned about to face the darkness and the wind. Her purse like a handcuff about both wrists, she gripped the rail with her hands and leaned over, as if to throw up. "You got my mitts, Mom," I said, swallowing most of the sentence down with a gulp of wind. It was bitterly cold, the gale gone round from a storm of rain the night before, and the yard around us was a field of frozen slush. I stepped closer to her and. with my hands in my duffel-coat pockets, buried my face in her coat, my forehead hard to the small of her back. I could feel her body beneath, her warm body shaking. I threw my arms about her, and fitted my body to hers. But, just as I began to feel that I could stay that way forever, she dropped her purse, and pulled so suddenly away from the rail that I almost fell. She said something, it sounded like "Bobby"; it might have been "goodbye." And then she ran down the steps and started across the ice. "Mom, your purse," I shouted but she kept on, the ice, now and then, giving way beneath her, the water splashing black about her boots. I hurried down the steps and, grabbing her purse from a pool of slush, started after her. I knew my mitts were in the purse, but I was in such a panic that I didn't think to stop and put them on. I ran, holding the purse, as if to keep it, like a baby, from the wind. And, to keep from slipping, I tried to find the tracks she'd made. Now and then I looked up and saw her, far ahead of me. She seemed strange without the purse, like someone not my mother. Her hands free and, for balance, high in the air, she might have been a dancer, or off to meet a lover hidden somewhere in the dark.

But, out on the road, she stopped suddenly and raised her hands to her face, like a woman who realizes she has run naked from her house. She stayed that way until, slipping and sliding, I came up behind her. Without lamps or the lights of cars, the road was dark, but I could see that she was crying. She was dabbing her eyes with a tissue, the wad of tissue white in her black, gloved hand. "Here," I said, and held out her purse like an offering. She smiled, took the strap in both hands and slowly pulled it from me. "What's wrong?" I said and, now that she was again my mother, began to cry. The wind gusted, and the cold, sweet smell of perfume wrapped round me like a hug. "Nothing," she said and, with her free hand, pulled my stocking-cap tight on my head. Then she opened her purse and handed me my mitts. "We won't tell your father, will we?" she said. I shook my head, though I was unsure what she meant. "What did Sister say?" I said. "Oh," my mother said, "Sister said nothing. Just teacher talk, that's all. I should know, now, hey?"

We began to walk home together, hand in hand, having, for the first time, agreed that some things are best forgotten.

Later that night, I listened from the doorway of my bedroom while, in the living-room, my mother and father talked about what Sister had said. As near as I could make it out, Sister had told my mother that I was suffering from something called "high IQ." Now, though by this time I was well up on every nuance of my father's bright-baby theory, I had never heard him use those words, "high IQ."

"Bobby's IQ is a little high," my mother said.

And my father, gravely: "How high is it?"

"They're not sure."

"They," implying that I was in sufficient danger to warrant the attentions of a whole team.

My father sighed, long and loud. It was a "disease incurable, death imminent" kind of sigh. "Well, what are we supposed to do?" he said.

"There's nothing we can do, really," my mother said, "just treat him the same, maybe try to make things more interesting for him."

I had heard enough. I closed my door and got into bed, and spent the night wide awake, for I knew if I slept I would dream. It never occurred to me to wonder how a nun would know I was sick. Nuns, priests, doctors, teachers, they were all the same, all bad news to me. They were grownups, whose sole purpose in life was to diagnose and chastise the ills of children.

High IQ. What part of me was climbing like a fever, higher and higher? What part of me was tending further and further from normal? I was too terrified to ask.

Over the next few days, my parents began to treat me very strangely. They repainted my room, from my dear, drab, sea-fog grey, to what I presumed was high-IQ blue. My mother hung more holy pictures, including one of the patron saint of child prodigies. And she kept asking me if I was bored. While my father and I were sock-surfing, she would interrupt every so often to wonder aloud if there might not be better things for me to do. As to whether there might not be better things for my father to do, the thought never seemed to cross her mind.

As it turned out, I was not quite the genius they feared. I did, at the age of eight, read romantic poetry, but only for the sad-sounding words.

The IQ crisis eventually blew over. As the days and weeks passed, and I did not begin to feel worse, it seemed my high IQ was in remission—surely such things were not unheard of—and I relegated it to an inner closet, piled it with other close calls, the bones of old bad dreams.

I found out that the possibility of my being accelerated two grades at school was considered but nothing was done because my mother intervened. A teacher herself, she had seen the effects acceleration could have, and would not have her child subjected to it.

When I try to remember school at Duley's, it is not the school itself I remember, nor much more than the names and faces of the teachers and the boys and girls in my class. Rather, I remember one boy I was made to be friends with, "made" in the providential sense, though not by God but by my mother, whose hand in it went undetected until after the boy was gone. "Who'll we get for you this year, Bobby," she said, "now that Gabriel's gone?" That Gabriel had been gotten for me was news. I thought it was I who'd been gotten for him. But, looking at my mother, I saw that she was serious. Her eyes, meeting mine, were full of guilt and worry. "Who'll we get for you this year, Bobby?"

Gabriel went round in a wheelchair. He and his family lived a few houses away from us. Come the end of March, when it was no longer necessary that a special van take him over the icy road, to and from school, my mother decided that it was time Gabriel and I became friends. "He's got no-one, Bobby," she said, "and he's such a nice boy. No-one understands him, that's all." She said people were afraid of the wheelchair. It was the chair that blinded everyone to the real Gabriel, that made them think he really was the awful little wretch he seemed to be. "How would you feel, Bobby, if you were in that chair?" she said, and went on to imply a causal relationship between my good legs and Gabriel's bad. She spoke of there being, somewhere in the universe, a leg factory, an assembly-line for limbs, and on that line were angels run so ragged, the poor dears sometimes made mistakes. Gabriel was a victim of supply and demand. "Be nice to him, Bobby," she said, "walk to school with him and talk to him, make sure he gets home okay."

And so, it seemed I was Gabriel's guardian. I used to meet him out on the road in the mornings. His mother would push him as far as our house, and then Gabriel, whose hands, as far as anyone knew, had yet to be formally introduced to the wheels of his chair, would look up at me and say, "Okay, Bobby, let's get this show on the road." My mother found this show of stiff upper lip nothing short of heartbreaking. "What a brave little boy," she would say. She would stand in the driveway and watch as I began to push the brave little half-ton boy half a mile uphill to school.

Gabriel was paralyzed from the waist down, and had no control over bodily functions, so the result of even the slightest exertion was often a long, slow, but not quite silent fart. My father called him Puff the Flatulent Dragon; and, on seeing him, would point a finger and observe: "But soft—what wind from yonder little boy breaks?" Sometimes, like a gymnast on the parallel bars, Gabriel would, with sheer arm strength, raise himself from the chair, and stay that way until he was sufficiently purged as to have no worry of embarrassment for at least a few hours. He even made money from it, for such a performance commanded an audience, and Gabriel refused to perform without inducement. Boys and girls would give him nickels, and then watch from an upwind distance while Gabriel went to work. Up in the air, his grey-flannel legs hanging limp, his shoulders hunched, his neck on his collar like an overflow of dough, his face bursting red, he would more or less deflate, and wait until someone shouted, "Emission Control, we have a lift-off," and then suddenly drop himself into the chair, with a groan and a loud sigh.

It was having to push I held against him. The road that went round the pond was unpaved, full of potholes and ribbed like a washboard. Gabriel required that I neither hit the potholes, nor zig-zag around them so much as to make him sick; and that I not go so fast that, upon a sudden stop, he would be catapulted from the chair, nor so slow as to make a sudden stop altogether uninteresting. On the main road, where there was pavement, I was expected to "burn out," which involved tipping the chair back and running with it like a wheelbarrow. Gabriel, hands on the arms of the chair, would press his upper body back, turn his head sideways and, his face pretending to the contortion of an astronaut's as I pushed him faster and faster, would shout: "One G, five Gs, ten Gs, fifteen Gs, twenty Gs, twenty Jesus Gs, Bobby, *twenty Jesus Gs*." Or, he would lie back and, with his face turned to one side, look off into space, as if watching the sky go by. Or he would make kamikaze noises, "at-at-at-at-at," gunning down with the Equalizer anyone who got in his way. The Equalizer was an ordinary walking cane, except that, when you pushed a button at the top of it, a nail came out like a switch-blade from the bottom. His father made it for him, after Gabriel told of a similar contraption he had seen in a James Bond movie. His father said it was only to be used in case of emergency. About every 30 seconds, Gabriel would shout "EMERGENCY," and start stabbing at the world, at a wind-blown blitz of candy-wrappers. "Take that, you Crispy Crunch," he'd say, "vile O'Henry, thou shalt die." He would hold the Equalizer like a lance, and have me charge oncoming transport trucks. And he was cruelly adept at impaling bumblebees. He would take them home still squirming. He would introduce me to them: "Bobby—Bumblybee. Bumblybee—Bobby." Holding the Equalizer with both hands and arching his head so he could see me, he would try to bring the writhing, half-dead things into contact with my nose.

It was the Equalizer that got one legend started. It was believed by the other boys and girls that, in addition to the Equalizer, Gabriel had a veritable arsenal of concealed weaponry. He had knives strapped to his legs, those harmless, yet somehow sinister legs. And he had an undepletable supply of rocks, painstakingly chosen on the basis of size, shape and capacity to injure. And there was that plastic bag, hidden somewhere in his clothing, which, unless you were nice to him, he would threaten to show you.

But it was the chair that marked him most. It was the symbol of his exemption, the thing that set him apart. And, because he was different, he was believed to have special powers. Natural laws did not apply to Gabriel; and Gabriel indulged his friends by pretending to the powers they said he had. They said Gabriel had visions. He had them. He would, in the midst of a crowd, suddenly close his eyes and, with his head rolling back and forth, as if his neck had turned to jelly, begin a prophetic mumbling. "Shhhhhh—" they'd say, "he's goin' into it." It was understood that if Gabriel, while in one of these trances, said your name, some great misfortune would befall you. I noticed that those whom Gabriel perceived as having done him wrong were, sooner or later, named. "Tommy," Gabriel would say, a pained expression on his face, "Tommy," as if he didn't want to name Tommy, but what could he do—it was a vision and out of his hands. "What happened," he'd say upon waking, "where am I?" Before the day was out, Gabriel and his band of boys would fulfil the prophecy.

One day, when we reached the schoolyard, Gabriel announced that he had mastered the technique of "goin' into it" at will. He began to use visions to settle disputes. Squirming in agony, face and body coursing with divine wisdom, he might say: "John gets to blow the biggest frog." These rulings were not questioned. It was the will of God that John blow the biggest frog. It was part of a master plan that must not be called in doubt.

Gabriel was not blind to the possibility of power and profit in

38

all this. He guessed that the boys and girls believed because they wanted to. (I did not believe because Gabriel, on the way home from school every day, laughed aloud at the others. Gabriel always needed an audience and, for this pulling of the wool, I was it.) Such material, mundane things as chocolate bars, chips and Coke began to have a profound influence on the oracle. And there was very soon evident a correlation between those boys who took Gabriel round the yard for rides, and those who made up his gang of avengers, those who were the instruments of retribution, but never subject to it.

Gabriel also came to have a way with girls. Because he was magic, and because they knew that, whatever his impulses, he couldn't act upon them, certain girls began to show Gabriel certain things up behind the school, near the woods, where they and Gabriel went by pre-arranged appointment. "Only Gabriel can come," they said, and on these occasions, Gabriel discovered remarkable and, heretofore, unguessed-at powers of locomotion. And what did Gabriel and the girls do? According to those, and I was not among them, who had nerve enough to go up to the woods and watch, Gabriel allowed the girls to take out one of his paralyzed parts and play with it. They, in turn, lifted and lowered certain items of clothing, or let Gabriel, with the Equalizer, raise their tunics front and back. And it was said the girls brought one, and sometimes two, rudimentary protuberances into teasing contact with his ears.

Afterwards, on the way home from school, Gabriel would claim to have performed that act I now know him to have been incapable of performing. At the time, I didn't have the vaguest notion of what he was talking about. Horrified, I tried not to hear while he made of his day a mound of forbidden words. He heaped them on his lap, and went through them like a haul from Hallowe'en. "Fuck—cock —cunt." All the while I was with Gabriel, I tried not to hear such words. I have a memory of myself as always on the edges, the sulking little fellow who did not take part, but took over when the taking part was done. The others saw me as they saw the wheels of Gabriel's chair—I was essential, but uninteresting. It was having to push I held against him, being exempted from his world as he was from mine, being allowed to see the strings on his puppet of fun.

It was for these journeys home that my mother brought us together. She said as much, years later, when, tipsy with relief over the fact that I no longer needed protection, she let slip some things she might not have otherwise. There was an ongoing feud when I was eight between the Pond and the Line—the Line was the road along which the houses of the old town were situated, and which had to be crossed to get to the Pond. I had not yet lived in enough neighbourhoods to earn the kind of diplomatic immunity I would later enjoy. In other words, I was fair game. Because I lived within a mile of school, I was not allowed to take the bus, so my mother figured the only way to get me home safely was to pair me with Gabriel, the one person at whom no-one would sink so low as to throw a snowball or rock. It worked like a charm. Each day, the boys on the Line broke ranks to let us through. In fact, it worked so well I might have been stuck with Gabriel for years, had not his life of Riley ended during the last week of school.

The graveyard was near the woods, up behind the school, and, to get to it, you had to cross the schoolyard. We were never forewarned that a funeral was coming through, but we were honour bound that if, while we were outside, one did come through, we would maintain a respectful silence, and keep clear of the far side of the yard, where hearse and train would pass. Gabriel was caught one day, behind some bushes, not 50 feet from the graveyard, by a solemn procession of mourners, caught in his chair like some sedentary satyr, surrounded by a trio of twelve-year-old nymphs who, though wearing tunics, had their panties in their hands. The show, tell, pull and play was well advanced by the time some poor, bereaved and unsuspecting soul looked left to see, there in the woods, the four of them, the three girls brazen, bare and bending over, and Gabriel, *little Gabriel*, with both hands full—such was the story I later overheard my mother tell my father. There was shock and there was outrage. It was said that, if not for the man from the funeral home, even more harm might have been done. He, it seemed, was used to such things, as if pubescent, bare-ass sex was just what one might expect on such an occasion, as if that, specifically, was one of the things he'd been trained to deal with. He motioned the procession to continue and, removing his jacket, ran with it, matador-like, toward Gabriel and the girls. He held it so as to "screen our aged innocent from our corrupted young"—such was the way the priest put it the following Sunday, in a sermon full of hellfire and euphemism.

Gabriel and the three girls were suspended and missed the last week of school. The girls' story was that Gabriel had been having trouble with his plastic pouch and they were trying to help him. As one of them put it, in a phrase that immediately became the stuff of legend, "the thing came off his thing and we were trying to put it back on." No-one believed this—there was the problem of the panties—but, for me, it was something to fill the void I'd encountered upon trying to imagine just what *had* happened to so upset everyone.

That last week, the playground was rife with rumour and misconception—boys on one side, girls on the other, exultant, and somehow complicit in Gabriel's crime. During recess, and before and after school, the nuns went about the yard, breaking up groups of three or more, urging everyone to run or sing or play, to do anything but talk. They were frantic. The student body was burning; it was on fire in a hundred places, and the flames, no matter how well put out, started up again. It must have seemed to them a whole generation of souls was threatened, for Gabriel and the three girls had dragged into the light of day a thing which, heretofore, had been kept in darkness.

I have no doubt that quantum leaps forward in sexual knowledge were made that week, and notions were formed, the disabusing of which would take years. The younger boys were afraid to ask questions, for to ask was to admit you did not know. They hung around the edges of groups, walked nonchalantly, if slowly, past the older boys, hoping to pick up that one bit of information that would make sense out of what seemed like an unholy mess of contradiction and absurdity. As for me, I made no leaps and formed no notions. Oh, I I was curious, precociously so, but, because I was only eight, I was last in the pecking order, chased away when I hung about for crumbs. My mother warned me not to listen to the older boys. "If anyone talks about Gabriel," she said, "put your hands over your ears and run away." A bell had been hung on Gabriel's name: keep clear, keep clear. Do not speak it. If spoken, do not hear it. And, of course, she made sure I did not see Gabriel after school any day that week. She had the maid keep watch at the gate, in case Gabriel tried to enter. Everyone at school wanted to know what Gabriel had to say about the whole thing, and, naturally, they asked me. All I could say was that I hadn't seen him.

I knew it was likely that I would never see him again, except by meetings that were illicit or accidental—and, if illicit, more his fault than mine, because my passion for his side of the story was half-hearted and waning compared to that burning one I had to be free of that damned chair forever. It was bad enough to have to push him half a mile, twice a day, five days a week, and to have to wait around at recess, and after school, while the other boys fought over whose turn it was to help the janitor lift him down the steps. But, worst of all, was having to always be so close. Gabriel was a joke I knew too well to laugh at, a great big ball of fun I couldn't have. What I hated was having to be with him, having, at the age of eight, to pimp for a gimp in great demand, having, ever and always, to listen to the steady stream of compensatory bullshit that poured from him. That it was compensatory I didn't know then; nor, if I had known, would it have made much difference. I wanted to be by myself, away from the world, not forced to a friend who was too much with it.

Too much with it. He seemed to be. How could I know that life in that chair was life encased in one-way glass. He could see out, but not get out—and no-one could see him. Having to climb the wall like a treadmill to make it move, needing always a push to get started, someone to roll you along—that must have been how it was. And not the Equalizer, not obscene boasts nor loud lies could break that glass. Nor could he, as on rare days he seemed to be trying, charm his way out with the church-morning pitch of his voice. How could I know that, though he'd grow, his closed black world would not; and that, one day, what space he'd had would fill with years, and he would be its dimensions, with nowhere to go and nothing to do but take again that same walk round his mind. I don't say it had to be that way, only that it was. Though he and his family moved to town that summer, my mother kept track of them through the years. "No legs," my father said, "but the heart of a sprinter." Cruel gift. When he was fourteen, Gabriel tried to kill himself. From that time on, he was in and out of hospitals. I don't remember him that way, but in the chair, watching the sky go by. And I imagine him thinking how, even at that speed, there was nothing to fear.

CHAPTER 3

My father distinguished between "places to stay" and "places to live." You needed a place to stay to find a place to live; or, as in our case, to find another place to stay. Worse even than having no place to stay was being "between houses."

At Lawton's, the house to which we moved next, we were "between houses." Aunt Dola and Uncle Rennie lived there and, because we couldn't find anywhere else, we put most of our furniture in storage and moved in with them. We arrived the first of September, and they were due to move, after Christmas, to a house they'd decided to buy. "Buy," my father told my mother, "buy, not rent."

Whether it was jealousy on our part, or the fact that we were paying rent to relatives, I'm not sure, but there was a definite tension between our two families. We went at one another with candy-coated daggers. My mother and Aunt Dola:

"You were busy today, were ye Dola?"

"Yes girl."

"You were too busy to wash my dress, were ye?"

"I was girl, yes."

"I suppose with supper to cook, now—"

43

"Yes girl. An' de tree extra pork chops, ye know."

"Are ye tired my love?"

"A bit girl, yes."

My father and mother had their own room, one which, until we moved in, had lain empty. I, however, had to sleep on the chesterfield. It had been Rennie's intention to have us, all three, sleep together, but my mother objected on the grounds that such things simply were not done. My sleeping on the chesterfield caused some problems. At nine every night, so that I could go to sleep, the television had to be wheeled from the living-room into Uncle Rennie's and Aunt Dola's bedroom. Aunt Dola would allow no-one but Uncle Rennie in her bedroom, and that included her four daughters who, from 3.30 onwards each day, would sit in front of the set, looking at once both spellbound and bored. Because of me, they had to go to bed at nine no'clock.

My father, who was used to watching television from his seven-o'clock forecast to the midnight news, was also forced to go to bed early. And my mother, who had always retired two hours before my father, had to get used to the fact of their being not only in bed together, but simultaneously awake.

The whole house was put out by my sleeping on the chesterfield. And that moving of the set from one room to the other, Rennie and Dola with a hand on either side of it, their heads bowed and shoulders slumped like pallbearers, and the four girls following behind; and my mother and father and I, watching, feeling as if all this would not be if it were not for us—that moving of the set remains for me a kind of tableau of our days at Lawton's.

The worst times for me were the mornings. Rennie worked with the Department of Highways, putting pavement down, and had to get up at six. The kitchen and the living-room were adjacent, so I could hear, quite clearly, everything that went on. Aunt Dola would rise with Rennie and, whispering, the two of them, him in workboots, her in steel-soled five-pound shoe, would clump from tile to tile while cooking breakfast. Once awake, I could not get back to sleep, so I lay and listened to the sound of Rennie and Dola whispering, as if trying to hush the bacon as it sizzled on the pan.

It was a long way from first light to sunset and rosary. Most evenings, we broke like camps at seven to say our warring rosaries: my mother, from Hail Mary to Glory Be, singing the song required of her by the Lord in this strange land; and Dola, praying plague and swarm of locusts, praying "let my people go." The rosary, for us, was not so much an event, nor a time of day, as it was a place in which, as in the confessional, you could say what you wanted, and not have to own up for it afterwards. My parents' room was adjacent to Dola's bedroom, and the wall between was paper-thin. Saying the rosary, we would kneel to the wall, three of us on one side, the six of them on the other, and we would, with impunity, and under cover of code, speak our pent-up minds. The winner was that side which, in tone and volume of voice, managed to sound more sinned against than sinning. "Our father who art in heaven," my mother would say, lunging at Dola with the Lord's Prayer. "As we forgive those who trespass against us," Dola would parry, with all the vengeance she could muster. My mother would raise her eyes to heaven and say, "hallowed be thy name, thy kingdom come," her face full of patient suffering, as if, not judging, no, only remembering the measly portion of potatoes Dola had given us at supper. And Dola would answer, "and lead us not into temptation, but deliver us from evil," in the voice of one who, though not inclined to temptation or evil, had every reason to be, and one of them was on the other side of the wall. It was hand-to-hand combat, a pious gouging of eyes. "Speak up dear, so God can hear you," my mother would say, as I pelted puny Aves at the enemy, still on my second decade while, on the other side of the wall, Flo was on her fourth. Gradually, as the rosary waged on, our voices would rise, until soon it became a shouting match. "Holy Mary, Mother of God," my father would roar, and Rennie would raise his voice accordingly, belting out a Gloria for all he was worth. Often, both sides would slow down near the end, because neither wanted to finish first. Finishing the shorter, though papally sanctioned, form of the rosary first meant having to decide whether or not to continue; and sometimes, when one side decided 55 prayers was enough, the other side found in that failure the strength to start down the road to 165. Later, the winning side would come out of their room, looking tired, humble and twice as holy as the other.

The girls and I carried on a cold war of our own. There was Ambrosia, the youngest, nine like me—our ages agreed, but nothing else. I was not allowed to call her Ambrosia. My father called her Hambrosia, but he would not let me do it. I had to call her Mary. I asked her once what Ambrosia meant. She was ready. Hands on hips, lips in a round for-your-information pucker, she said in a sing-song voice: "Food of the gods; anything delightful to taste or smell; beebread." That did it. Ambrosia was that from then on for me, a great big bun of bee-bread, all the more remarkable for having powers of speech and locomotion.

Ambrosia hated me because, by getting good marks, I made her look bad. We were in the same grade and so, the inevitable comparisons were made—and Ambrosia did not come off well by them. Ambrosia was famous as the first student ever in a grade higher than five to record a final mark not higher than ten. Upon looking into the reasons for her score of 6% in mathematics, it was discovered that her difficulty derived from a misconception she had formed in Grade 1, which had somehow gone three years without correction.. Ambrosia had been told by her Grade 1 teacher that a good way to learn addition and subtraction was to remember that they were opposites. Now Ambrosia had mastered subtraction—it meant to "take away." *Ergo*, addition, as the opposite of this, must mean "don't take away." Eight don't take away six equals eight. Ten don't take away three equals ten. Indeed, ten don't take away 16,452 equals ten. Once this misconception of hers was cleared up, Ambrosia began getting the forties and fifties of which we had always known her capable.

Ambrosia had not failed any grades by Grade 4 because she made up her deficiencies at summer school every year. Perhaps it was being made to miss her summer holidays that soured her on the world. Ambrosia had no interest in anything except television and Mr. Freezes—semi-frozen sticks of flavoured gruel, encased in plastic, one of which she would put in her mouth and, sitting in front of the

TV, with her hands on the floor beside her, suck slowly on it for hours. She would sit through whole TV shows, the tube hanging intravenous-like from her mouth, the slush oozing into her. Absolutely immobile, she might have been a display in some science museum: *Osmosis: push button for demonstration.* The button pushed, the window in the wall would light up, and there would be Ambrosia, osmosing Mr. Freeze for the edification of young and old alike. Ambrosia took things into her body as if by some process independent of her will. She was, at the age of nine, living the life of a passive sponge. And sometimes, while she was sitting so, watching TV, she would stare at me, her black eyes glazed with hate, and looking out from her face like raisins from a hot-cross bun—as if it was I who had nailed her to the floor, I who was forcing Mr. Freezes down her throat, I who had started her body on the way to becoming the balloon it now was.

Ambrosia had ways of fighting back, though. She knew that more was expected of me than of her, and she was a tattle-tale of unusual ability. She told on me in that sing-song way of hers, with an excited intake of breath after every third or fourth word:

"Aunt Agnes."

"Yes Mary, my love."

"Aunt Agnes, guess what."

"What Mary?"

"Bobby done a sum wrong on the board, he did, he done it wrong, and he never even knew until Miss told him."

Sometimes she played for keeps.

"Uncle Ted."

"What?"

"Uncle Ted, did Bobby tell?"

"Tell what, Mary?"

"Did Bobby tell he failed a test? He did, he failed, 'coz when he gave Miss his scribbler there was nose all over it."

"Nose" was the word Aunt Dola let the girls use when a reference to snot was unavoidable. The word in our family was "piggie." Ambrosia was not lying. I had a cold that day and there *was* nose all over the page. I passed in a page of piggies, flat shiny streaks of

47

green which I tried, unsuccessfully, to erase. Miss circled each piggie with red pencil and wrote "−5" beside it. I had all the answers on the test right and, if it hadn't been for the piggies, would have gotten 100%. There were, however, eleven piggies and, at five marks per piggie, I failed a test for the first time in my life— I got 45.

Ambrosia told my mother about it, too. "You'll have to be more careful, Bobby dear," was all she said, to the disappointment of Ambrosia, who was standing wide-eyed and gloating beside her, munching squirrel-like on something hidden in her hands. But later that night, as the three of us knelt for the rosary, my mother was inconsolable. "It's my fault, Teddy," she cried, "I should have made sure he had a handkerchief."

"Now Agnes," my father said, "don't be so hard on yourself. It's nobody's fault, it's just one of those things, that's all. Anyway, if you ask me, five marks per piggie is a bit much."

"Yeah," I said, injustice welling up like an ache in my throat, "it's only two for chocolate." It was an incident I was long in living down. At the Christmas concert that year, the Grade 4s put on a play about the Beothuck Indians. I was given the part of Little Running Nose.

Then there were the twins, Cheryl and Sharon, in Grades 6 and 5 respectively, as Sharon had failed one year, summer school and all. For Cheryl and Sharon, the only thing more reprehensible than a boy was a boy who was not as old as they were. Because they were eleven and I was nine, I was contemptible, not a form of life as they knew it. I was an object, inanimate, neither more interesting than the coffee-table, nor less deserving of a kick if I happened to get in the way.

They watched TV on the floor, lying on their bellies, hands cupping their cheeks, the joints of their jawbones popping like pistons, working wads of Double Bubble, gob-stopping hunks of gum so large as to strain credulity. If Cheryl asked, "Who took my bubble-gum?" she meant that package not yet unwrapped. But if Cheryl, a note of panic creeping into her voice, said, "Where's my gum?" she meant that highly personalized, tooth-indented wad that, even now, might be stuck to some windowsill, or the bottom of a bureau drawer, slowly ossifying. A wad of gum, to be impressive, had to be large, but a quality wad had also to be aged and cared for.

"Sher dis is nuttin' Mom," Sharon said once, beginning to put back in her mouth the three-foot strand of gum she had just pulled from it inch by inch, "you should see Betty Brewer's, her is de best, dere's still some in it from Grade 4. Dere's even some Banana Boat in it, and dey don't make dat anymore."

It was from a show called "Ben Casey" that Cheryl and Sharon got the idea to call me a "brain tumour." "I'm not a 'brain tumour,'" I'd say. "Yes ye are," they'd say, without taking their eyes from the TV, giggling, and wiggling their derisive little bums.

And finally there was Flo, known at school as Menstrual Flo. Flo did not hate me more than she hated the rest of the world. I was deserving of hate for increasing by one that number of people who might some day learn her secret. I didn't know what "menstrual" meant. I knew what "chthonic" meant, and "irrefrangible," but not "menstrual." My mother for my sake neutered the universe. She wove a web of conscience round my mind and, every day when she got home from work, went one by one through the words it caught, wielding guilt like a fly-swatter.

"Did you hear any new words today, Bobby?"

"No."

"Are you sure?"

"Well. What's hole?"

"Hole? H-O-L-E?"

"I think so."

"You mean like a hole in the ground?"

"One girl said, 'Kiss my hole.' The other girl said, 'Can't kiss a hole, can only kiss around it.'"

"*Mother of God*—now Bobby, listen to me. That's a dirty word, a dirty, filthy word, and you're not to say it or think of it again. Do you hear me?"

"Yes."

I didn't know what "menstrual" meant, so Flo was a mystery to me. I had no idea why she did the things she did; why, when the groceries were delivered to the door, she would run out ahead of everyone else and, seconds later, come running back, her arms about what seemed to be a random bag of groceries, and would look wild-eyed at us, as if our part in this was to try to tackle her before she made it to her room; or why, sometimes, minutes after slamming the door of her room behind her, she would come out, screaming "WRONG BAG, WRONG BAG," and chase everyone from the vestibule, so that she could find the right bag; or why, with alarming regularity, she would call out to her mother from the bathroom:

"MOM."

"What?"

"Mom, can ye come 'ere?"

"What for Flo?"

"Mom, please."

"Where are ye?"

"Mom, can ye jus' come 'ere."

"Flo honey, what for?"

"MOMMMMM."

"Well, why didn't ye say?"

Nor did I know why Dola and Flo, moments after such an exchange, would emerge from the bathroom, Dola hiding Flo like a stolen sweet at her side, and the two of them would walk, in a tip-toeing parody of silence, to Flo's room, with all the brazen confidence of cartoon characters, as if a firm belief in their own invisibility was all that was required to make it a fact.

Poor Flo. Quite simply, she was terrified. Probably, she thought that she was breaking new ground, that her period was something for which history had no precedent. Probably this was a thought that Dola did nothing to discourage.

Boys would buy packs of pocket Kleenex, just so they could colour them red down the middle and present them to Flo on the bus. "Dis yours Flo?" they'd say, "ye must have dropped it gettin' on." Flo, her arms in fervent hug about her books, would sniff and shake her head, and look out the window, as if, out there, was a world where such things could never happen.

"But it must be yours Flo," a boy said once, loudly enough for all the bus to hear, "it has your name on it, see." Holding it by the string to which it was attached, the boy dangled the Kleenex in front of her. But Flo would not look, so he passed it around.

"Dass Flo's, hey?" he said, his voice full of mock helpfulness, "it got her name on it, right here."

"He's right Flo," some girl shouted, "dass your name all right. It even got your address and telephone number. Flo Martın, Sounder's Bay Road, Kellies, 322-1197."

The boy went back to Flo.

"See. It must be yours Flo. We can mail it for ye if ye like."

Flo shook her head.

"It's yours den?"

"Yes."

"What?"

"YES."

"Do ye want it?"

"Yes."

"Sorry. Finders keepers."

Flo began to cry.

"Losers weepers."

"Please."

"We'll mail it for ye."

"No. Please. Don't let Daddy see it."

The boy laughed and, holding the Kleenex high, made her lunge three times for it, and made sure that, when she got it, her hand closed round the red part.

"*Don't let Daddy see it, don't let Daddy see it,*" the children chanted on the way home.

Flo gathered us all together, Cheryl, Sharon, Ambrosia and me, when we got off the bus. "Don't nobody tell," she said, still crying. "Mary, you won't tell, will ye? If ye do, I'll tie ye by yer pigtails to a post."

The next day, the schoolyard was littered with pocket Kleenex, all coloured red down the middle, all with Flo's name, address and telephone number in the upper left corner. As Flo's luck would have it, it was a dry and windy day and, from time to time, when I looked

51

out the window, I saw columns of Kleenex, three stories high, swirling about the building. Caught in updrafts, they reared before the window like twisters, or like something, perhaps, from one of Flo's nightmares—the world a whirling vortex of sanitary napkins. At lunchtime, Flo walked home, and did not return to school the rest of the week.

Over the fall, the wads of tissue turned grey and, grounded by the rain, collected in the grass on the edge of the yard, or lay soiled in roadside puddles, Flo's name and number fading slowly from them. They hung round for years, in spring still there when March pulled back the snow, raw memories that would never heal.

It was at Lawton's my father started watching the Weathergirl. Actually, it was Rennie who first started watching her. She did the weather on the CBC—which channel, by this time, we were able to get quite clearly—and did it, Rennie said, better than my father; or, at least, looked better doing it. My father wondered what she had that he hadn't. "Good legs and go-go boots," Rennie said. Not to mention a skirt which, when she reached for Whitehorse or Rankin Inlet, left those legs and boots a paling pace behind.

"No hard feelings Ted," Rennie would say when, every day at seven, he rose to change the channel.

"Aw c'mon Daddy," said Cheryl and Sharon the first time, "we wanna see Uncle Ted."

"Do ye now?" Rennie said, and, picking up Ambrosia, who had not said a word, by the arms, carried her kicking to my father's chair. "There he is," Rennie said, "Uncle Ted. Take a good look." Ambrosia, suspended in mid-air, looking solemn and confused, stared at my father, as if to let him know that she was not fooled into thinking this was anyone's fault but his.

Not until just before Rennie and Dola and the girls moved out was my father able to sit through one of the Weathergirl's forecasts. The first few weeks, he could not even stand to listen.

Once, rather than sit and watch her, he gave in the hall a repeat performance of the weather he had taped at four. The girls and I sat on the floor in front of him, and Ambrosia did the introduction:

52

"And now—bombebom bombebom bombebommm—Ted O'Malley. To tell us today about tomorrow." My father, improvising a map of North America on the wall behind him, miming a piece of chalk, commanded, with arms upraised, a great constellation of Highs and Lows. He waved the chalk like some maestro of the atmosphere; and when he was done, we applauded, "BRAVO, BRAVO." Bowing low, he walked off to his room.

He did this several days in a row, and might have made a habit of it, had not Rennie complained that all the noise was drowning out the Weathergirl. And so, those weeks, those months, sitting and watching with us, while my mother was in the kitchen having tea, my father changed his mind about the Weathergirl. I did not see this, of course. I saw only that, as the days went by, he minded less and less being made to watch; and that, when Rennie and Dola moved out, and we, at last, hooked *our* TV to the antennae, he went on watching—and, over the next five years, watched every Weathergirl forecast from start to finish, all the while slipping slowly away to that nebulous place we called "the other channel."

My father and mother needed one another to bring down the dark, as curtains to close upon a window. The day Dola and Rennie left, my mother cried. It was a Saturday, the first Saturday of the new year, and it was dark by four in the afternoon. She and I were alone in the house. My father was off somewhere with Rennie, celebrating Christmas for the umpteenth time. The only lights were the blue lights of our tree. I know why my mother cried, because I heard it, too—a sound like sadness coming in, as if through a crack in the house. I wonder how long, by then, she had been hearing it, and if Rennie and Dola and the girls, for a time, had drowned it out; and if she had been hoping it had gone away. Now, in the new silence, it was back.

My mother cried for a long time, not loudly, but full of a strange, articulate dispassion, like a woman who no longer believed that others could hear her, like one contained by the sound of her own voice. She cried for hours, sobs groping like hands in the dark.

The world was changing. What had been a field of battle between my mother and father was becoming a no-man's land. What they'd had was an agreement to disagree, and were joined somehow by that—opposed, but linked by tug of war. Now, like armies who no longer remember why it was they first took up arms, they began to wander aimlessly, and to look at one another across the distance with puzzlement and reproach.

For instance, my father, on Saturday nights, liked to watch the hockey games, and my mother and I would watch with him. He would go about the house, just before the game, getting those things he deemed essential for full enjoyment of it: beer, chips, pretzels, his red, white and blue No. 9 Habs sweater—and my mother and me. My mother was comic relief. I was statistician. I hated hockey, then, and would sit reading on the floor until called upon to regurgitate some of the numbers with which he had crammed me full. "Bobby," he would say, "how did Rousseau do in '65?" I would close my eyes, screw up my face and recite: "Rousseau, Robert: G 30; A 48; TP 78; PIM 23." I neither knew nor cared what "G" or "A" or "TP" stood for, and would run away whenever he threatened to tell me.

Now my mother approached hockey with a kind of cheerful bemusement. She considered it a silly sport, but was not, by that, unduly upset. Rather, she indulged my father's obsession as one might certain forms of madness—with kind smiles, and comments and questions phrased so as to make one sound interested without in any way compromising one's own sanity. "What a goal," my father would say, and my mother, who had not looked up from her knitting for the past 45 minutes, would now do so and, with eyes focused with seeming fascination on the set, shake her head in wonder, as if to say, "My God Teddy, is there no stopping this team?" Some nights she asked questions in a tone of voice that might fool you into thinking she knew what she was talking about. She might wonder, for instance, as one *afficianado* to another, why the team in the black-striped shirts never carried sticks, and why there were only three of them, when the other team, who, incidentally, did carry sticks, were allowed to number twelve. My father would laugh and refuse to answer; and my mother would smile to herself, as if, though of course she would never spoil his fun by saying so, she had just discovered a failure of concept in the game itself.

At Lawton's, after Dola and Rennie were gone, my mother no longer sat with us and watched. Instead, at 9.30, when the game came on, she would go out to the kitchen and stay there for hours, reading, or brooding over a cup of tea. My father would shout out to her from time to time, to let her know she was not forgotten.

"Some game, Agnes," he'd say.

"Yes dear," my mother would answer.

"You wouldn't believe Béliveau tonight Agnes."

"Why, what's he saying?"

"Intermission soon. Be out and see ye then."

I think each, for the other, was coming less and less to life, and when they met about the house, it was as if for the first time, as if each, in the mind of the other, was dying fifteen times a day.

A priest, of whom my mother was a distant relative, and who served a city parish, began to make regular visits on Tuesday night, for toast and tea. Except to say hello or ruffle my hair, the priest was not much interested in me, so my mother, when he came, packed me off to bed. My father's company, however, was required, a fact of which my father was well aware. But he wanted revenge for being left night after night to watch hockey with a number-crunching nine-year-old. My mother, on Tuesday, the hour before the priest arrived, tried not to let my father out of her sight, but, better than half the time, he escaped. Sometimes, he fled the house altogether, went to see Rennie, or went, he claimed, walking in the woods, in the snow and the dark. Other nights, he locked himself in the bathroom, and claimed to be taking a bath. He would let the water run for hours, flaunting the fact that he had not put in the plug. My mother, the first few times he tried this, left the priest in the kitchen and made genuine attempts to bring my father out. I know, because I got out of bed and, opening my door a crack, watched and listened. Down the hall, my mother would rattle the knob on the door of the bathroom as silently as possible, and whisper through the wood. "Teddy, Teddy come out. Teddy, what will Father think?" But my father did not much care what Father thought. His aversion to priests, once it began to manifest itself, was extreme. My mother would tell him the priest had to use the bathroom, but my father wouldn't fall for it. She would head back to the kitchen and, just before she got there, put a bounce in her step and a lilt in her voice so that the priest would not suspect anything. She must have spent her days inventing ways one might be indisposed. She told the priest my father was sick. She told him he was tired, he was out, he was busy, he had just gotten into the tub. After a while, she gave up trying to bring my father out, though she was careful not to let the priest see this. She would go as before to "see what's keeping Teddy," but now she neither knocked nor whispered; she just stood outside the bathroom door, so silent my father must not have known she was there, and looked up at the ceiling.

That winter, my mother was promoted from the classroom to the school board. She was fired, really, in a way that only my mother could be, by being given a raise and a better job. She was made an assistant superintendent, a reward, my father said, for a teacher than whom there had been none stranger in all the history of Heavy Heart High. As assistant superintendent, she would make more money—more than before, and more than my father. She wanted to save the extra money, and hurry near the day we could have our own home. But my father, who, instead of acknowledging that she was out-earning him, talked of the money as of something that had, lately and happily, begun to fall from heaven, sat at the kitchen table and calculated that, thus far, he had spent two years of his life "inside a bloody bus." It was, he said, time to buy a car.

At Lawton's, we lived on a road called Luby Line. This was a new neighbourhood of a dozen or so young families, and "next door" was often a mile away. I made real friends on Luby Line. There, all the children were younger than me, first- or second-graders, most of them, to whom the walking cerebroid, Bobby O'Malley, was something of a legend. I was not afraid on Luby Line, not quick, as at school, to curl up at the drop of a whisper, or sideways look, or laugh behind my back. Whether the talk , the looks, the laugh were meant for me I neither knew nor tried to find out. I clung to myself as to a piece of driftwood. But the boys on Luby Line, my God-sent, five- and six-year-olds, were like lumps of clay. I could make them do whatever I wanted, explain the world to them any way I wanted—abolish natural laws and make up new ones. There was Barney Boomer, Harold and the Bunquin Hollow, Floods and Just Plain Joe. My father called us Mr. Big and the Fatal Four. On Luby Line, with the Fatal Four, the world seemed far away.

"So," my father would say, whenever Floods came to the door, "so ye wanna see Mr. Big." Floods, hands on hips, would look up at my father and make a Bogart face. "Outta my way, fat man," he'd say. Floods—hence his name—wore pants too short. The spring after Dola and Rennie left, we played alleys a month and a half, waiting for the snow to leave the woods. In April, the Line was a mound of melting mud, with plates of yellow earth pushing up like ice-pans in the middle, the road running back to swamp and summer before our very eyes. For alleys, Flood was a mott-maker. Smacking his fist into the muck, in the earth up to his elbow, he would tightly close his eyes and laugh with his mouth wide open whenever the muddy water splashed up in his face.

Barney Boomer was so-called because of his strange obsession with body-checking. Barney boomed everything: cars, rocks, concrete walls. It was said that he had never seen a hockey game in his life, that his passion for impact was innate. The wonder was he never seemed to hurt himself. Oh, he was often dazed, and might, sometimes, after booming a building, remain prone for a disturbing period of time. But always he would get up and, grinning, wander drunkenly about.

Then there was Harold and the Bunquin Hollow. Why a dog should be called the Bunquin Hollow, no-one but Harold's mother thought to ask. She wanted Harold to call the dog something else, some name she could repeat at parties without alienating guests, without enhancing what she claimed was an unearned, but already widespread reputation as a woman gone slightly mad. While other wives were opening their doors at night and calling reasonably to Rover, telling Spot it was time to come home, she was shouting,

"Here the Bunquin Hollow, here the Bunquin Hollow," like some lunatic loose in the suburbs. She tried "Here the Bunquin," and "Here the Hollow," but to anything less than his full title, the Bunquin Hollow would not respond.

Harold and the Bunquin Hollow were a unit, inseparable. The Hollow was a shepherd mutt, as of some once-great, now fallen family. My father said there was in him "the blood of kings and the blood of the common dog." In what my father called "the worst possible department," he was hopelessly confused. He would mount, in public, anything except a member of the opposite sex of his own species. Cars, poles, people's legs, the Bunquin was seen astride them all, hind legs lewdly thrusting. Passionately joined to a fence-post, he would look around to see who was watching and, when his eyes met yours, would seem ashamed, beseeching understanding for this uncontrollable urge of his. He was a constant source of embarrassment to the mothers of Luby Line, because the question, "What's that dog doing?" was one often asked by their children. I asked it myself, more than once, but never got an answer. My mother called the Bunquin "that woman's animal," in reference to the rumour that he and Harold's mother were, in some ways, much alike. The Bunquin went about with head hung low, and looked at you with upraised rheumy eyes, as if he hoped that, forgiven in advance, you might not kick him so hard. But it wasn't kicking that had reduced the Bunquin Hollow to such a state—it was Harold. Harold's hero was Tarzan, and Harold had a rubber knife and a leopard-skin loincloth to prove it. Though the Bunquin Hollow came up to Harold's chest, Harold liked to wrestle with him. Summer and winter, in loincloth or duffel-coat, Harold leapt on the Bunquin Hollow and, holding him round the belly, rolled him over and over. Yodelling like Tarzan, he would work his knife-hand free, and hold it, prior to plunging, high in the air. He would wait until the Hollow was on top of him, belly up, four paws in mute surrender, tongue panting, and then he would look down at us until, like emperors of old, we turned thumbs down, at which signal he would stab the rubber knife into the Bunquin's belly.

Just Plain Joe was the first of the Fatal Four I met. I came upon him one day in the woods, sitting under a tree; despite its being late September, he was wearing only shorts. Sitting still, his skin so pale, he might have been a mushroom. He seemed to be asleep, and a huge bag of "nice-one" alleys lay between his legs. Now and then, with eyes still closed, his head against the tree, he pressed his legs about the bag, and rubbed and rolled his thighs, his bum on the moss going up and down, the alleys crunching loudly.

"What are ye doin'?" I said.

His body jumped, and he looked at me as if I had yanked him from a dream. Then he grinned and put his hands on the bag of alleys. "Guess," he said, flush and dream fading from him, "jus' try an' guess how many."

I shrugged. "Six hundred?"

He smiled and shook his head. "One thousand," he said, "three hundred and seventy-seven."

Just Plain Joe, or J.P., as we called him, was proud of the fact that his bag of alleys was the biggest on Luby Line. And he grew to like me because I was biggest, rumoured smartest and a veritable repository of world records, one of which I would give him as one might a lollipop to pacify a baby. "C'mon Bobby," he'd say, tugging on my sleeve, "gimme one." Unless told a world record, he would start to cry. But once told one he would take it off somewhere and, lying down with hands clasped behind his head, knees drawn up and with a pillow tucked between his legs, grunt over it for hours. "Grunting," we called it, and J.P. grunted a lot, on his back, on his side, always on the moss, grinding, grunting, red in the face, pedaling the pillow, as if in pursuit of something he never could quite catch. I would tell him, for instance, that the tallest tree in the world was the California redwood, at 750 feet, and he would go off and grunt about it. I doubt if he knew more about what he was doing than we did. In mid-grunt, his mouth and eyes would open wide, as if he could not believe what was happening, as if some deeper implication of the number I had given him was just beginning to show itself. The moment always passed, however, and he'd soon be back to bum a number. "C'mon Bobby," he'd say, "gimme anudder one." Other times, he'd ask me to come grunt with him.

"Ye wanna come grunt?" he'd say. I would tell him no, though in truth I liked the look of it. I was my mother's little bloodhound, able to sniff out mustn't-touch-its, able to tell a thing was bad, without even knowing why.

On Sundays, once the roads were free of snow, my father took us driving, up the Shore, sometimes, on rainy days, on fine ones down to Sounder's Bay, around the ponds a mile east inland. My mother rarely came with us, so we invited Harold's Mother along. J.P., Barney, Floods and I called her Harold's Mother. She said we could take our pick between that and Mrs. Upton-Downton-Huntington-Smith. Her real name was Paula Dunne, *née* Benson, but, to her husband's ongoing mortification, she corresponded and introduced herself as Mrs. Upton-Downton-Huntington-Smith, and would, with tongueless cheek, refuse to speak to anyone who called her anything else. It was for her invention of this name, and her ability to cast names like spells on people, she became known as the Wicked Witch of Luby Line. It was said that you had to be careful and keep your distance, that she could not name you if you were more than a hundred yards away, but that if you came within her zap-zone, the Wicked Witch of Luby Line would do a devil's baptism, sprinkle you with deholied holy water, or the pee of spooks and goblins—and give you a name that would stick for the rest of your life.

She was a witch for the way she looked, too, though tall and lovely, possessed of a body she never had got used to. Her brown hair was somehow always wet, and hung in deprecating curls about her face. She had arms and legs so long, her shoulders hunched in compensation, and her clothes pulled up her back, as if she was hanging by her collar from a string. Her chest was more deep than full, so concave it made her breasts seem small. She looked loose and unmade up, as if she might some day simply go to pieces. A witch, my father said, who needed a broom, not so much to ride as to sweep herself together.

My father didn't mind her coming with us on those Sunday drives. Nor did Harold's father, who, according to Harold, worked so hard all week long, he couldn't seem to get out of bed Saturdays until it was dark. On Sundays, having been up all night drinking and staring fixedly at a test-pattern, he usually went to bed when the rest of the family was heading out to morning mass.

The car was a purple Vauxhall, for which my father would not tell how much he paid, and which looked like a bloated Volkswagen —or, as he put it, "a hearse in a hippie funeral." The Fatal Four and I, the Bunquin Hollow and all, rode in the back, my father and Harold's Mother in the front. Or that, at least, was how we sat before the car got going. We boys did all we could to restrain the Bunquin Hollow. We sat on him, the five of us, like huge dead weights about his neck, tried with our bodies to block the space between the two front seats, but to no avail. When the car began to move, the Bunquin Hollow would come suddenly to attention. Ears up straight, apprised of peril, he would touch his nose to the dome-light and move his eyes from side to side, as if cooly assessing the situation. Once the car was cruising, however, the full weight of the paradox would hit him: he was doing 50, yet somehow standing still. Such mad mechanics was more than he could bear. To restore order to the universe, *he* must go 50 miles an hour—which, by leaping in grim and silent panic from windshield to windshield, he tried to do. Now pawing the front dash, now skating up the back window, toenails clicking like castanets, he would, every few seconds, catch sight of himself in the rear-view mirror, and stop and look and, inspired by the vision of panting terror that looked back at him, go again; and would, thus, in five minutes, climb the scale to the highest pitch of panic, and then suddenly stop and go to sleep. Or, sometimes, in his horror to see the world so much in motion, the Bunquin Hollow would pause in the front seat to embrace my father. His forelegs coyly about my father's neck, his rear end on the steering-wheel, he would blow the horn each time he licked my father's face. Once, we were stopped by an oncoming policeman, who professed himself surprised that a car driven by a dog looking the wrong way was able to stay on the road. Something had to be done, so one Sunday we cornered the Bunquin Hollow in Harold's house, and forced him, at the point of Harold's rubber knife, to remain still while we put a blindfold on him. Later, in the car, he sat quietly, head high and facing forward, the blindfold somehow lending him a strange and solemn dignity, which caused Floods to turn toward him every few minutes and say in his Foreign Legion accent: "Cigarette?"

We went hiking, sometimes, along the shore of Gull Pond, on the way to which we had to cross a river. There was a makeshift bridge, too narrow for cars, so from there we went on foot. Once, on the way back, crossing that part of the bridge which consisted only of two telephone-poles, laid side by side like railway tracks, Harold's Mother somehow found herself, one high heel on each pole, unable to move. She stood there, all six feet of her, her long legs spreadeagling space, heels dug in but slowly slipping, her dress behind a wind-wagged tail. "Oh my God," she said, "oh my God," her fists and breasts in spiteful terror going up and down. "I'll save you Paula," my father said. As Harold remarked later, it sounded like a movie.

Harold's Mother had been crossing behind my father. The rest of us, including the Bunquin Hollow, had already crossed. When we heard her scream, we turned around and there they were, the two of them, standing face to face, my father on the plywood part of the bridge, Harold's Mother on the poles:

"Paula?"

"Ted?"

Probably, almost certainly, it could have been done some other way. Probably, it never occurred to my father to simply reach out and pull her to safety. Instead, he lay belly-down on the plywood and, extending his arms, took hold of Harold's Mother's legs, just above the ankles. She screamed with each intake of breath, "Ahh-ahh-ahh." And no wonder, for as she confessed later, she had closed her eyes the minute she got stuck and had kept them closed, and so when my father grabbed her by the legs, she thought some "river thing" had come to claim her.

"TED," she cried, *"Ted, my God, what are you doing?"*

"I'm saving you," my father said.

"Saving me?"

"Yes, for God's sake, saving you, what do you think I'm doing?"

Harold's Mother opened her eyes and looked down at him. "I think it's all a plot to get a look up my dress."

They both began to laugh, Harold's Mother hysterically.

"Make a run for it," my father said, "I won't let go."

"WHAT?"

"Make a run for it Paula."

"Make a run for it Mom," Harold shouted.

"Make a run for it Harold's Mother," the rest of us said together.

She rolled her eyes, as if to say "I swear to God." And then she ran. And my father, helping her, seemed to lift her legs as she came toward him—until at last she hit the plywood and toppled like a wind-up toy; her knees about his ears, her face fiilled the space between his boots, and her high heels came off in his hands. We all cheered and, more or less astride my father, she began to crawl toward us. She did not stand until she reached the bank, at which point she turned round and, taking my father's head in her hands, planted a kiss on top. When he gave her the shoes, she touched his head with one high heel and said, "I dub thee Sir Pants-a-lot." We all laughed. Harold's Mother raised her dress then and, smiling, curtsied low, one long leg behind her. Looking up with eyes aflutter, she said, "I shall be your Lady Anywhere, a damsel in dis dress." My father went white and tried to laugh, but Harold's Mother took his hand. "And I should tell you now," she said, "I shall require quite a lot of saving." We cheered again as my father, red-faced now, pulled his hand from hers and started up the bank toward the car.

We were like a family, I, my father, Harold's Mother, the Fatal Four and the Bunquin Hollow. We saw a lot of each other. Almost every Sunday, we drove along the Shore. We sang songs, and played games like "Pin the Tail on the Bunquin" and Harold's Mother's favourite, "Embarrass the Boys." As we were driving along, she would slowly turn her head and, making what she called her "Bella-Boris face," would say in the voice of a baritone ghoul, "Guess what time it is."

"*Oh no—*"

"Yes, it's time to play 'Embarrass the Boys.' Mmm-ya-ha-ha. Pull over Pants-a-lot."

"We're not going in," I'd say, "you can't make us." This might have been true if not for J.P., who started bawling every time they threatened to withold ice cream, or abandon us on the road. "Embarrass the Boys" was a game they played on unsuspecting store-keepers. In the store, my father would shake hands with the man behind the counter, but would say nothing. The man would look at Harold's Mother. She would call him down the counter and whisper: "That's just his way. He can't speak, but he likes to say hello." Then Harold's Mother would extend *her* hand. "I am Mrs. Upton-Downton-Huntington-Smith," she'd say, "and this is my dog, the Bunquin Hollow." The man, eyebrows by now quite roundly raised, might wonder why the dog was blindfolded.

All in all, it was not very nice, but my father and Harold's Mother were so caught up with one another, they never seemed to notice.

I saw them once, not doing it but having done, lying on a blanket in the woods. It was summer, Sunday afternoon, and the trees were full of hag-hair, up high so thick the sun could not come through. It was dark, their bodies white against the green. She was lying on her side, faced full-length away; somewhere, the other side of that wide bare back, my father was laughing. But all I saw was, now and then, his hands, on her, telling her things I could not understand.

She was with him when, later, he came into the house, naked beside him when he kissed my mother's cheek. She was there, a mix of sweat and the musk-sweet smell of flowers, my mother must have wondered where she came from. Most of that night I could not sleep, for wonder of her body on the moss. And when, at first light, I did nod off, I left one world behind. For it was of her and her dress I had my dream. When I woke, I thought I'd wet the bed, and that my pee had, overnight, turned thick and changed its colour. From this, I shrank with the usual horror and put it from my mind.

That summer we tried for something as high and final as Babel, took up each day some long-standing challenge of nature, number, time and space. We cut down all the trees in Kellies—or thought by noon the job was done because we'd managed three. We roamed the

64

woods to gather together all the blasty boughs that ever were, and made a mound so high and wide we could not get the last ones up; and saw, going home, as many again, and on the hills whole groves of orange. We tried one day to stop a river, dropping stones down one by one. By dark the pool was still so deep we could not see the bottom. We counted crows, a murder that looked a half-mile long, and we gave them each a name. But, when we were done, they changed places and made us start all over again. We tried to make a city of moss. The moss came up as clean as sod. You could bare a square of the forest floor for the site of a house in minutes, and make poles of pulled-up trees, and leave the knots to hang the moss on. We made ten houses and, a morning in August, found them gone, found plots of faded earth. J.P., at the completion of each new house, asked its number, then went inside to grunt. It must have seemed he was in the number, the walls of moss like"six" around him. When the houses were gone, and he had to rely on his own imagination again, he was like an addict getting by on a lesser kind of dope. We bought him the *Guinness Book of World Records*, and by the end of the month, he was doing a page a day.

One day, frightened by what my father was doing, I decided I would run away. J.P. cried, and said he wanted to run away too. I told him that it was his turn next, that instead of all of us running away together, we would run away one by one, so as not to draw attention to ourselves. The plan was for me to go deep in the woods, and there build a moss house where no-one would find it. Not even the Fatal Four were to know where it was, so that, no matter how much their parents tortured them, they could not tell on me. Every even hour, I was to leave at least one message, under a tree by a rock on the edge of the woods. The Fatal Four, taking turns, were to come and get the messages every odd hour, and were to do whatever they said.

The problem with this was J.P., who, instead of waiting his turn, hid all day behind the rock and grabbed up all the messages, so that he could use them when *he* ran away. As my father said later, the messages, in the order in which they were written, were like the record of a mind dwindling down to madness. From the relative stability of the early-morning, "Bring more buns," to the first incipient sign of panic, "What's happening?" to the noontime note of dark despair, "Trust no-one–not even the fat man," to the euphoric, almost lyric delusions of two and four o'clock, "It's nice here–it's so nice I'm never coming back," to the final, suicidal shout at six: "Tell them I'm dead."

J.P., when he read the last one, displaying an ingenuousness I would have thought beyond even him, ran home crying and told his mother I was dead. This was at seven, by which time my parents had not begun to worry because Harold had earlier told our maid that I was going to his house for supper. J.P.'s mother called my father and asked him to come over. When he got there, she and her husband were puzzling over the notes on the kitchen table. "He's run away, Ted," she said, "and J.P. won't say where." J.P. by now was bawling loudly, protesting that he did not know where, and wondering why *they* wanted to know, since in any case I was dead. "He's not dead J.P.," my father said. "He is," J.P. said, "I think he starved to death." My father then called Harold's Mother, who threatened to give Harold the nickname that she had, for love of him, been withholding all these years, unless he told them where I was. Harold broke down and brought them to the rock. They posted J.P.'s mother there, in case I came back with another note, and my father, J.P.'s father, Harold's Mother and the Bunquin Hollow began to comb the woods.

I, by then, was hungry and thirsty, and long past wondering what had happened. I was sitting in my house of moss, feeling sorry for myself, crying now and then, whenever my mind called up some better-than-average little-boy-lost-unloved-in-the-woods image. I would show them. I would wait until it was dark, and then strike out for home and become so hopelessly lost they would never find me. Along the grid, where moss and pole did not quite meet, I could see the sky, like a mesh of light thrown over the house. Watching it fade, I fell asleep. When I woke, the night was down so close I could not breathe nor move. The air itself was black and thick and wrapped like arms around me. The hag, to those who have not known her, cannot be described. Awake, but somehow still locked into sleep, so self-contained you cannot move, you know the hag is off to one side, watching. And it could be her breath, or a sound as of a dress so long it sweeps the floor, that lets you know she's coming. I heard her outside, walking, at first slowly, around the house —at my feet, then past the open door, then at my head, then down along the wall and, once around, on her way around again. And then she was walking faster, and soon so fast the sounds were all one sound, not loud, but like some winding whisper that, at any moment, might stop and rush inside. Just when all seemed lost, there was another sound in that one and, unlike it, growing louder. It was my name, called out over and over, lowered like a rope into my sleep. "*Bobby—Bobby—Bobby*." Sobbing, eyes closed against the darkness, I got up and ran straight through the wall, into my father's arms.

When we got home, I told my father about the dream. He said he had lately begun to think there were three kinds of dreams— nightmares, nicemares and nomares. Nightmares were bad dreams, nicemares good dreams. And nomares were dreams which, upon waking, you knew you'd had but couldn't remember. I wasn't sure what he meant by nomares, so he told me to imagine a movie which, once they left the movie-house, no-one could remember—all they knew was that they'd seen a movie, nothing else. They could go to that movie over and over, forever, and never know it. He said it was possible there was only one nomare, which everyone had from time to time. Everyone had the same nomare, but no-one could remember it. Wouldn't it be funny, he said, if the only thing everyone had in common was something that no-one could remember?

And before I went to sleep, my mother held my scratched-up face in her hands, and wondered if becoming an altar-boy might not make a man of me.

CHAPTER 4

We moved the middle of October, to a house in the old town. Leaving Luby Line, I rode a chair in Rennie's truck, high atop the furniture, waving goodbye and crying my eyes out for all the world to see.

For the Fatal Four and I, a kind of friendship lingered. Having to walk to school again, and now, in junior high, forced into a timetable out of synch with theirs, the only time I saw them was some days after school when, turned out by the janitor, they waited an hour on the steps, sometimes cold and wet. It wasn't so bad in the fall, but I remember looking out one winter afternoon while putting my boots on and seeing them there, their backs to the wind, stamping up and down as if they had to pee. It couldn't go on. By January, only J.P. waited, Though we said a dozen goodbyes, he kept on coming back. I tried leaving by another door, but after a week he figured out what I was doing, and was there waiting when I came out. "J.P.," I said, "after today you don't have to wait any more, okay?" "Okay," he said, and two days later he was back again. It might have gone on forever, except that one night, lying in bed, I realized what was happening. He was counting on me to come up with a way of ending it that would not make it seem he was betraying me. So the next time we met, I told him that every day from now on I had altar-boy practice after school. And he smiled, more happy, it seemed, than he had ever been.

Our new house was White's. The day we moved, my mother stood in the front yard at White's and, with her box of hair in one hand, her purse in the other, raised them up like offerings. "Oh Teddy," she said, her arms spread wide as she ran toward the door, "let's live here forever." On the topmost step she stumbled and, arms still spread, stretched out full length, her face upraised in accusation. "Not bad Agnes," my father said, "have you been practising long?" The TV legless in his arms, he hurried up the steps and went inside. My mother had Rennie, his truck not yet unloaded, go ask the priest to come and bless the empty rooms. I felt right away that, though the walls and floors and windows were bare, that house had something in it. And as we followed the priest from room to room and he, like an exterminator, sprinkled holy water everywhere, I discovered what my father would call "spookie hot-spots." That house by day was full of ghosts, pockets of chattering silence that moved about. I felt them most whenever I looked out a window. It was like looking out with someone else's eyes.

For a while, we were not unhappy. My father discovered that, by strapping two pillows to his backside, he could slide down the stairs with minimum injury. The pillows he chose were large and, when tied together, and their corners fixed with reins of rope, like tobog-gans. My father, sitting, knees drawn up, forearms vertical, tight to his chest, his fists beneath his chin, pulled the reins both front and back and was sandwiched safely inside. He made a sled for me, too. His he called the Teddy-tank; mine he called the Bob-sled. He offered to make one for my mother but, smiling, she declined. While my mother, in the hallway, sat and watched, my father and I had races. Every night after supper he would let loose with several closed-fist trumpet blasts of pari-mutuel music. My mother, sighing stoically, would go to her chair, and I would run to my room and, grabbing the Bob-sled, wait at the top of the stairs. My father had me give him a two-step head start because of what he called my "lower co-efficient of friction." Down we would go, side by side on the stairs until, at the bottom step, we would be airborne for a while. Then, landing, we would shoot across the linoleum and, dropping the reins, crash feet first into the wall. Sometimes, so as to make a rattling noise, my father would scream going down, and his voice would have in it a kind of resigned hopelessness, like that of someone falling from a great height.

Once, as we were getting ready for a race, my father lost control of the Teddy-tank and, pulled round by inertia, went down the stairs backwards. I watched from the top. All the way down, his mouth and eyes wide open, he looked at me as if he thought it likely he would not see me again, or as if hoping, by the expressions on my face, to guide himself through the obstacles below. When I winced, however, all he did was scream, and shortly afterwards, smashed into my mother's chair, sending her flying onto the floor in a great flurry of skirt and wool and knitting-needles.

From that time on, to avoid further surprise attacks, and to keep property damage to a minimum, my mother volunteered her ser-vices as a buffer between the Teddy-tank and the wall. (I was so skinny, I posed no threat, even to Gyproc.) From where she waited, on hands and knees at the end of the hall, most of the stairs were obscured by ceiling and shadow, so when my father shouted "GO," and he and I, a moment later, came roaring out of the darkness, she must have had but scant seconds to react. Having not only to stop my father but also to avoid a collision with me, she would keep off to one side and, sitting back on her haunches with arms outstretched, lunge laterally like a soccer goalie. Most of the time, she would catch my father on one shoulder and send him spinning harmlessly toward the other wall. Sometimes, though, she panicked and, shout-ing his name, threw herself at him, and with arms about his neck, was dragged along behind him like an anchor. Every night, when it was over, she would get up off the floor and shake her head, as if in disbelief that a woman who did this by night could by day be an assistant superintendent of education. (An afternoon a few months later, my mother would come home early from work and, opening the door, step into the hallway just in time to hear my father and Harold's Mother start from the top of the stairs. My father and Harold's Mother, naked in the Teddy-tank, would come roaring out of the darkness, she in front, squealing loudly, with knees pressed tight to her bouncing breasts, he behind her, his arms about her belly. And there would be a moment when, though they could see my mother below, they could not stop what they were doing, but would have to go on doing it, on down to the bottom while she watched.)

My mother, since the night my father found me in the woods, had spoken several times with the priest about my becoming an altar-boy. There were some problems. Altar-boys, it seemed, were con-scripted; they did not enlist. And the priests, and the nuns who did what amounted to a scouting report on all boys coming of altar age, were unimpressed with me. The priest showed my mother the nuns' report, and my mother made a copy and confronted me with it one night before the races. The nuns, for the past year or so, had been rating me on a scale of one to five in those ten qualities deemed by the priest essential in the modern altar-boy—the Virtues, as my father called them. My father, in the Teddy-tank on the kitchen floor, in foetal racing position, the pillows draped round him like gigantic diapers, made disapproving noises with his tongue as my mother read the charges against me:

VIRTUE	SCORE
1. Is of a happy disposition and cheerful with others	1
2. Is willing and able to work with others	1
3. Welcomes discipline; knows it is good for him	1
4. Knows that elders know better than he	1
5. Is willing to take on responsibility	1
6. Takes part in mass; sings hymns; knows Confiteor	1
7. Is punctual	1
8. Is neat and clean; has comb, handkerchief, etc.	2
9. Has strong sense of purpose; knows where he is going	1
10. Gives general impression of holiness	1

My father punctuated my low score on Number 10 with a loud clucking noise, and freed one finger to wag it back and forth. My mother looked at him. "Teddy, for God's sake," she said, "get up off the floor." He released the reins of the Teddy-tank and, getting up, went into the living-room. My mother looked at me.

"Well?"

"Well what?"

"Well, what have you got to say for yourself?"

I shrugged.

"You have to get between 25 and 30 before they'll even consider you for the altar. You got 11."

"I didn't know they were keeping score."

"Don't you get smart now."

"I'm not."

"Well—all right then. Bobby, they don't think you're bad or anything. It's just that—well, the way Father put it, you're always off in another world. You're a dreamy little boy, he said. Are you?"

I supposed that I was.

"Well then. What are we going to do about it?"

"I dunno."

She took my hand.

"I have a surprise," she said.

"A surprise?"

"Yes. I've talked to Father about it, and he's decided to give you a second chance. If you can get your score up to 25 by after Christmas, he'll let you join the altar-boys. And remember Bobby, the sisters will be watching."

I tried hard, I really did. I did everything she told me to do. "No wonder they think you have no sense of purpose," she said. "Straighten your back, Bobby, straighten your back." I tried, but she was dissatisfied. "Pretend you have a halo," she said, "and unless you walk straight, it'll fall off." This worked a little better. Whenever I saw a nun, I walked as if with a piece of plywood in my shirt; and if the nun said hello, I turned only my head toward her, and went on by, like a soldier past a grandstand.

"I'm sure you sing hymns Bobby," my mother said, "haven't I heard you singing hymns?" "No," I said. "Well, you should sing then. When you're in church, sing loud and look up at the ceiling." My back ramrod straight, I sung loud and looked so hard at the ceiling I couldn't see anything else. "Careful dear," my mother said, "you'll hurt yourself," and, putting her hand on my head, pushed it down about ten degrees.

"The best way to be on time Bobby," she said, "is to get there much too early." Thus began my parents' practice of dropping me off in the schoolyard at 7.30 every morning on their way to work. My mother somehow arranged to have the janitor let me ino the basement, where I would sit at one of the old desks and go back to sleep.

"Try smiling," she said. "You should smile more Bobby. When

you look happy, you'll feel happy." I smiled. My body stiff as an android, I smiled relentlessly. I smiled in the classroom until the teacher asked me what was so funny and, when I wouldn't tell her, gave me extra homework.

"You should let people know you like them Bobby," my mother said.

"But what about I don't like them?"

"Then make them think you do."

"How?"

"Well. Be helpful. Do the boards. Stay after school. Join something."

I did the boards every day, and I joined the Glee Club. It was awful. We had to sing and look sad. At the Christmas concert, we opened with "Barbara Allen," and it made me feel so mournful I started to cry. By the time Barbara Allen "bursted out a cryin'" I was bawling loudly. And I continued to do so for the rest of the evening, front row centre, a picture of grief, lending, as my father said, "a somewhat inappropriate dirge-like quality" to such up-tempo favourites as "She'll be Comin' Round the Mountain" and "Will the Circle be Unbroken?" By "The Ode to Newfoundland" I was weeping uncontrollably. I put the damper on what was, otherwise, a rousing rendition of "O Canada," and closed by singing "God Save the Queen" as if I had just got word the queen was dead.

The nuns gave my mother a progress report the first week of December. It was bad news. After almost a month and a half of intensive training, my score had climbed only 3 points, to fourteen, still far short of 25, and with less than a month to go, it looked like I wasn't going to make it. Some desperate, radical measure was needed, some overnight transmuting miracle. I would go to bed Bobby O'Malley, and wake up the Golden Boy. "That's easy," my father later confessed he said to my mother in bed, "tell them he's decided he wants to be a priest." He said he meant it as a joke, and that it seemed she ignored or did not hear him.

But on the last day before Christmas vacation, the priest had me come to his house for cake and a cup of tea. He said my mother had told him of my decision and, though he was glad to hear it, he felt he should say how important it was that I first think long and hard, and then make up my mind. As always, the priest had got my tongue and I could not say a word. But then, I wouldn't have anyway. I was not about to ask a priest what in God's name he was talking about. Nor, when I figured out what he was talking about, was I about to tell him that my mother was a liar. He danced his way round "priest" and "priesthood," withheld them, as he might withhold the sacraments from one not yet baptized. He said that becoming an altar-boy was the best thing I could do. It would give me a chance to learn more about the Church. He told me to pray for guidance. He said he would pray, and so would my parents, and all the nuns. And he hoped I'd know by Christmas next if I really had the call. He went on and on. By the end, I was piled so high with explanations and cautions and words of advice, I knew I would never find a way to tell him the truth. As he spoke, it was as if he had something in his hands that he did not know was mine, and which I, until now, had not known was missing. He was turning it over and over, assessing its possibilities, and I wanted to reach across and grab it back. Instead, when I left, I left it with him, as if it wasn't anything I couldn't live without.

For Christmas, I was given a scarlet soutane, a white surplice and red-and-black tartan slippers. Dola and Rennie and the girls came by Christmas night, and I, in my suit, was put on parade, made to walk and turn about and raise my arms to show the sleeves. "It's the rage in Rome," my father said, to snorts of laughter from Cheryl and Sharon. Ambrosia refused to watch. She went off to the kitchen with a box of chocolates, only to return an hour later, looking as if she had rubbed them on her face and fingers before eating them. Hands pressed tight to chocolate cheeks, she whispered something to my mother, who smiled and called me over. "Bobby," she whispered, cupping her hand and putting her mouth to my ear, "Ambrosia wants to know if she can wear your uniform." Ambrosia was beaming and licking her fingers. "She better wash her hands first," I said. "And her face." Ten minutes later, Ambrosia was off to the bathroom with a bar of soap and my altar outfit. In another ten, she emerged to loud applause, holding her breath, as we realized later, so as not to pop any buttons. The soutane was such a tight fit, she walked about stiff-legged, unable to lower her arms to her sides, like an over-inflated cherub. She sat, all but paralyzed, on the chesterfield, able only to move her head from side to side. Her hands in her lap, she managed to hold out for an amazing length of time. Had we not, after her triumphant entry, turned to other things, we might have noticed, as we seemed to do in retrospect, that all the while she sat there, her face grew redder and redder, that after two minutes she began to squirm uncontrollably, and that whenever we looked at her, she smiled by bulging her eyes and pressing her lips even tighter together. We might have noticed that, by some super-human effort, she got herself on the floor, and there began, quite unobtrusively, to lose consciousness. It was my mother who saw her, who, though not one to stick her nose into other people's business, wondered if it might not be a matter of some concern that Ambrosia was turning blue-black in the face. Dola shrieked, and Rennie, bending over his daughter, asked her what was wrong. Clawing and kicking the air, on her back like an overturned beetle, Ambrosia was beyond answering. "It's the soutane, Rennie," my mother said. Rennie, with thumb and forefinger, plucked the collar from between Ambrosia's chins, and frantically popped the button. Ambrosia, with a series of long deflating gasps, came back to the world of the living. And ten minutes later, I was again dressed as an altar-boy.

It was my mother who announced I was going to be a priest. Cheryl and Sharon spent the rest of the night inventing phony confessions. They fell on their knees in front of me, saying "Bless me Bobby, I have sinned," and followed me around the house, demanding penance.

To be a brain was bad enough, but to want to be a priest was worse. At school, I was given a name rumoured to have been invented by Harold's Mother—"Rev." The altar-boys wrote on my church-cellar locker, "The Reverend Robert O'Malley." At home, my father called me "Your Holiness." "If it please Your Holiness to pass the salt," he'd say. "What does Your Holiness make of the gravy?"

Among the altar-boys was a tall, pale, Jesuitical young man with the unlikely name of Archie Bishop. Archie Bishop liked me because he, too, was going to be a priest. And I liked him. I liked him for the way he fouled up the Confiteor. Because of a severe speech impediment, he could not get the Latin right. It was a language, as he put it, "with an appalling numbuh of etheth." Archie could pronounce neither his "ss" nor his "rs." Everyone called him Archie-bird, pronouncing it Ahchiebud. "I thay, ithn't that Ahchiebud Bithop?" they'd say. Archie would answer, "Ahchiebald, not Ahchiebud." Often, at mass, he would get flustered, and not only mispronounce the words, but forget them; or, as on one memorable occasion, lapse into unintentional mockery, saying, instead of *"mea culpa, mea culpa," "mea mea, culpa culpa,"* for which irreverence he was slapped by the priest in full view of the congregation.

Archie wore grey slacks, white socks, black shoes, what he called "my bwutteth blue blathuh" and the only knotted necktie St. Stephen's had ever seen. He also wore cufflinks and carried a briefcase. He came to school with coloured leads, matching pen-and-pencil sets and a souvenir lunchbox from Ste.-Anne de Beaupré. He arrived every morning at five before nine, stepped out of his mother's car and, briefcase in hand, strode briskly up the school steps, like an executive on his way to work.

When you were with Archie, he acted as if something very important was happening somewhere else, which, if it were not for the fact that he was with you, he would be taking part in. He would look at his watch and shake his head in exasperation, as if people he was supposed to meet were forever failing to show up. Even in an empty room, he would stand on tiptoe, as if searching for a face in a crowd. He looked, my father said, like someone next to last in a line a million long, waiting to have his picture taken by what was rumoured to be the last camera on earth. I had never seen anyone so self-conscious. "Relax Archie," I'd tell him, "relax." "Welactha-thun Wobert," he'd say, "is jutht a wathte of time."

We became such good friends that we were able to talk to one another about what he called "the facth of life." I was having wet dreams. I believed that, inside me, something was wrong, that every night vital fluids were draining from my body. I got up the nerve to ask Archie about it and, lazily turning from page to page of the *Summa contra gentiles,* he assured me that such emissions were not unusual.

Women's breasts, I asserted, had milk in them, and were not, as was widely believed, subject to enlargement by prolonged holding of breath.

"Cowwect," Archie said, and told me how he had once seen his sister's breasts. "You'hh awah of the nipple of courth," he said. I assured him that I was.

"Girls have babies," I said.

"Yeth," Archie said, "they do."

As it turned out, Archie knew something about everything except the sex act itself. It was a most informative afternoon. Masturbation he described as "the heinouth pwactith of pulling onth penith." He said that, looking at girls, he sometimes got erections. I confessed that I, too, had had this happen. Blushing, he looked at his book, and told me what men and women did together. I was mortified, but also glad that, finally, someone had said it.

I had often wondered, before becoming an altar-boy, what went on behind the mass, what the sacristy was like, what was on the other side of all those doors that opened out on the altar. It hardly seemed possible that, for those who took part, there was any life apart from this, that among those essential to the celebration of this mystery was a boy for whom no-one could think of a better nickname than Rat.

When, after mass, the priest and the altar-boys left the altar, I wanted them wrapped in consecrated cloth and put behind glass, as at school we were told was done with the sacred vessels. My first day as an altar-boy, before going down to dress in the cellar, I looked round the sacristy and I knew the mass, for me, would never be the same again. The days that followed were like days backstage at a magic show, watching how the tricks were done.

I was terrified of the priest, certain that never in a million years, in front of him and a church full of people, would I be able to

77

handle the cruets of water and wine without spilling or dropping or breaking them; nor ring the angelus bells without making it sound like the advance of a colony of lepers; nor manage what, even now, seems to me should have been one of the twelve tasks of Hercules—the untangling of the four chains of a thurible, so as to raise the silver cap and put some incense in.

The priest was never more to me than a massive mound of vestments, from which there darted, now and then, a hand so big it could pick a boy up by the bum—but which, more often, was aimed for the back of his head. The priest went about some days and swatted us like so many flies. One minute you were standing, minding your own business, doing your best not to look at him; the next, you were reeling, head ringing, across the room, victim of a surprise attack. There was no motive, neither malicious nor punitive, in any of this. It was done randomly, almost unconsciously. He might have been a doting devil, having fun with a flock of cherubs. On his good days, most of us were punch-drunk before mass even started. Ducking was permitted, as were multiple swings on his part, but there were no time-outs. He might have his hands on your shoulders, telling you what he wanted done, and—SMACK—he was picking you up off the floor. My father said that no-one not wearing a hockey helmet should stand within ten feet of him. He didn't think it was funny, this strange impulse of the priest's, and advised that the next time he hit me I should hit him back—"One good sock in the sacred groin, and you'll hear no more from him." My mother, when I told her what the priest was doing, saw it as a kind of endearing nervous tic which, if brought to his attention, might embarrass him. It was quite exhausting, really, having to be always on guard, not only in the sacristy, but during mass as well. Those not serving mass were relatively safe, but, during the Preface, when he was required to stretch out his arms, the priest was known to come round with his hands from behind, and give one or both of the servers so subtle a tap on the head that not even the practised eye of a nun could pick it up.

Asked to describe his character, I could not. He never spoke, except to scold, or pass on some instructions, never acknowledged our existence except as things to be batted about. It did not occur to me to wonder if he was like or unlike other priests, or like or unlike other men. He was "the priest," the only one Kellies had had in my lifetime, the very definition of the word. Even when my mother began bringing priests home, my view of him went unchanged. He was "the priest," the others imitations. The younger priests took up a place in my scheme of things similar to that taken up by post-Vatican-II Catholics in my mother's, and by post-expansion hockey players in my father's—they would never, no matter how good, be of the supremely great.

What struck me most about priests was their calculated loneliness, and the idea they had that the man was closest to God who was furthest from his fellow men.

Our priest was of the old school. He asked nothing of his congregation but absolute subservience, to him and, where those few were concerned who recognized the distinction, to God.

He was asthmatic and had, as far as I could tell, about one attack per week. He wheezed from sentence to sentence, and was frequently out of breath. At all times, he carried on his person a pocket respirator that was so large he had to remove his false teeth to put it in his mouth. This he would do in one urgent motion at the onset of an attack—yanking out the plate with one hand, he would insert the respirator with the other; and, as if in sympathy with his mouth, his eyes would bulge. He would find a wall and, resting against it, seem oblivious, transported, focusing inward on the subsiding pulse of his body. That one moment, eyes closed, head against the wall, his great chest heaving up and down, he ceased to be the priest. Exultant, drunk with relief, he forgot himself and us. His face, contorted by the respirator, his mouth as if pulled round it, would all at once relax and soften to a smile.

Before every mass, we dressed in the cellar, and waited there until the priest called us to the sacristy. The "cellar" was that part of the church basement which was lit by a lone bulb. It was not defined by walls, but by darkness pressing round. There *was* one wall that went downside the stairwell. Along it sat the senior altar-boys. The rest of us sat opposite, our backs to the darkness, hoping that nothing was coming up behind us.

The church basement was a kind of resting-place for statues. Statues broken or superseded were put there, and sometimes we got up the nerve to turn round and search the darkness for them. You had to look a long time, until your eyes grew accustomed to the dark, and then, one by one, they would appear. And each one came clear gradually— head and torso first, then outstretched arms, then the line of a cloak and, finally, a pedestal. If you looked long enough, you could see them all, a host of saints in silhouette, a gathering of shadows.

It was said that a nun who misbehaved was banished to the basement and was never seen again. She was there, somewhere, among the saints, crying, lighting candles. One morning, the janitor came downstairs, and found an ancient paschal candle burned down next to nothing, and a thurible, smoking incense, hanging from the rafters. A little fellow named Loyola got to the cellar first one morning, and the next boy to arrive found him in the sacristy, rambling on to the priest about some headless Virgin that had chased him up the stairs. Loyola got a going-over for that. One day, while he was sitting on the benches, the senior altar-boys grabbed him from behind and, dragging him off into the darkness, tied him to a limbless torso and left him there ten minutes.

Not that I fared much better. One day, Norman, the oldest altar-boy, came downstairs after mass with a handful of little plastic pouches and gave them all to me. I remember what was written on the back of them, though, at the time, I did not understand it: "This package contains one (1) multi-coloured, lubricated, long-ribbed prophylactic."

"It's your turn," Norman said.

"For what?" I said.

"To put the candle-covers on."

"The candle-covers?"

Norman explained that, after a Requiem Mass, all the candles on the altar had to be individually covered as a sign of respect for the dead. "I better show you how to do it," he said. I told him I would appreciate it. Under the careful guidance of Norman, I soon had one of the candle-covers in my mouth and, to shouts of encouragement from the other boys, was blowing it up to the required beach-ball dimensions. "This," Norman said, pretending to read aloud from the back of the package, "is a preliminary stretching technique, to ensure that the cover can accommodate candles of all sizes." Inflated, the candle-cover looked like a hairy balloon. It was remarked that not since Rat's introduction to the candle-cover had a beginner so successfully mastered, in one try, what was generally acknowledged to be a most complex procedure. Norman continued: "Holding tip of candle-cover between thumb and forefinger, allow air to escape slowly. Hint: a proper rate of escape is that which produces a high whining sound and causes the candle-cover to vibrate." Holding the candle-cover at arm's length, I let some air escape, then looked round to see if they thought I had done it right. They looked at one another, some nodding, some doubtfully shaking their heads. Opinion was divided. More than half thought I had done well enough, but the rest, though not unappreciative of my effort, wondered if I had got the sound just right. It was vital, they said, that the high whining sound be produced, or else the candle-cover would wear out prematurely. Now my sound, though interesting, had not been high and whining. I had not whined but warbled, and a warble would not do. And what about the vibration? Had the candle-cover vibrated? It had, it hadn't, no-one could say for sure. It was agreed that I should try again, and I was told not to lose heart—Norman himself had tried five times before succeeding. Norman thought he should tell me, however, that if all the air escaped from the candle-cover and the desired sound was not produced, the candle-cover would be ruined. It could not be reinflated. It would be of no use whatsoever, and the priest, who kept count of his candle-covers—and at such a price, who could blame him— would not be pleased when he found out that one was missing. I might have panicked, had not all of them been so supportive. They had me stand beneath the bulb in the middle of the floor, and they crowded round to cheer me on. "C'mon Rev, no sweat," they said, "you can do it Rev." But as it turned out, I could not. Several times, in their opinion, I made the candle-cover vibrate, and several times

I produced the high whining sound, but, heartbreakingly, it seemed a simultaneous effect was more than I could manage. I watched in horror as the candle-cover got smaller and smaller, and soon, on the verge of tears, I was saying things like, "I'm sure I got it that time, I'm sure I did." Much as they would have liked to, they said, they simply could not agree. And after such a promising start, too. They shook their heads. By the time the candle-cover was down to the size of my fist, by the time it began to look like a spiked plum, I was unabashedly bawling. The cellar went silent as Norman stepped forward and put a hand on my shoulder. Everyone crowded in close. "This is it Rev," Norman said, "this is your last chance." "C'mon Rev," the boys said, "you can do it Rev." As stories would have it later, I stood there a good two minutes, focusing on that candle-cover, holding it at arm's length between thumb and forefinger, afraid to release that last precious handful of air. And then I closed my eyes, gritted my teeth, turned my head away—and let the candle-cover go. When I opened my eyes, everyone was looking at everyone else. "It was close, wasn't it?" Norman said. They agreed, yes, it was *very* close. "But not close enough?" Norman said. They nodded. But not close enough. Mournfully, slowly, they formed a line, and each in turn shook my hand. Some of them looked me in the eye, as if to say that they would be of greater comfort, if only they could speak.

It was Archie who saved me, Archie who, all throughout my initiation, had sat, watching, on the stairs. As the other boys began to leave, I gathered up the candle-covers and headed for the sacristy, intent on making a full confession to the priest. No longer crying, resigned now to my fate, I was going to give him his candle-covers, promise to pay for the one I'd ruined and say I hoped he understood why I was leaving the altar and never coming back. But Archie grabbed me and made me wait till the others were gone. "Wobuht," he said, "you have given new definithun to the wuhd gullible." I had, he said, been "twicked." But he managed to cheer me up by telling me that Loyola, who, a year before, had fallen victim to the same gag, had been further duped into going to a drug-store and buying a box of candle-covers, so that he could replace the one he had spoiled, and practise at home on the rest. Loyola's mother was said to be still recovering from the shock of coming home to find Loyola in the kitchen, applying prophylactics to the legs of her table and chairs.

Candle-covers came up a lot in conversation the next few weeks, and I tried to find out what they really were. According to what my father called his "Concise Cryptic Dictionary," which I borrowed without his permission, a prophylactic was "a method or measure preventing disease." According to Archie, it was a "manthpethific contwatheptive, fwowned on by the Church."

Archie was eager to take me under his wing. We would walk, during recess, slowly about the schoolyard, father confessor and novice out to take the air. Hands clasped in front, he nodded sagely at the things I said, smiled wistfully, as if remembering the early days of his own vocation

Archie, though a year older than me, was in my class at school. He had failed Grade 7 the year before because he had indulged in too much of what he called "ecthtwacuwiculah weading." "I'm weading Aquinath," he'd say, as if this was a task he was performing, not because he wanted to, but because the great monk him.elf had chosen him for it; and as if, because of the strain it placed upon him, he must be conceded some measure of weirdness, some exemption from the mundane requirements of life.

Grade 7 was a piling-up place for those who went from grade to grade more by way of pardon than promotion, because it was there the pardons ended. The only way to get by Grade 7 was to pass, and so it was there the refuse of the system collected. Grade 7 was the largest class, with an average age three years higher than that of Grade 9. Boys almost of drinking age and girls engaged to be married made up one half of the class; the other half was made up of boys and girls my age.

In March that year, Grade 7 got a new teacher. He was Jimmy McGraw, a former Christian Brother, a trouble-shooter sent by the Board of Education up and down the Shore from school to school. He was, in my father's words, "a big, mean, raw-boned bastard." He was an idealist who, when the world failed to measure up, struck out at it in rage. All he asked of a shack was that it be a crystal palace—and when it proved itself a shack, felt fully justified in tearing it down. Worst of all was having to watch while he set himself up for heartbreak. For the more hopeful he seemed, the more ingenuous his latest plan for a new and better world, the greater was his rage when, once again, he failed. I remember his face, spite-hot, flushed, blinking back the bitter tears; and the way, when mad, his back to the board, he raised one leg behind him and pinched his heel until his thumb went white; and how he looked that winter when at last he went for the strap, as if never before had he been let down so hard.

His strap we called the Lad. He kept it on his desk. A long, pink, tongue-like thing it was, with a handle, and hurt-enhancing holes from top to bottom. It was said that he'd made the Lad himself, and that it could make your hands bleed. But at St. Stephen's, no-one knew if this was true, because Jimmy McGraw had yet to use it. It lay there, on his desk, half of it hanging over the edge, kept from falling by a nail down through the middle. The mere presence of the Lad maintained order. Jimmy McGraw put down revolt by going closer to it, walking round it, stopping near it, by raising it to better view on the flat of a wooden ruler. Grade 7 was never so well behaved as when Jimmy McGraw was in charge. Among the nuns, there was talk of a new era, one in which there would be no dropouts, no ditch-digging graduates.

Near the end of the month, however, he made the mistake of dividing us up into groups. He gave each group a name. There was to be competition among groups and, within groups, co-operation, all for one and one for all, a sharing of knowledge and ideas such as St. Stephen's had never seen. Our group he called the Cougars. There were ten of us, and our circle of desks was put at the back of the room. My fellow Cougars were Smack MacDougall, so named for the sound produced by the coming together of a yardstick and his unusually flat-bottomed bum, and, as my father unkindly put it, "seven other male morons." There was also Philomela, known as Philly, who, at seventeen, was the youngest Cougar next to me, and who was famous as the only girl in Kellies who would fart in the presence of boys. Smack was one of six Cougars pushing twenty. One *was* twenty, and one, Mike Mahoney, was rumoured to be 23.

The Cougars came from older families, and older families in Kellies tended to be poor. Sister Sharon, our principal, liked to tell us there was nothing wrong with being poor. There were those, she said, who were poor and proud, making do with what they had and not complaining. But, though she never mentioned it, there were also those who were poor and not taking it very well. The Cougars were of this group. They came to school wearing waders and smelling faintly of manure.

The Cougars didn't like me, nor the stated fact that I was there to motivate them, to inspire them, to, in some way, rub off on them and make them smarter. On tests, they were to see if the sum total of their marks could exceed mine. The nine of them together once got 56 in Geography, for an all-time high average mark of 5.6%. Most of the time, Smack and Mike and the other Cougars tried to get zero, but zero was one of the two marks Jimmy McGraw would not give. The other was a hundred. Each, he said, implied perfection. If, as often happened, the Cougars passed in blank sheets of paper, he gave them one mark for neatness. The most common Cougar grade was 1%. And if, as often happened, I got everything right, he gave me 99, and gave the missing mark, as he said, to someone who needed it more. It was because of this that Mike Mahoney, who thought to make himself ineligible for the neatness bonus by passing in sheets of paper both blank and crumpled-up, began to blame his inability to get zero on my stubborn refusal to make a mistake. When, despite his crumpled paper, he got 1%, he claimed that it was mine, and said that if Jimmy McGraw could give it away, he, Mike Mahoney, could give it back. He would roll his test paper into a ball and stuff it in my book-bag. "Dere," he'd say, "I got zero, an' you got a hundred." "Give Mike back his mark Bobby," Jimmy McGraw would say, and I would fish it out and put it on Mike's desk. Again Mike would give it back, and it sometimes went on like that for minutes on end, the ball of paper going back and forth between us. One day, Mike got so exasperated, he took out a match and set fire to his test paper right there in the classroom. Jimmy McGraw put it out, and then made Mike put the ashes in his pocket. Mike claimed that, burned up like that, it wasn't a mark any more. But Jimmy McGraw said a mark was like matter—it could neither be created nor destroyed.

Jimmy McGraw liked to read our marks out loud and, whenever my mark of 99 was announced, the Cougars, as if passing round an invisible joint, one after the other made sucking sounds, and then, joining arms above my head, their heads upraised like howling dogs, sucked in a kind of chorus, or strange college cheer.

For a time, Jimmy McGraw let all this go. It was true, he said, that at first glance the Cougars seemed a worthless lot. They did appear to be rough and lazy, without ambition, disobedient, having respect for nothing and no-one, least of all themselves. But he spoke of the redeeming characteristics which, thus far, they had so successfully kept hidden. It was to the uncovering of these redeeming characteristics that Jimmy McGraw dedicated himself. Anyone but he could have seen that it was hopeless. The next few weeks, the Cougars were worse than ever. It was inevitable that Jimmy Mc-Graw would go for the Lad. What could not have been foreseen was that he would choose to start on me with it.

One day, boiling with frustration, he decided that my getting only 85 on a test was the last straw. I looked up and he was suddenly standing over me, red-faced, the Lad in his hand, shifting his weight from one foot to the other as if he had to pee. "Get up," he said. I was so scared, I couldn't have gotten up for all the money in the world. And, as it turned out, I didn't have to.

Fights in the classroom were not unusual at St. Stephen's, and there had been much talk among the Cougars about who would have the guts to take on Jimmy McGraw. The moment he told me to get up, Smack, without hesitation, grabbed him by the arm and pulled him head-first inside our circle of desks. Smack and Mike got out of their desks and jumped on him, not hitting him, just holding him down, and then a couple of the other boys took the Lad away from him. It ended that way because, when they let him go, he knew there were more of them than he could manage. His face full of rage and spite, he walked out of the classroom and he never did come back.

After that, as if they decided that, having been deemed worthy of a strapping, I couldn't be all good, the Cougars greeted my marks with mock congratulation, laughing loudly and pounding me on the back.

It was around this time my mother lost her purse. After mass one Sunday morning, she left the church without it, and when she went back to get it, it was gone. In the space of a couple of minutes, it disappeared. She wondered who would be so brazen as to walk out with it. "Imagine," she said, "stealing in church." Someone who had just been to mass, maybe even Holy Communion, took her purse and walked out with it—walked out, past the priest, who was shaking hands at the door. Nonsense, my father said. Had she forgotten, her purse was not just any purse. It was *the* purse, First Purse, on which all others had been modelled. Her purse had not been stolen. It had ascended into heaven where, even now, it was on display in the hall of fame, the first inanimate object to make it past the Pearly Gates. God had looked down on that black handbag, lying there forgotten, and decided he had to have it. My father's blasphemy notwithstanding, my mother said, it *was* a special purse. She'd had it since she was married, and she couldn't imagine life with some replacement. So that settled it. Thereafter, my mother went without a purse. She used her pockets and the glove compartment of her new car.

The new car had to do with the fact that it was also around this time she caught my father and Harold's Mother sliding on the stairs. I came home from school one afternoon to find the car in the yard, and my mother and father sitting at the kitchen table. I knew that something must be very wrong to bring them both home early from work. They were sitting at opposite ends of the table, not speaking. The silence between them was hours old. My mother smiled at me, the way adults at funerals smile at children, as if I were an imbecile, whose delusions of happiness must be left intact. She had been crying, but not much. "Go on upstairs Bobby," she said, "your father and I have something to talk about." It was in my room that day, lying face down on the bed, that I first began to wonder how it all started. Harold's Mother had nothing to do with my parents downstairs, so drained of love they could not manage an argument.

The terms of the treaty which my mother and father reached I deduced from certain changes that were made. They began sleeping in different rooms. The explanation for this, as given by my father one night while we were sliding on the stairs, was that my mother had, after all this time, gotten fed up with his snoring. They bought another car, an Austin Mini for my mother, so that they could drive to work alone; or, as my mother put it, "so that my comings and goings will not inconvenience your father."

My mother's comings and goings greatly increased. She joined the Catholic Women's League and the St. Stephen's Sisters (known in Kellies as the SS), a group of married, middle-aged women who got together once a week to talk about abortion and baked goods. She began to work long hours, coming home sometimes late at night. She was made Assistant Director of Curriculum and Texts for high schools. "Think of it Bobby," my father said, "a whole generation of Newfoundlanders influenced by your mother." He said the only thing she talked about any more was her work. She wanted *Huckleberry Finn* to be a required text in all Roman Catholic high-school English courses. Students would be asked to rewrite certain passages, correcting the grammar and spelling. In the curriculum listings she brought home, this part of the course was known as: "'Without You Have Read'—Huck Finn Goes Back to School." She began preparing an interdisciplinary course, based, she said, on the belief that learning can be fun. It was to be called "PT and Poetry." Among those exercises suggested for boys was the writing of a description of a basketball game in blank verse. My mother had not yet decided whether to call this exercise "The Language of Layups," or "Play by Play the Shakespeare Way." The girls, it was hoped, would rise to the challenge of "Home Metronomics," a course that would teach them to compile anapestic recipes, and make grocery lists more interesting by the use of alliteration and internal rhyme. (Months later, my father professed himself "re-assured" when both "PT and Poetry" and "Home Metronomics" were rejected by the Board of Education.)

Despite her work, my mother stayed home two nights a week so that my father could go out with Harold's Mother—not that Harold's Mother was ever mentioned. They were unaware that I knew anything about her. My father, Tuesdays and Thursdays, would shower and shave after supper, singing loudly all the while —songs like "My Way" or "Cape St. Mary's," anything upliftingly sad. Now and then he would come out of the bathroom and shout from the top of the stairs. "Agnes, did you see my shirt?" And my mother would answer, "Yes dear, it's ironed, in the closet. And I pressed your pants for you too." She was taking better care of him than she ever had before. It was a marvelous arrangement, really. My mother ironed my father's clothes, and Harold's Mother messed them up.

The only way to describe my father's behaviour back then is to say that he acted euphorically guilty. Sometimes, when he was getting ready to go out, he let me in the bathroom. I would stand and watch him at the sink. Whistling, splashing aftershave, he would now and then wink at me. I did my best to make it hard for him.

"Where are ye goin'?" I'd say.

"Bowling."

"Can I come?"

"Not tonight."

"Can I have your scorecard then?"

"Okay."

For the first little while, he thought he could get away with saying that he forgot the scorecards, but I kept at him. "I'll call you up and remind you," I said, but he said no, that was all right, he'd remember from now on. Soon he started bringing them home, five or six ten-frame scorecards, filled out most convincingly, the scores neither so high as to make me incredulous, nor so low as to make me ashamed. "See," he'd say, pointing, "three strikes in a row there." I would get him to tell me all about it, how close the game was, how his friends had done. And I would test him, now and then, by asking him if he thought he had done better this week than last. My father's imagination and memory were taxed to the limit. On weekends, when he spent a lot of his time in his room, I think he was filling out the score cards and making up the names of the men on the other terms. There was one man, Tom Two-Sixty Sullivan, whom we agreed was an ace bowler and my father's arch-enemy. We planned strategy against Sullivan in the bathroom. And the next morning we'd go over the scorecard, analyzing my father's victory, or on rare occasions, his defeat. It was, as my father said, years later, quite a sad charade, and not confined to him and me. "Teddy goes bowling twice a week," my mother told her fellow SS members. She bought him a pair of bowling shoes for his birthday.

My mother must have told the SS a *lot* about my father because, the nights they met at our house, the ladies crowded round him when he came downstairs, marvelled at him, as if he were a member of some soon-to-vanish species, or the latest thing in husbands. Silent, smiling at him and at one another, they would escort him to the door. My father confessed he found it quite unnerving. If it happened that they came some night when he was staying at home, he and I would go upstairs. My mother forbade us to go sliding when the SS were in the house, but, when it came near time for them to leave, we would assume racing position at the top of the stairs. Now and then, while going from the kitchen to the hallway, one of the ladies would hear us and look up, and my father and I, inside our pillows, would free one hand and wave. The poor soul would flash a painful smile and turn quickly away, as if she had caught us in some act of personal hygiene.

In the midst of all this, my nightmares got worse. They recurred as they had at Mortrey's, except that now they were empty, hag-ridden dreams. Every night I would open my eyes, as if awake, and hear that same sound, as of a dress so long it sweeps the floor. Contained, like something set in stone, every pore plugged up by dark-ness, I believed the sound was death itself come creeping. My mother consulted the priest, who said the hag was a kind of spiritual claustrophobia, the soul entombed, buried alive in the body. He came to the house and blessed my bed. I put on my altar outfit and carried the sceptre and holy water, while he went round and said some prayers. But, despite his prayers, the dreams continued. A next-door neighbour, when my father told him about my dreams, said he'd heard the hag only came to those who slept on their backs. He said that men, in olden days, got rid of the hag by going to bed with a belt on backwards—if, in their sleep, they rolled on their backs, the buckle woke them up. My mother decided that, instead of a belt, we would use a cross. The one she chose was made of metal, full of points and edges, and even had a crown of thorns. They wrapped it in cloth so that it would not be cold against my back, and my father fixed it to a piece of rope, which they tied around my waist. That one night I wore it, I did not have what my father was calling a "hag-attack." But neither did I get any sleep, so afraid was I of impaling myself on the cross.

The next night, I went to bed without it, and the hag-attacks began again. My father, as his room was closest to mine, was the one who most often came to my rescue. The way he told it, he would lie awake, or lightly asleep, waiting for me to scream—and, when I did, would jump out of bed and come wake me. Often, by the time he got there, I had thrown myself on the floor, where, still asleep, I was wrapped up, wrestling blankets. My mother began to put pillows and cushions on the floor beside my bed, so that, when I threw myself out, I wouldn't get hurt.

Word got round at school that I had the hag, and no-one would have much to do with me. Who could blame them? A twelve-year-old demon-possessed genius with aspirations to the priesthood was not my idea of good company, either. I was a source of entertainment and terror for the younger children. They would gather in groups and put themselves in front of me so that, when I got close enough, they could have the pleasure of screaming, "THE HAG, THE HAG," and run off in all directions. Sometimes they dared one another to see who would go closest to me. It was quite off-putting to have about a hundred little boys and girls tiptoeing toward you from all sides, or to look up and find half a dozen outstretched hands about to grab the cap off your head. As for the older children, they would come up behind me in the schoolyard and shout "BOO" as loud as they could. Some, whenever I came near, made a cross with their index fingers and, holding it in front of their faces, backed away slowly. I was told that an old wart-faced woman was always walking behind me with arms outstretched. Often, when someone pointed her out, or said "Hey Rev, who's dat behind ye?" I would look over my shoulder and go round and round like a dog chasing its tail. "C'mon Rev," they'd say, "you can catch 'er," and they would applaud and laugh as I went round faster and faster. The hag and I became known as "Rev and the wife." People, when they said hello, did so to both of us: "Mornin' Rev. Mornin' Ma'am."

Those days, I hated to turn my back on anything. I'd stand against a wall, or some place where I could see my reflection, just to make sure there was no-one behind me. And at night, in my room, I sat up for hours, afraid to get in bed, knowing that, if I did, the hag would come.

What with being so constantly on edge, and going so long without sleep, I was soon a nervous wreck. In class I couldn't concentrate, or even sit still. It seemed to me that the boy behind me was always touching the back of my neck with something, so I kept turning around to catch him. It was the day the boy behind me stayed home sick, the day that I, nevertheless, continued shooing him away and telling the empty desk to "knock it off," that the teacher decided it was time to write my parents a note.

They kept me home a few days. My father stayed home with me, and we spent most of the time sliding on the stairs. The first day, my father took me to see the local doctor, who took something of a tongue-in-cheek attitude toward me after my father announced loudly in the waiting-room—he said, afterwards, he meant it as a joke—that his son was suffering from "chronic crone syndrome." The doctor put down my hypertensive phobia to adolescence, "pubescent exuberance," as he put it, and my nightmares to midnight snacks, about which, he said, I had fooled my father and mother, but I could not fool him. He gave me some pills that he said would help me sleep, and they worked wonderfully. Four nights in a row,

I fell into a deep dreamless sleep. After the fifth night, the night the pills no longer worked, my mother noticed that I was looking much better and sent me back to school.

It was that first day back I joined the "pilgrimage." Mike Mahoney was organizing a pilgrimage to Mattie's house. Mattie, the seventh son of a seventh son, lived at the end of the Old Line. Seventh sons of seventh sons were believed by some Catholics to have "a gift." My mother, for instance, although she never mentioned Mattie, thought highly of other seventh sons who lived along the Shore. They were men whose prayers on behalf of others were said to find favour with God—it was thought that those who believed in them might have their ailments cured, and people with everything from toothaches to kidney stones asked their help. Mattie, however, who had been in and out of the mental hospital in St. John's all his life, was something of an embarrassment, a parish joke. "One sod short of a lawn," was how my father described him, but it was not his craziness so much as his lack of scruples that bothered people most. He only prayed for those who gave him money, and he sold candles and "holy" water that he, himself, had blessed. People went to see him just for the fun of it; for $3 he would take them into his house and get on with what the priest called "a lot of blasphemous mumbo jumbo."

Mike said he would ask Mattie to grow him a beard, and Philly said she wanted one too. Norman said he wanted to get rid of a wart. But though it was all a joke to them, something my mother believed in was good enough for me. I told no-one but I was going in hope of having the hag-dreams stopped. I asked Archie if he would come, and he said he would, not to take part, but to keep me company. Ambrosia, who said that, since Christmas, she'd been snacking too much, decided to come along, too, declaring that she would ask Mattie for "will-power." "Dis better be fun," she said, looking at Mike, "if it's not, I'm gonna tell."

The six of us set out for Mattie's the afternoon of the last Saturday in April. It was four miles from the school, where we met by prearrangement, to Mattie's house. We walked all the way in silent single file, Ambrosia bringing up the rear. Archie and I looked back now and then to make sure she was still with us. She must have thought it was to some kind of Church we were going, for she was like an apparition on the road behind us. In white pumps and white panty-hose and what, later, bemoaning its ruination, she called her "short bright white dress," the folds of which, with thumb and forefinger, she held out as if ever about to curtsy, she was trying to tiptoe uphill through the muck. So as not to fall backwards, she was leaning out over her shoes like a ski-jumper and, at the same time, was taking frantic steps so as not to fall forward. She was wearing a bonnet, also white, which must have been Dola's bridal bonnet, for it was fixed with a huge veil which, despite her attempts to keep it pinned in place, kept falling down, enclosing her like a tent.

It was mid-afternoon when we got there. Mattie's house, a small pink shack, was almost overgrown by trees and bushes. There were old tires all over the place—there were no vehicles, broken down or otherwise, in sight, yet there were tires of all manner and size.

Mattie must have been watching us from the window, for the storm door swung open when we were still a hundred feet from the house. A little man appeared and began, in a gravely silent manner, to make directional signals with his hands, as if we were a truck he wanted parked in a particular place. "Hello Mattie," Mike said, but Mattie said nothing. He waved us backwards, forwards, side to side, a little to the right, a little to the left. He made a stirring motion with his finger, and seemed pleased when we began to walk in circles. It was easy enough, at first, to do what he wanted, but after a while the signals became increasingly ambiguous, and he began sending them faster and faster. He made a cranking motion, switched suddenly to a cat's paddle and then began a mimed juggling of what seemed to be an enormous number of objects—his face, all the while, wearing an expression of utmost earnestness. It wasn't long before the six of us were stumbling and bumping into one another and falling over tires. Ambrosia was having a particularly bad time of it. The veil kept falling down, so that she could neither see where she was going, nor pick up Mattie's signals. The rest of us kept bowling her over, turning her upside down in the tires. Most of the time, her great hose-encased bottom was in plain view. "Where in the blue blatheth doeth he want uth to go?" Archie said, trying desperately to keep his glasses on. "Shhh—" Mike said, "he'll hear ye."

One hand on his hip, Mattie held out the other hand as if to stop a bus, and shouted "DON'T MOVE" in a way that made me think there must be land-mines all around us. Stopped, we were scattered all over the place, standing, facing him, except for Ambrosia, who was upside down in a pile of tires, her bottom rising from them like a hubcap.

I was at last able to get a good look at him. He couldn't have been more than four feet tall. He was wearing the upper half of what, it seemed, had once been a Santa suit. Minus belt and white fur fringe, it looked now like a cowl, Mattie like a diminutive monk. I discovered later that he was wearing a pair of hip-waders many sizes too big, over which the cowl hung down, so that not even his feet could be seen. The effect of the waders was extraordinary, especially on someone unaware of them. His legs were lost inside them, so that he was barely able to lift his feet, and he could not bend his knees at all. He moved by way of imperceptibly tiny stiff-legged steps, of which the cowl betrayed no evidence, so that he might have been gliding along the ground like a float in some Lilliputian parade. Of Mattie's face, I remember only its look of perpetual surprise, as if, each time he blinked, a curtain came down on the past, and he was forever waking on a world he had never seen before.

He came rumbling toward us and stopped in front of me. Hands on his cheeks, his mouth wide open, he began jumping up and down. My first impulse was to run, but then I saw that it was the sight of Ambrosia that so disturbed him. By now, she had managed to right herself and, having lifted the veil just high enough to see out from under it, was staring at Mattie as an abandoned bride might look at the groom. Mattie went over to her. "So me duckie," he said, "what might Mattie do for you?"

Ambrosia went back behind her veil.

"Ask and it shall be given," he said.

Ambrosia shook her head.

"Ask," Mattie said.

Ambrosia hung her head and turned away.

"She wants to lose weight Mattie," Mike said, laughing. Mattie waved his arms frantically, as referees do to indicate "no goal." Then he pointed at Ambrosia. "Confess," he said, "confess."

Ambrosia began to cry.

"Leave huh alone," Archie said.

"What might Mattie do for you?" Mattie said, turning to him. When he found out that Archie had only come to watch, he ordered him away from the house, saying that the near presence of a disbeliever would make "miracles" impossible. Then, beginning an almost imperceptible progress toward the door, he had us follow him.

When we were inside he told us that the rule of the house was "no money, no miracle," and he pointed to a half-size statue of Christ in the corner. Going closer, we saw Christ to be a piggy-bank with a coin-slot in its head. We gave our money to Mike and he pushed it through the slot. Mattie had us write on pieces of paper the "miracles" we wanted. "Ask and it shall be given," he said.

He took Mike and Philly upstairs where, as they later reported, he had them repeat, over and over, something called the "Prayer for Hair." Me he had kneel in the kitchen and told me that, once he was out of the room, I should pray to the following saints: St. Francis of Paula, founder of the Order of Minims, whose feast day this was; St. Symphorosa and her Seven Sons; the Seven Holy Founders of the Servites, and St. Felicitas and her Seven Sons. Most of my prayer I forget. I only know that it began, "O hear me Minims," and ended with a reference to the hag. It was very dark in the kitchen—there were no windows—and what with Mike and Philly in the bathroom, giggling and loudly reciting the Prayer for Hair, I started praying too. And our voices, theirs and mine, grew louder, and louder still, until suddenly, the kitchen door slammed shut and I was left in total darkness. "Mike," I shouted, "Mike, let me out." There wasn't a sound. Terrified, I groped about in the dark until I found the back door which, as I learned later, had not been opened in twenty years. It was a storm door, with a latch so caked in rust I couldn't lift it at first. I pulled with all my might, and it was the fact of its being so stuck that saved me, for when it came suddenly open I went backwards with it, and the great branch that, with a roar, came bursting in, altogether missed me. The door, however, hit my head and banged me against the wall, and for several moments I was dazed. As if from a great distance, I heard Ambrosia scream. It was not because of the tree she screamed, and it was not for being half knocked out I heard her from far away. She *was* far away, down in the basement where, having gotten bored with Mattie's pre-scribed and, to this day, secret recipe for will-power, she had gone in search of Norman to see how his wart was doing. As it turned out, it was not to rid himself of warts that Norman had come along, but to have enhanced the size of a certain organ. Ambrosia found him, standing at a thigh-high table, sunk to the roots in a Mason jar of holy water, Mattie's "'Lastic 'Lixir." It was then she screamed and ran back up the stairs. By this time, Mattie, Mike and Philly were in the kitchen, and Ambrosia and Norman soon joined them. I was still behind the door, and it must have been that no-one noticed my feet, because Ambrosia started bawling about how I had been eaten by a tree. Indeed, the kitchen half-filled with that cragged ten-tacle, and no sign whatever of me, it must not have seemed unlikely that she was right. They ran to the front door and outside to search for me, before I could announce my continued, if dazed existence. When, moments later, I finally did come out from behind the door, I turned the wrong way and went head first into a tangle of snags and broken branches. My feet came clear of the floor, and the tree, with all my weight on it, began to go up and down. I was in the process of disentangling myself when Archie came in and shouted "Jethuth Cwitht" so loud I slipped for fright and fell back in. He then began to pull me clear with a fervour somewhat in excess of that required. Turning round, he took one of my feet in each of his hands and ran, as if with a wheelbarrow, toward the hallway. "Well, thath gratitude for you," he said later, when I wondered if, in get-ting me out, provision could not have been made to have my epi-dermis come with me. Both my arms were badly skinned, as was one side of my face. "Don'e wuwwy," Archie said, "you'll heal. You'll be a new man in no time."

He and I left the house just in time to scare away what wits poor Ambrosia still had left. Taking one look at my bleeding face and arms, she threw off her bonnet, veil and all, and started running down the hill.

Neither Mike nor Philly managed to grow a beard, but Ambrosia got her wish. She lost about 50 pounds before, as my father said, "bottoming out at a svelte 165."

And Norman got his. By some trick of light and 'Lastic 'Lixir, that part of him in the Mason jar had impressed Ambrosia as being much larger than it really was. By the time she got through telling her friends, Norman had grown so large in legend that what we called his "too-small smackeroo" no longer mattered. (It was rumoured years later in Kellies that the fact that no-one told Ambrosia that Norman, as she described him, was anything out of the ordinary, left her with a rather too-generous notion of male endowment, and caused no end of trouble between her and the sub-Norman man she married.)

And I got my wish——for the hag never did come back.

Book Two

CHAPTER 5

That September began what my father called our "Protestant period." For want of anywhere else to go, we moved to the Protestant part of town, about half a mile from Luby Line. It was an area that was unofficially segregated, a kind of ghetto, I suppose, where the Protestants, and people of other outnumbered persuasions lived. The house we lived in goes unnamed, because no-one lived in it after us. A Protestant family owned the house before us and, when my mother had the priest come and bless the empty rooms, my father muttered something about "chasing the heathens out with holy water." When the priest was gone, my father discovered that he had "missed the kitchen sink." The kitchen sink, he said, was still Protestant. We would have to do the dishes in the bathtub. He ran upstairs and found to his horror that at least five, and possibly as many as fourteen bathroom tiles were still Protestant. With a felt-tipped pen, he put a "P" on the ones that looked suspicious. We were not to step on these, he said, lest our feet catch fire. Going downstairs, he declared one corner of the living-room "100% Protestant," and built a barricade of books around it. He then went around the house, writing "P" everywhere, while my mother, with Ajax and cleaning-cloth, followed him, saying, "Go ahead dear, have your fun. Bobby's old enough now. His father doesn't frighten him any more." My father, in retaliation, named my mother's bedroom the "Martin Luther Memorial Room."

The stairs, my father decided, after a painful experiment, were too steep for sliding, so we retired the Teddy-tank and Bob-sled.

For generations, the core of the Protestant community in Kellies had been four or five interrelated families, who went by the name of Hamilton. Hamilton was synonymous with Protestant, and every Hamilton had red hair—orange-red that is—and up until High School, I thought it was for this reason Protestants were called Orangemen. Orange hair, pale skin and freckles—the marks of a Protestant. Dola would say of Protestants that they had so many freckles they were "one big birth-mark." Protestants were not born with freckles, we were told. They got them growing up. "Sin-spots," Dola called them, but the prevailing opinion was that they resulted from dirt-clogged pores. Protestants, as we all knew, never washed. The only thing that saved them from total filth was getting caught in the occasional shower of rain. I remember at Lawton's, whenever it started raining, Dola would say, "Here comes a bath for de blacks." Her way of saying that it had been raining for some time was, "De Prodestins must be down to last year's dirt by now." A particularly heavy downpour caused her to exclaim one night, "My God Rennie, if dis keeps up, dere'll be nuttin' lefta de Prodestins but fog and freckles." If, in the daytime, it stopped raining, she would tell us to go out and count the freckles. She said that, after a storm, there were freckles all over the place. I remember Ambrosia and I, walking about with eyes fixed on the ground, hoping to find a freckle, on hands and knees in the wet grass, searching. Ambrosia would claim to have found one and, when I came to look, would say, "He got away." She had permission from her mother to eat any freckles she found and, sometimes, after a backyard expedition, would refuse to eat her supper on the grounds that, having had a feed of freckles, she was full. Rennie worried that, young as she was, she might be mistaking "snails or worms or God knows what" for freckles. They explained to her that freckles did not exist, except on someone's skin, and could not, *could not*, by any amount of biting, be removed.

It was hard to pin my mother down on Protestants. She claimed not to mind moving into the Protestant neighbourhood, but I wonder. Once, when she was angry, she referred to Protestantism as "the unfortunate misconception of one misguided monk–a German monk I might add." My mother's view of Protestants was that they were more to be pitied than persecuted. She reserved for Protestant children, born to the double burden of original sin and heresy, a special compassion. She did not, as Dola did, say that Protestants, when they died, went to purgatory and stayed there until the soot burned off their souls. She did not say it, but it must have been something like that she believed, for when I pointed out that burning would only make more soot, she explained that the fires of purgatory were "the cleansing kind." The average Protestant, according to Dola, burned about a million years—"until they become nice crisp Catholics," my father said. I asked my father once if it was a sin to shoot a Protestant, and he said, "It depends." I asked my mother if she thought purgatory was segregated. "Why should it be segregated?" she said. "The people there have their sins in common." It was a matter of some contention whether everyone went to purgatory, at least for a little while, or whether there were some so good that, when they died, they went straight to heaven. My father said the latter was true, and in that saintly category were included such people as the Virgin Mary and my mother. But my mother said that "everyone except Jesus, Mary and some saints" went to purgatory. My father replied that, unless there was a part of purgatory where people went to have their sins purged by sitting too close to a stove, she was surely wrong. He asked my mother to imagine the SS ladies being burned alive. My mother warned against a too-literal interpretation of Catholic dogma. Fire, she said, was a metaphor for some "more subtle, but no less purgative agony."

"Like throwing up?" my father said. "They should call it regurgatory then." He imagined a million retching sinners, a million sinners throwing up for a thousand years. In regurgatory, he said, we'd all be on a boat and seasick, heaving our sins over the side— "and everywhere, the smell of fatback frying."

"Hardly subtle," my mother said.

In the early days of Kellies, there had more or less been a range war between Catholics and Protestants. A man was killed. Another had his ears cut off. A Catholic who tried to convert was horsewhipped. By my time, the war was a cold war, though there were incidents—beatings, and once, a rape of a Catholic girl by Protestant boys, bent on revenging something her father had done. The old hostilities flared now and then and, when they did, it wasn't safe, especially if you were a Protestant, to walk the roads. At such times, the priest and the minister met and talked, and differences were settled that way. But most of the time Protestants and Catholics simply ignored one another. Whenever we saw a Protestant coming, we crossed the road.. What I remember most clearly is, in the summertime, hearing the Protestants playing outside, while we were saying the rosary. It always seemed they stayed out later. After dark, shouting voices way off in the woods, or on the road getting louder and louder until they passed your house, were said to be Protestant voices. Heathens, that's what Protestants were, who went wild when the sun went down.

Protestant girls were said to be loose, their red hair a badge of promiscuity. It was said that Catholic boys, walking the roads, were often enticed into the bushes by them. I know that, when I walked the roads, I never looked straight ahead, though you were supposed to. I was always hoping to see a Protestant girl, peering out between the branches. When I was *very* young, I was terrified, afraid to go near the road. It was said that if you wandered off the road the Protestant girls would get you. You were okay as long as you stayed on the pavement, but if you even happened onto the shoulder or, God forbid, into the ditch, you were a goner. And it was said that, after dark, not even the pavement could protect you. After dark, the Protestant girls came right up on the road and dragged you off into the woods. Everyone said you had to watch out for "the black bush in the bushes." Was it, I wondered, a poisonous bush; did the black come off on your clothes? There was a rhyme, not to be recited unless in broad daylight, with both feet firmly on the pavement:

Little Black Bush
Come blow my horn
I'll make you as white
As the day you were born.

If the little black bush did not respond, you said

Black Bush, Black Bush
In the tree
Black Bush, Black Bush
Can't get me.

and then ran as fast as your legs could carry you.

The word on Protestant boys was different. They were not randy, but stupid. Dola referred to them as "brutes." And they were greedy, too. Misers. "Prodestins," Dola said, were "tighter dan a cow's hole at fly time." It was said that Protestant storekeepers kept their children home from school so they could use their fingers for counting.

Dola saw our moving into the Protestant neighbourhood as the natural next thing, just what you'd expect from a family whose father was out chasing women. By now, my father's affair was common knowledge, and Dola seemed to believe that the entire family's resistance to temptation was lower because of it. At our new house, as if we were in need of periodic injections of goodness, she and Rennie and the girls often came to visit.

She made it clear what she thought of my father. With all of us gathered in the kitchen, the girls and I sitting on the counter, my father and mother and Rennie at the table, Dola would put her chair in the middle of the floor, stretch her bad leg and, looking at her orthopaedic boot, hold forth in a kind of code. Always on record, though never spoken, was a statement of my father's absolute worthlessness. Everything that Dola said was, in some way, a qualification of this statement, everything prefaced, "The sins of this man notwithstanding." "Now mind you," she'd say, as if picking up on something that had been said, when, in fact, these were the first words spoken, "Now mind you, dere *are* good men in dis world." My father would squirm, the girls would giggle, and we'd be there for hours. Dola, in making these remarks, was not hoping to start a conversation. The proper response was silence, and we were more than willing to give it. But if, by chance, a conversation, not about my father's affair, did get going, Dola would end it by throwing out some irrelevant remark, some cryptic, yet transparent statement, and we would sit in silence, with heads bowed, as if pondering what she'd said. "Still, now, it could be worse," she'd say, in the midst of a discussion of last night's hockey game. We would nod and look at my father, as if to say, "Yes, I suppose it could be worse, but it's hard to imagine how."

For Cheryl and Sharon, my father's affair with Harold's Mother was a prurient mix of hilarity and mystery. They would never have thought of *their* father and mother doing what *my* father and Harold's Mother were doing. Intercourse was to them a grossly dirty, though funny thing—the equivalent of eating piggies. And it was the idea of adults engaging in such activity they found mysterious, the idea that those who made sure they did not do "it" were doing "it" themselves. They found it fascinating that adults had secret sins, and that those sins were, if anything, even more undignified and disgusting than those of children.

Flo was still Flo, trying to shake her sex as if it was some hot and shameful fever. As far as she was concerned, people had affairs so that she would be embarrassed by them. It was, in fact, solely for her embarrassment that sex itself had recently been invented. Whenever Dola lunged at my father, it was Flo who winced the most.

As for Ambrosia, she was as righteous as her mother, if somewhat confusedly so. She never spoke when others were around, but, when alone with me, she'd say, "Your fawder's committin' adultry." Adultry. The failure of an adult to act like one? Some way of being bad peculiar to adults? "Cheryl said dat someone seen 'm goin' to de hotel," she'd say, and study closely my reaction. She seemed to think there was only one hotel and that it was the only place you could commit "adultry"—indeed, she seemed to think that it existed solely for that purpose.

I became quite a figure in the community that fall. My call was confirmed by the priest. There was no test of its authenticity, no final interview I had to pass. I was not required, as my father had been saying all along I would be, to hang by my thumbs in public and explain the gospel to passersby. I did not, contrary to his assertions, have to ascend the altar and, facing the congregation, hold in my hands two burning lumps of charcoal. Also dispensed with was a ceremony that would have had me carry a cross up and down the Shore, while all of Kellies followed, throwing stones. The priest simply informed my mother by phone that, from what he and the nuns had lately seen—there was, for instance, my uncomplaining, almost saintly tolerance of persecution—I had, indeed, been chosen.

My mother decided to celebrate. Rennie and Dola and the girls came over, and some of the SS, and there was a little drinking done. They drank a toast to me. My mother cried, and they drank a toast to her. Ambrosia smuggled a glass of sherry upstairs and drank it in the bathroom—and spent the rest of the night announcing, to no-one in particular, "I don't want to be a nun." Once, when we were alone in the kitchen, she looked at me and said, "You're not gonna be a priest, are ye?" She seemed to think it was something I'd cooked up to get attention. And she had never heard of the word "seminary." She thought it was to the cemetery I was going. She thought that, for seven years, I would wander in the graveyard, and then emerge, a priest. I think the prospect made her nervous, afraid of what a world in which spending years on end in graveyards was not only sanctioned but encouraged might one day require of her.

My father and Rennie got drunk. Every time Rennie swore— and Rennie swore a lot—he looked at me and said, "Beggin' yer pardon Bob."

Dola cried too and, after her second sherry, allowed how "maybe now certain members of dis family'll settle down." I don't think anyone heard her except me.

The priest came by about the middle of the evening, but stayed on the porch where everyone went to shake his hand. He made the sign of the cross and we all blessed ourselves. When he was gone, it was back to the sherry. My mother, having had a glass herself, let me have one. My father gave me a glass of beer and sherry mixed, "berry," he called it. It was afterwards said that, in the midst of the party, I arose and attempted a speech, which started "I'd just like to say," and ended with what my father termed "an obscure, but highly enlightening reference to scripture." In between, I used such words as "humble" and "undeserving" and "overwhelmed" and "proud." It was also said that when, near the end of the evening, I rose again and, in a voice loud enough for everyone to hear, professed myself "mixed up" and "scared" and started to cry, it was put down to excitement and sherry. And there, in that room full of understanding smiles, my mother rose and led me to bed. That night, I had what my mother and father happily called a "normal nightmare."

On the altar, I had already started serving, but now, with my call confirmed, I was chosen to do all the difficult things—weddings, funeral masses, christenings. In addition to going to mass in the morning, I was going to Prayers at night. I remember at Prayers that fall how, after dark, the almost-empty church, so hollow sounding, smelling of smoke and incense, made me feel like a part of a community of solitary souls. All of us there, together and silent in the darkness, hardly aware of one another, looking away from one another, at the Stations on the wall. At Prayers each night, the priest said, Christ was killed so that He might rise in the morning. Christ, at morning mass, was resurrected; at night, after Prayers, we left Him in the tomb. He said that, for the Christian, life was a continuous cycle of hope and dark despair.

It was my mother's idea that I begin to help out at bingoes and card games. My mother didn't go to bingoes and card games herself. She said that the people who really needed the money should be allowed to win it. "The people must have their jackpots," she said. She couldn't see anything wrong with my going, however, as long as I didn't play. Monday and Wednesday nights respectively, I went to bingo and card games after Prayers. At bingo, I sat on the stage and, when bingo was called, forayed into the audience to give the winners their money. A good many women went to bingo, but so did boys and girls, and a group of men who played poker down in the back. I felt foolish sitting there, with all of them looking at me, the grownups smiling approval, sizing me up, trying to figure what kind of priest I'd make; and the children, pointing, laughing. To parents, I was living proof that not all children were thieves and thugs. It was because of me they expected more from their own children—and it was because of that their children hated me.

The worst part was going through the crowd with the money. Men would get me in headlocks and pass me, thus, along the row, as if in some strange "wrestle the boy who would be priest" ritual. Youngsters would grab at me and say, "Hey Bobby, gimme a dollar," or make the loud sucking noises I was, by now, used to. And the women, when I got to the row where bingo had been called, would refuse to tell me who had called it. "Guess," they'd say, smiling, as if they imagined that, so serious and grave a child was I, this little game was the highlight of my week. "Mrs. Clarke," I'd say. "NO," they'd say, "guess again."

"Mrs. Smith."

"No."

"Mrs. Stead."

"No, yer not even warm."

This would go on until they noticed the look of distress that was coming over my face, and then, winking at one another, they would tell me who had won.

At card games I served sandwiches and cookies. "Save me a snowball," the ladies would say on the way in. The card games were worse than bingo because I had to spend a lot of time talking to people. It seemed every woman in the place imagined that I liked her especially. It became common belief that I brought good luck, so I was rotated round the hall from week to week, made to stand at certain tables at certain crucial stages of the game. They all took turns with me. It was considered an advantage to "have Bobby tonight."

It did not seem to be widely understood among the ladies that I would need seven years of seminary training before becoming a priest. They looked on me as a kind of priest's apprentice, "Learnin' de trade, are ye?" Mrs. Mackey always said, smiling. It seemed they thought that I would get the knack of the sacraments after a while, and learn to say the mass in that holy sing-song way. The Latin, of course, would take a little longer, and I might be in high school before I was able to give a decent sermon. They considered themselves lucky to know so well someone who was going to be a priest. Dola, who never missed a card game, imagined that, with me as a priest, her death and entry into heaven would be made that much easier, the way a stay in the hospital is made easier if there is a relative on staff. Harold's Mother was sometimes at the card games. She and some younger ("impressionable," Dola said) women from Luby Line came about once a month, a little drunk, for a very loud game of cards. She always said hello to me, but nothing more, and it was never asked that I stand by her table. Dola wouldn't have let me, anyway, not even to serve sandwiches. "Ye wouldn't tink she'd show 'er face," Dola said.

At school, I developed a kind of compensating wit—over compensating, I suppose. I made people afraid of me. It was Grade 8, and boys and girls were getting interested in one another, but, because I was going to be a priest, I was considered to be above all that. So I decided that, if people were going to stay away, I would make it seem it was what I wanted. I ignored boys, and spoke to girls as if they were the last thing in the world that I could have any interest in. I hoped that, somehow, indifference and arrogance would make me attractive. I hoped, by seeming contemptuous, to make myself mysterious; by my apparently total lack of interest in others, to pique their curiosity, intrigue them, draw them closer. There were sock-hops, but I didn't go to most of them—and when I did go, it was awful. Those one or two girls with whom I might have been friends, I didn't dare ask to dance. Instead, I went around saying things like, "The people in Kellies are clueless." I was, my father said, "an oasis of intelligence, an island of culture, alone among men. In short, a snob." At sock-hops, Archie and I would sit and watch, and wonder what on earth one said when dancing with a girl. How was it that the most inarticulate, brutish boys could, as it seemed, manage such eloquence when they got a girl in their arms? It was a long while before I figured out that it didn't matter what you said, just as long as you said something. I couldn't imagine that girls were generous, receptive, that there was a game going on that wasn't all that easy to play, and that, unless both sides did their part, it would fail. I thought girls held on to everything they had—words, lips, sex—and it was the boys' job to take those things away.

That fall, we practised for the Christmas concert. There was to be a play within a play, the nativity story, as told by a young married couple to their children on Christmas Eve. The play would open in modern times, the family sitting round the fire. In this introductory scene, the father would begin to tell the Christmas story, and then the curtain would fall. Minutes later, it would come up again on Joseph and Mary in the manger. At the end, an epilogue would bring us back to modern times.

My teacher that year was Sister Haymond, and she was in charge of the play. Assigning parts, she made every possible unpopular choice, except in making me Joseph. I was generally acknowledged to be perfect for the part. Mary, Sister Haymond said, must be played by someone with that name. Not counting Ambrosia, whom no-one but the members of her family called Mary, there were two Marys in my Grade 8 class: Mary Smythe, a pretty, uppity blonde, and Mary Hart, a big girl, who had a wart on the side of her nose, and hands as grey as old rope. As luck would have it, Mary Hart was chosen to play the Blessed Virgin. Mary Smythe, Sister Haymond said, would play "the modern mother." I was by no means indifferent to these choices because, as St. Joseph, I would have to kiss the Virgin's cheek, and I would much rather have kissed Mary Smythe's cheek than Mary Hart's. Kissing Mary Hart's cheek, I would come perilously close to the wart. (Mary Hart was Mary Wart to people who didn't like her, and that was almost everyone.) To top it off, Sister Haymond revealed that the boy playing "the modern father" would get to kiss Mary Smythe full on the lips. A good-looking fellow named Tony McGillivray was chosen for that most coveted part.

The play, Sister Haymond said, would centre around the kisses. "The kiss of Joseph and Mary, chastely on the cheek. The somewhat less chaste kiss of father and mother, lightly on the lips. Chastely on the cheek, lightly on the lips, opposing ever so neatly the saintly purity of the Holy Family, and the restrained, respectful passion of the modern Catholic family." Unfortunately, not everyone shared Sister Haymond's enthusiasm. Mary Smythe's father, for instance, wanted to know how lightly was the lightly his daughter would be kissed. And it was generally acknowledged that "full frontal kissing" was a bit much for Grade 8 boys and girls. In an editorial, Kellies monthly paper allowed that, "Perhaps in this, the bard's advice is best: 'If it were done when 'tis done, then 'twere well it were done quickly.'"

Bowing to pressure, Sister Haymond announced that the "modern kiss" would not be rehearsed, and would be left out altogether at the matinée for the younger children. "Instead of kissing," Sister Haymond said, "father and mother will smile affectionately." So as not to "unbalance the drama," the chaste kiss, too, would neither be rehearsed, nor included in the matinée. There would be but one kiss of each kind, "chastely on the cheek," and "lightly on the lips," during the main performance. This seemed to satisfy most people. Tony McGillivray was disappointed, of course, and went around saying that, if there was only to be one kiss, he would make the most of it. It was hoped among the boys that Tony's kiss would bring Mary Smythe down to earth, "melt her snows," as my father put it. Mary herself was said to be dreading the kiss. She was said to have a boyfriend on the mainland, where her family vacationed every summer. Having a boyfriend on the mainland was about as stuck-up as you could get.

My father referred to the upcoming kiss as "the ravishment." He would not, he said, for anything in the world, miss the ravishment of Mary Smythe. He wondered if it could be arranged to have this sort of thing done on stage once or twice a week in Kellies. My mother, on the other hand, was the only person in Kellies who opposed even the chaste kiss. "My concerns, I assure you, are purely hygienic," she said. She had long believed that people were contagious, "not just when they're sick, but all the time." She said the body was a breeding-ground; it was a little-known fact that each of us carries around inside us at least one of every kind of disease-causing germ know to man. "Our own germs can't hurt us," she said. "Disease occurs when people start exchanging germs." She said we had to keep a proper distance between ourselves and others. We must imagine ourselves encased in a sterile bubble, and let no-one come inside it. "Remember the bubble, remember the bubble," my mother liked to say. "If someone comes too close, step back." What about married couples and families, I wondered. My mother said that, by the grace of God, a man and a woman became "immune" to one another at marriage. "I'm immune to your father, and he's immune to me." It worked with children, too. "We're immune to you, and you're immune to us. Isn't that wonderful?"

The problem with Mary Hart, my father said, was that her germs were bigger than mine. Her germs were "bully germs" that had been lifting weights and jumping rope since birth. My mother denied this, saying that Mary's germs were not bigger, "just more numerous." People said I was so holy that, when I kissed Mary Hart, her warts would disappear, then reappear on me. I didn't believe any of this, of course, but it made me think a lot about warts, and I was by no means opposed when my mother came home one day with something called Wart Guard and, every morning afterwards, rubbed it on my face and hands. It was a white cream that, when applied to the skin, vanished. My mother said it was best to start using it right away, so that, by the time of the concert, a good resistance would have formed. She said that, on the night of the concert, I was to kiss Mary Hart with my mouth closed tightly. And afterwards, my father said, I must douse my head with disinfectant, or pour boiling water down my throat. Or better yet, why not hose down Mary Hart before the play, or get an exterminator to give her a good going over?

My mother, of course, could have refused to let me take part in the play. Indeed, it was originally intended that, at the end of the play, the Christ child would rise in gown and golden halo and say, "God bless us, every one," and my mother had hoped that I would get that part. But as it turned out, it was decided that a doll and not a live Christ-child would be used. As Sister Haymond said, any child old enough to stand and speak would not make a credible baby. "Anyway," my mother said, "it's not every day a person gets to be St. Joseph." My father reminded me that I was playing the part of the most uncomplaining cuckold who ever lived. My mother read from her *St. Joseph Daily Missal*: "Jesus, Mary and Joseph exemplify the proper relations that should exist between husband and wife, and parents and children. We should often ask them to sanctify our families by their example and intercession." And she had me learn by heart the Litany of St. Joseph. Once, when my mother was not there to hear, my father pointed out the strangeness of using, as an exemplary family, one made up of a man and a woman who never made love, and a boy who grew up to be God.

We practised three times a week throughout November. We had to make our own costumes and, as she was afraid that we would damage or lose them, Sister Haymond decided there would be no dress rehearsal. My parents did not make my costume until the day of the concert, a Saturday. My mother borrowed a wig from one of the SS, and decided to make me a beard from the box of hair under her bed. I said I didn't need a beard, but my mother said St. Joseph had to have one. She went to her room and, locking the door, made the beard by pasting bits of hair onto a piece of cloth. When she was done, it was big enough to cover half my face, and it had what my father called a wizard's whisker that hung down to my chest. She put it on me right away, using glue, and string that looped about my ears. Then she put the wig on, and then a robe she made from a blanket by cutting holes for my head and arms. To complete the costume, my father lent me a pair of his sandals. There was still an hour before we left, but it was decided that I would leave the costume on and wear it to the concert. My mother was afraid the beard, if taken off, would fall apart. She said I could take off the wig if I liked, but, as my father pointed out, I would look even weirder without it. My father sized me up and said that, unfortunately, I looked, with my complexion, more like a bearded lady than a man. We sat and watched television, and he kept asking my mother, who was in her room, getting ready, if she had noticed that, lately, I'd been looking old. Was it, he wondered, altogether normal for a thirteen-year-old to have a beard—or to wear a blanket for that matter. He knew what it was, he said. It was the new biblical look that was all the rage at school. I tried to ignore him, but he kept at it. I was about at the end of my rope when, to make matters worse, Rennie and Dola and the girls dropped in. Ambrosia had her costume in a bag, but, when she saw that I was wearing mine, begged Dola to let her put hers on. Dola relented, and Ambrosia went to the bathroom, from which she emerged, minutes later, wearing a snowsuit, inside out. It was lined with wool, and she did, indeed, look like the lamb she was supposed to be. Her black boots looked like hooves, as did the baby shoes into which she'd halfway forced her fingers. At rehearsals, her bleating had been rated exceptional. She had been chosen to be, not just a lamb, but the lamb that had to bleat and move the most, "the prime lamb," my father said. She got to crawl around and look at the baby Jesus, and didn't just have to lie there, sleeping, like all the other lambs. "Show them the head Mary," Rennie said. Ambrosia reached into her bag and took out the head of an over-sized toy panda bear. Emptied of its stuffing, it hung limp on her hand, like a puppet. "It was her favourite Teddy bear when she was little," Dola said. "We found him in the attic today." Ambrosia nodded, sadly it seemed, then put the head on. Where the bear's big eyes had been plucked out, spaces were left too large for Ambrosia's eyes, so a lot of her face was visible on either side of the plastic nose. "The only hard part," Dola said, "was the ears. We had to take the old ones off and put some new ones on." The new ears were made from hollow slips and were too large. Cheryl said they made Ambrosia look like an Easter bunny.

"Bobby looks nice, doesn't he girls?" Dola said. It was generally agreed that, though I looked nice, I looked more like Moses than St. Joseph. My mother said that was all right, just as long as I looked like *someone* holy.

Our play, which ran only twenty minutes, came on after the Glee Club and the tap-dancers. We waited off-stage in one of the dressing-rooms, cramped and warm. Ambrosia, to the mortification of the lady in charge of the Glee Club, practised her bleating quite loudly. "Baaa-aaa, baaa-aaa." My beard smelled of mothballs. It got in my nose and made me sneeze. Mary Hart and I tried not to look at one another. She was wearing bed-sheets, blue and white, and holding a plastic baby Jesus in her arms. When we finally did go on, the play went well, up to the point where Mary, sitting, holding the baby Jesus, turned to me and said, "Kiss me Joseph, so that, for a moment, we three may be one." I was standing beside her, and she was to lean a little toward me, so as to seem, Sister Haymond said, "not just kissed but kissing." To the audience, it must have seemed that Mary Hart, holding the baby Jesus with one hand, grabbed me by the beard with the other and, pulling my face down to hers, kissed me, not chastely on the cheek, but deeply, passionately, on the lips. (As my father said, "You wouldn't think Joseph and Mary, married this 2000 years, would still carry on like that.") But what actually happened was that, extending her cheek, Mary leaned too far and started to fall, and grabbed me by the beard to save herself. Consequently, I missed her cheek, and got her on the mouth. It was my misplaced kiss that kept her from going over, because the beard, though it held at first, came off in her hand the moment her lips met mine. And what, to the audience, must have seemed passion, was both of us pushing to get her back into the chair. We had to push, lest our faces slip apart. Not wanting to let on that anything was wrong, I did not use my hands but, to keep my footing, held my arms out like a surfer. And Mary did not use her hands, because she dared not drop the baby Jesus, nor acknowledge the beard by dropping *it*. Nothing touched except our lips. We might have been two acrobats, performing some rare feat of balance. My arms out straight, my face shoved her face back until she rolled into the chair.

While this was going on, the only sound in all the hall was that of Ambrosia bleating—and, in the bleating, there was an undercurrent of giggles, which she was trying to suppress. So infectiously risible was this combination of bleats and giggles, there was, very soon, a tremendous release of laughter, as from people who'd been holding back for years. It started at the back and moved like a wave to the front, like an avalanche of forbidden fruit. It came roaring, not in giggles but great guffaws, and broke upon the stage. Even the nuns and the priests in the front row laughed. My mother would have it, later, that my father was one of only a few people who found it funny. But according to him, she too laughed loudly. "Outrageous," was the word she used. She said the reaction of the audience was "outrageously disrespectful." "Go on," my father said, "everyone laughed except Mary and Bobby and the baby Jesus." We, he said, seemed stunned, and looked out at the audience, as if *its* drawers had dropped, not ours.

We managed to finish the play. The audience settled down when, at a signal from Sister Haymond, Ambrosia stopped bleating. It was the birth of Christ, slapstick style. My father said, later, when the Wise Men came on stage, he expected them to pull out pies and cream the Holy Family. For Tony McGillivray and Mary Smythe, it was a hard act to follow. It was generally agreed that their kiss was nothing next to ours. It was done, in that final scene, so lightly on the lips, no-one batted an eye. Afterwards, Sister Haymond went out and bravely announced that the play had ended. No-one got blamed for the fiasco. Concerning Mary Hart and me, my father said it was "hard to know who ravished who." My mother got her beard back and, to her relief and mine, I did not develop warts.

Except at school, I hadn't done any reading for a long time. After Christmas, I started again. Books were worlds I could escape to, and I read my favourites over and over. One book I read was *The Mountain and the Valley*. I was in love with the notion of declining like David Canaan, tragically, romantically. That winter, whenever it snowed, I went out and climbed the hill behind the house. And I lay down and, closing my eyes, let the snow fall on my face. I imagined what it would be like to stay there and never go back—to be found afterwards, frozen to death, or to emerge in the spring, like a secret from the snow. The priesthood began to seem like a wonderful way to go, the call like a luminous tumour, growing inside me. And I was in love, and that was mixed up with it, too. I was in love with Mary Smythe. Because of Mary Hart, I knew what a girl's lips felt like; and, in my mind. it was easy to match one Mary's kiss with the other Mary's face. Whenever I recalled the play, I recalled kissing Mary Smythe. I thought of how her legs looked, pink with cold, when, in the mornings, she pulled her slacks down from her tunic. I imagined us engaged, then having to break it off because I had decided to join the priesthood. I imagined no great anguish, no heart-rending goodbyes—only silent suffering. I was a hero. I saved her from gangs of boys. I hurled myself in front of a train to knock her out of the way. And I imagined meetings—the two of us, sensitive loners walking after dark behind the school, unaware of one another, and then, somehow, colliding and falling together into snowdrifts. . .kissing. . .holding hands. . .each discovering that, after all, there was someone just like us.

We didn't get to see my father on TV much. He either wanted to watch the Weathergirl, or avoid forecasts altogether, so sick was he of Highs and Lows by the time he got home at five. But sometimes, when he was late getting home, my mother and I did watch him. "It's time to turn your father on," my mother would say. Watching him made me feel uncomfortable. When he was on TV, I could see how hard he was trying, how hard he had to try. Early in the writing of this book, I saw him new, unique, not defined by his connection to me. I saw him that way back then, too, but with one difference. He seemed, not so much strange and separate, as insignificant. When you see someone you know on TV, it is easy to see them as strangers do, to render them general, to fancy that they mean nothing more to you than to everyone. It was frightening to think my father did not fill the place in everyone's universe he filled in mine. Watching him reminded me that one day he would die. I wished I could see my mother on TV. I was sure that, then, I could love her the way I loved my father. It's hard to love someone you think will live forever.

There was no fence on one side of our house. The yard gave way to a road that had been half-built, and which we shared as a drive-way with our neighbours. There was no telling where our half of the driveway ended and our neighbours' half began. We kept to one side and they kept to the other. In between, there was a lot of unused space. Digging out the driveway that winter, it was in that space we piled the snow, so that, by January, there was a wall down the middle so high we could not see over it. Now and then, while we were digging, a shovelful of snow would come flying over the wall and land on top of us. My father and I would promptly throw some back. And soon, the air would be filled with flying snow. Out of breath, our faces drenched, hardly able to open our eyes, we would keep up the assault until, inevitably, the person on the other side started to laugh. And you could tell he was trying not to laugh, for he did it intermittently, gasping in between. His laughing got us laughing, and our laughing made him laugh louder. At the point where he was so incapacitated by giggles that all the snow was going his way, we would stop shoveling. And then the laughter on the other side would fade—not so much decline in volume as grow gradually distant until, with the sound of a door opening and closing, we knew the battle was over. My father called the person on the other side the Unknown Shoveler, though of course we did know who it was. It was Mr. Gulliver—Mr. Gulliver the Shoveler we called him when we got to know him—who was not allowed to laugh because he had a hernia. He could, he told us, shovel snow and lift large objects, run a mile or climb a tree, but he was not allowed to laugh. My father used to threaten to tell him jokes. I remember Mr. Gulliver running toward his house with his hands over his ears, my father in hot pursuit. Mr. Gulliver was black—not black as in Protestant but, as Dola said, "black as in the ace of spades." Mind you, he was Protestant, too, "black inside and out," Dola said.

Since September, we had seen Mr. Gulliver and his family coming and going, but we had never said more than hello. On Sunday mornings, if it was fine, he and his wife and their four children would walk to church. (The Protestant church was about a mile down the road, as far from the Catholic church as it could be without leaving town altogether.)

One day in January, while we were shoveling, a voice on the other side of the wall said, "Too bad dis snow's not black. We could make it feel inferior and it might go away." This was followed by the sound of receding laughter, the sound, as we learned later, of Mr. Gulliver running inside. It went on like that for quite a while. Mr. Gulliver would get off a good one-liner and then run away before, by laughing, we made him laugh harder. Those first few weeks, he made fun of himself relentlessly, whether to put us at ease, or to parody our misconceptions, we were never sure. In Kellies, blacks were accorded the kind of irony often reserved for midgets—as if blackness was an unfortunate, but highly comic, accident of birth. A kind of good-natured prejudice was extended toward them. The generally held Christian view was that Negroes were

God's children too, and deserved as much happiness as, by keeping to themselves, they could acquire. Mr. Gulliver, those first few weeks, said things like, "I works in de warehouse, where no-one 'cept de cats can see me." He was big and totally bald. People called him Kojak. "I could be Kojak," he'd say, in a Louis Armstrong kind of voice, "'cept I don't like lollipops."

"Am I white Mr. Gulliver?" I would ask him. "Honey," he'd say, "you're as white as a polar bear's bag."

"Is it gonna rain Mr. Gulliver?" I might ask.

"Cats and dogs," he'd say.

"And when there's no more cats and dogs?"

"Downpour o' pigs."

"And when there's no more pigs?"

"Honey, when dey's no more pigs, it's gonna rain rhinoceros."

Mr. Gulliver was from Halifax, and had moved to St. John's about when I was born. Later, he left the city and came to Kellies, and had lived in the same house ever since. His wife who, except to go to Sunday service, never ventured out of doors, wore an expression, if not of terror, then certainly of watchfulness. Walking on the road, she looked about her, as if she expected that, any moment, something would come darting from the ditch.

It was a strange friendship that my father and I had with Mr. Gulliver. We never saw the inside of his house, and he never saw the inside of ours. We never met except in the middle of the driveway. It was there we would go on Saturday, about two in the afternoon, to play pepper-squash curling. My father flooded the driveway, and made a curling-rink, using a nail to cut concentric circles in the ice. The grooves he cut he filled with snow and stamped it down. For stones we used pepper squash, first boiled, then frozen solid. For brooms, we used regular household brooms. The first day we played, Mr. Gulliver laughed so hard he had to go in. But the next day we got a game going. There were problems of course. The brooms, for instance, were much too long, so we had to hold them halfway down, and, while sweeping, be careful that the upper part didn't hit us in the head. My father and I, the first time, were knocked about the eyes so badly we afterwards wore goggles. Mr.

Gulliver, who was taller, tended to get hit on the neck and cheeks, which, he said, he didn't mind. There was also a problem with the pepper squash. They tended, upon colliding with anything, to break quite neatly in half. And there was no back-stop at the end of the driveway, so they sometimes went sailing across the road and under the wheels of cars. On any particular day, the game was over when all the squash were broken up. My father and Mr. Gulliver took turns buying them and flattening their under-sides so they would glide along the ice.

I loved it when it was my turn to throw the squash, because then I could watch my father and Mr. Gulliver, out of time with one another, sweeping up a storm, the brooms going like windshield-wipers. The two of them, with heads held back, and eyes half-closed and blinking with every sweep of the broom, went down the drive-way side by side. Because of the over-sized brooms, it was hard to work up sweeping speed, and my father and Mr. Gulliver looked, not so much frantic as deliberate, as if they were more interested in getting the ice clean than in moving the squash along. I doubt if it was the kind of thing Mr. Gulliver, left to his own devices, would have been doing on a Saturday afternoon. Sometimes, as he was sweeping or throwing the squash, a look of puzzlement would come over him, as if it had just occurred to him to wonder why he had lately taken so readily to doing things that, before, he would not have been caught dead at. On the other hand, it may have seemed to him quite in keeping with natural law that something so frowned upon as mixing races and mixing religions should result in aberrant behaviour. As for my father, he seemed to think that this, and only this, was the proper thing for a black Protestant and a white Catholic to do together, as if it was by the lack of pepper-squash curling they had all this time been kept apart; or as if, because it was un-heard of for such people to be friends, it was only right that their friendship involve activities altogether unheard of.

People talked about us, but not much else. On Saturdays, they passed back and forth in front of the house, looking up the drive-way. But they never stopped to watch, never said anything. I think Mr. Gulliver's being a *black* Protestant may have made things easier. There seemed to be a feeling on both sides that, because he was black, it didn't matter quite as much—though this was not the view taken by my mother and Mrs. Gulliver. I would have said pepper-squash curling was an activity sufficiently weird to render irrelevant the question of what company you kept while doing it. But not so. My mother was full of euphemistic complaint. She complained about the rapid disintegration of her brooms, about the way the driveway looked, littered with straw and fragments of squash. She asked my father if he thought it was right to play with food. Imagine, she said, two grown men meeting every Saturday afternoon for the sole purpose of destroying pepper squash. She urged that he ask himself this question: "Would I, or would I not, be ashamed to play this game in the presence of people from Biafra?" Mrs. Gulliver's objections were basically the same. She was also worried, however, that, because of the curling-rink, emergency vehicles would never make it up the driveway; and that, attracted by the squash, "animals" would come creeping down from the woods at night; or that, worst of all, the children would learn to like the game, and would come to her begging money to buy squash. Mrs. Gulliver kept her children inside on Saturday afternoons, and pulled the curtains so they could not watch us from the windows. My mother, too, stayed inside, and SS women started coming to sit with her on a regular basis, as if, in these most troubled times, she must not be left alone. Rennie would drop Dola off at the house, and sometimes stay to watch a game—until Dola, noticing that the truck was still in the yard, would come out and remind him that the girls were at home alone. Once, Mr. Gulliver's little boy came running out, and Rennie picked him up beneath the arms and, holding him high, said, "Have you got a blackbird in dem drawers?"

Somehow, my mother succeeded because, after a while, my father stayed in on Saturdays, sending me out to the wall to explain to Mr. Gulliver why he couldn't come out. Without my father, Mr. Gulliver and I didn't know what to say to one another. Pepper-squash curling wasn't much fun with just one sweeper. "Yer daddy's busy, is he?" Mr. Gulliver would say, over and over, as the two of us stood outside in the cold. "Yer daddy's busy, is he," or "Busy is he Bobby?"

We tried to make a game of it, finding all the variations. "Is he busy Bobby?" "Busy, Bobby, is he?" "Daddy's busy, is he Bobby?" I could see he was disappointed, and he could see how sad I was. My father should have come out one of those Saturdays, should have said something to Mr. Gulliver—some acknowledgement of parting was needed. But he seemed not to notice that anything was ending. Perhaps he never really gave in to my mother, but only put off coming out, thinking there was time, until there began to grow around him, like a brake of thorns, that inertial solitude we all hate to fight. At anyrate, one Saturday when I went out to the wall, Mr. Gulliver wasn't there. And though I waited an hour, he did not show up.

By May, the wall had melted, and my mother, giving us each a garbage-bag, sent my father and me to pick up the pieces of squash, the rotting bits of stalk and peel, the remnants of the winter.

That summer, I found out that I would be accelerated past Grade 9 and go straight to Grade 10 in town. "Accelerate," became my mother's favourite word. "Bobby, you're being accelerated," she said. And indeed, I was, head over heels down a sudden slope in time. My mother said she was still "opposed in principle" to acceleration, but thought it marvellous how easily and justifiably an exception could be made in my case. For one thing, I was old enough now to deal with it; for another, I was "brilliant."

My father agreed. He said I was so brilliant, my friends had to wear sunglasses.

My mother said that everything was arranged. I was to leave for the seminary "not this June, and not the next, but the next one after that." "The date is set," she said.

It was a strange summer, a succession of Prayers and masses, bingoes and card games. Since we'd moved, I hadn't seen much of Archie, except on the altar. Whenever we met that summer, he seemed remote, almost unfriendly. He had been counting on the two of us leaving together for the seminary, as had I. Now both of us would go alone, and I would go first, and steal his thunder. "Anti-climacth all the way," Archie said, referring to the day in three years' time when *he* would leave. It had been hard for him all along, because it was generally believed that I would make a bishop, and that Archie, if by some miracle he managed to get himself ordained, would not make it past priest. "I'm thtupid," he said, "and I have a thpeech impediment. I gueth I won't make Pope." The coming year, going to school in town and, so, spending less time on the altar at St. Stephen's, I would hardly see him at all. It struck me how, all my life, I had been leaving people and places behind, and yet saw those people and places every day. The truth was that I had left nothing behind, but had had, in the midst of many friend-ships, to see friends fade to mere acquaintances, and homes to houses, overnight. It seemed that if I stayed in Kellies long enough, I would start all over again: first friend, first house, second friend, second house; and would, the rest of my life, go round and round, not really knowing anyone, not really living anywhere.

CHAPTER 6

There was no high school in Kellies. St. Stephen's was what my mother and her friends at the Board of Education called K-9—"a dog of a school," my father said, but it really meant kindergarten to Grade 9. The high school in town was Brother Arthur Noonan High, "the Barn," as we called it. My father said my mother sent me there a year early just so she could have a high-school student in the house on whom to test her curriculum ideas. This was not true, of course, but once the school year started, she *did* sit me down from time to time to ask my opinion on various things. She began to call me "the Voice of Youth." "It's time to hear from the Voice of Youth," she'd say, and beam at me, as if I was some oracle of adolescence, some archetypal teenager. It made me feel very strange, and I hoped it wouldn't get out to my fellow students that I was in part responsible for the courses and text-books they so dearly hated.

The Barn, just down the hill from Heavy Heart High, was an all-boys' school, renowned for its high academic standards and strict code of discipline. I did not like the idea of switching from St. Stephen's to The Barn. For one thing, although other boys from St. Stephen's were going with me, they had all been in Grade 9 the year before, and I didn't know them very well; for another, at the Barn they used what my mother called "the Tiers of Intelligence" system. My father, harking back to the bright-baby theory, called it "PDB, the Principle of Declining Brilliance." Boys with bloated IQs were put in Tier Ten, and my mother was informed a week before school that I had made it, "with IQ points to spare." She said I was the first student ever from St. Stephen's to make Tier Ten, and she was overjoyed that I was "finally running with thoroughbreds." "A nag no longer," my father sighed. Most of the boys from St. Stephen's were put in that tier which, for years, had been known as the Bay Boys—Tier Five. I anticipated that being in Tier Ten would cause me a lot of problems. I thought the boys from town would think a bay boy was a bay boy, whether he was in Tier Ten or Tier One. And I was sure that the boys from St. Stephen's and the other schools along the Shore, would think that anyone in Tier Ten was a townie, a brain, a brown-noser. I was sure that, hated by both sides, I'd be an outcast. We of Tier Ten were called the Wise Ones and, as it turned out, it was not so bad. Most Wise Ones were, like me, relieved to find that they were not the rare, queer birds they had been made out to be. It was nice to be in a class where you did not have to be ashamed of being smart, where you could talk about things you were genuinely interested in, without alienating fellow students. I made friends quickly, and the boys from St. Stephen's pretty much left me alone. About the only time I saw them was at lunch in the cafeteria, and on the bus going home. They were more than a little intimidated by the Barn, and it seemed they did not know what to make of someone who was doing well there. It struck me on those bus-rides home, sitting usually by myself, that a gap had begun to open between me and my home town. Having lived all their lives in one place, within one tradition, the boys from St. Stephen's were suddenly switched, suddenly found themselves among strangers. Whenever I saw one of them, looking lost in the corridors, I felt like telling him that *here* I knew the way, and I would be glad to show him. But, to the boys from St. Stephen's, I would always be the Bobby O'Malley of the hag and candle-covers. It was at the Barn I first began to think of Kellies as my home town. And I knew, leaving it every morning, that I would one day leave for good. It seemed strange to think that it was a place outside of me, that it was real, and would remain when I was gone.

At Brother Arthur Noonan, there were lockers in the halls instead of coat-hooks, long rows of metal and marble. The corridors were always cold and, lacking windows, always dark. Early mornings, sometimes, you could see your breath—down the line of lockers, a hundred breathing boys.

The first week, we underwent Noonanization. This involved daily gatherings in the gymnasium, for lectures on the history of the school. We were told that, writing before the turn of the century, to his superiors back in Ireland, outlining his progress in establishing a Christian Brothers school for boys, Brother Arthur Noonan envisaged a school that would not turn out the kind of men "who have about them that air of ever wanting more than God or man can give. Here, on this rock-bound Elba of the North Atlantic, here, under the ceaseless howl of storm and gale, give me a boy who will make his mark on the rock."

We gathered every Friday in the gymnasium for the reading of this letter and to recite what we called the "Noonanisms," a long list of things that a Noonanite must and must not do.

Also, at these gatherings, we sang the school song, called "Nay, Stay Brother Arthur":

Brother Arthur Noonan High
As we stand and sing your song
Let us pause and breathe a sigh
We've not seen him for so long.

　　Though he be gone
　　His name lives on
　　Praise God, praise God.

Brother Arthur Noonan High
That man's name you proudly bear
Will not ever really die
Just as long as you are here.

Though he be gone
His name lives on
Praise God, praise God.

Brother Arthur Noonan High
We are only passing through
We'll be leaving by and by
But we will not forget you.

According to school legend, the song, as it was first written, had a fourth verse. No-one had ever seen the fourth verse, or heard it sung, but it was somehow known to have existed, and was said to have been the best by far. Someone known as Brother Ubaldus Hedwig was said to be writing a new verse every week, extending the school song *ad infinitum* in the hope of coming up with a suitable fourth verse, one as good as the unknown one by the unknown master. Hedwig had, by the time of my arrival, been writing fourth verses to "Nay, Stay Brother Arthur" for twenty years, without success. The school song was now 1040 verses long, all of which Hedwig was said to be able to recite from memory. Everyone knew that Hedwig was, in fact, our principal, Brother Gilmore, who put an hour aside now and then to write verses for special occasions.

Going to an all-boys' school was new for me, but not for most Noonanites who, up until Grade 9, had gone to the School of St. Peter's Chains, just up the hill from Heavy Heart. So, although the Barn was new to them, they had known each other for years. They had never had co-ed classrooms, or even female teachers. The Brothers believed it was better that way. It was impossible, they said, for boys to learn with girls around. How could they concentrate? Inevitably, those who were willing to waste their breath and argue with the Brothers cited bay boys as examples of co-educated males who had not gone wrong. "What about O'Malley," the boys in my class said, "he's been in the same room with girls for eight years. It hasn't affected him." The Brothers would smile and say that that remained to be seen. When bay boys weren't being teased, their favours were courted. We were someone to whom the school traditions and city surroundings, which the townies took for granted, seemed quite special—and so we made the townies *feel* special. I remember one little fellow proclaiming his amazement that I had never been to lunch at Rice's restaurant. Everyone, he said, had been to lunch at Rice's a thousand times. He was incredulous when I told him that I had never even heard of Rice's.

Those townies who had few or no friends saw in us bay boys a chance to start over. I was beleaguered the first month, on the one hand by outcasts and loners, on the other by those who wanted to warn me against them. I don't say it to my credit, but I was a regular within weeks. I knew who to talk to, and who to stay away from. I wanted friends. I wanted, at long last, to make it with the crowd. That I was bright, or even that I was going to be a priest, bothered no-one. Half the class were incubating vocations of one kind or another. Grade 10 at Brother Arthur Noonan High was about the happiest year of my life. There was something about the place and time that made me nostalgic for it, even while I was there. Maybe it was the way the Brothers kept throwing it up to us that we were on the verge of manhood, that, in a very short time, we would be out in the big world, having to make it on our own. "*Ye shall never pass this way again*," the banner that, in two years' time, we would hang in the gym on graduation night, was our motto from the first day. The Brothers were acutely conscious that our stay at the Barn represented the system's last chance, that whatever we had missed over the past nine years must be crammed into these two, that we must be made to absorb enough nourishment now to sustain us through the years ahead. The Brothers liked to tell of how, almost every day, one of their former students, often one who, during his stay at Brother Arthur Noonan High, had been much chastised and punished, came into the office to shake hands with Brother

Gilmore, and to thank him, and to tell him that, many times since he had left the Barn, the lessons he learned there had stood him in good stead. Few of us thought that the Brothers were making up the story. The affection they reserved for reprobates and upstarts, the zeal with which they beat them up, the way, when strapping them, they looked them in the eye, as if to see there, awakened by the blows, the seed, the nascent moral fibre that, in time, would make them men—all this convinced us that the story was either true, or had been around so long, the Brothers could not remember making it up.

I remember Brother Gilmore walking up and down between the tables, lunchtime in the cafeteria, looking at us as a boot-camp sergeant looks at his troops, knowing what we could not know—that many of us were soon to fall in battle. It was an unscrupulous world outside, full of men and women not like us. There would be much temptation. Would we have the wisdom and strength to withstand it?

There was tremendous *esprit de corps* among Noonanites. We were taught to think of ourselves as the moral elite. The world outside was run by men whose teachers had let drop the reins of discipline. The Barn might have been the last bastion of decency, beset all round by infidels and Protestants. The proof of our moral superiority was what Brother Gilmore called "our general excellence." We did everything better than everyone else. We were told that three things were important to a Noonanite: ethics, scholastics and athletics—the Three Ics, as we called them.

Brother Arthur Noonan High was the school that everyone loved to hate. Even the other Catholic schools hated us, but it was the liberal, non-denominational schools that considered us arch-enemies. Demonstrating a marked lack of originality, we called them the Artsie Fartsies. To them, we were Micks and Jocks and Jerks, what they called the Other Three Ics. There was a song about us that consisted only of those three words, or variations on them, sung to the tune of *"Frère Jacques"*:

Mick, jock, jerkie

Mick, jock, jerkie
Mick, jock, jerk
Mick, jock, jerk
Mickie, jockie, jerkie
Mickie, jockie, jerkie
Mick, jock, jerk
Mick, jock, jerk

It was at sports events we got our revenge, especially at basketball games. Some afternoons, I didn't go home on the St. Stephen's bus, but hung around after school to watch the games, and had my father or mother pick me up at five. The Artsie Fartsies wouldn't sing the "Mick, Jock, Jerkie" song when they came to our gymnasium, nor when we went to theirs. They sang it at the hockey games, though, because those were played at public stadiums, where you could get away with anything. What irritated the Artsie Fartsies most was our refusal to run the score up against them. At basketball games, we were usually leading by 40 points at halftime, so we would bench our first-string players and, in the second half, alternate our second and third stringers, and have them play defence only. It made for boring basketball, twenty minutes of blocked shots and pseudo-sportsmanship. It was humiliating for the Artsie Fartsies, and they would fill the second half with ceaseless booing. Our teams were called the Noonan Niners. For years, girls from Heavy Heart had been cheerleading for the Noonan Niners, though it was widely rumoured by opposing schools that they were really Noonanites in drag. The Noonan Niner All-Hearts were the most conservative cheerleaders in the city. They wore red-and-white knee-length dresses, the hems of which were weighted with ball-bearings, to prevent, as their principal put it, "that unsightly display of leg and underpants which girls from other schools give so shamelessly." On rare occasions, the hem gave way and the ball-bearings broke loose. Once, at a rival gym, an All-Heart was horrified, upon noticing much ducking and dodging in the opposite bleachers, to find that, every time she jumped, she was sending ball-bearings sailing across the court. The All-Heart cheers were pretty average: "Niners,

Niners, all the way, Niners, Niners, what a play. YaaaaaAAAY NINERS." Opposed to the All-Hearts were the girls from Gregg Academy, award-winning cheerleaders. When Gregg Academy came to play, the Barn gymnasium was full, but no-one watched the game. Known as the Greggettes, they were unofficially the Gyro Girls. In short white skirts, tight tops and pale-blue panties, they were most diverting, to fans and players alike. For a while, they were banned from the Barn, and were only allowed back upon agreeing to remove all pelvic thrusts from their performance. When at other gyms, however, they went on thrusting and attracted quite a following of Noonanites.

Tier Ten was a class of caricatures. Such a bunch of smart-alecks were we, of such prime wise-cracking age, we refused to take anything seriously, including ourselves. And though, throughout the year, there began to form groups of five and six and seven boys, within which, the next year, closer, truer friendships would result, Grade 10 was one long merciless lampoon. I was known as the bay boy bound for the priesthood. It was said that, when I was a priest, I would not wear a habit but a sou'wester, and would carry a codfish with which to bless my congregation. But things could have been much worse. There was Tommy Bates, for instance, who sat in front of me. Tommy was the son of a prominent Water Street merchant and, because his father was rich, he was the "rich man's son." Three years before, when Tommy was attending the School of St. Peter's Chains, his mother died, and Tommy's father sent the butler to bring him home. The poor man was so nervous that he forgot to knock on the classroom door. He simply opened it and said, "It's your mother Master Bates." Tommy had been called Master Bates before, many times, and the boys had long ago stopped laughing. But, on this occasion, the strange mix of sorrow and absurdity, the sudden flippant sadness, the bathetic plunge from "mother" to "Master Bates," was more than they could stand. Tommy would remember that, when they heard about his mother, all his friends, if only for a moment, laughed—and then were so embarrassed by it, some of them, they started to cry.

There was Max Devine, condemned by his name and the size of his nose—"Love is a nose / but you better not pick it / it only grows when it's on Devine."

There was Joe English, who made the mistake of professing an interest in ceramics. In class elections at the end of September, Joe was elected president-for-life of the Brother Arthur Noonan High Ceramics Society which, as Brother Gilmore said, "does not now, nor ever will, exist."

There was Little Lawrence Englehart, who came from across town and, not having attended the School of St. Peter's Chains, was able to keep secret for three weeks the fact that he was small enough to fit inside his locker. In October, Little Lawrence was rescued from his locker half a dozen times by Brothers coming down the hallway during class. Having screamed himself hoarse, he whispered his combination numbers through the locker vent. Once, a Brother refused to let him out until he told who had locked him in. But Little Lawrence would not tell. He *never* told, and people respected him for it. After a while, he started getting in lockers voluntarily. A student coming back from lunch or gym to get his books was often horrified, upon opening his locker, to have Little Lawrence come leaping out and grab him by the throat. It became very important that no-one know your combination, especially not Little Lawrence who, if he found it out, would go directly to your arch-enemy and offer his services for a fee.

There was Kiwi Williams, whose four brothers had gone to Brother Arthur Noonan High, all under the name Kiwi Williams. Kiwi was the family nickname. Kiwi's father, known as Kiwi One, owned a fruit store, and Kiwi was said to entertain a certain kind of passion for certain kinds of fruit. We called him "pumpkin poker," and "melon mounter." We pointed at him in French class and said, "J'accuse d'abuse banana."

There were boys about whom things were said that were not meant to make you laugh. There was Alastair (Alice) Skiffington, who had once, at the School of St. Peter's Chains, gotten an erection in the shower. There was Bag-Rot Pearse, whom no-one ever called by any other name than Bag-Rot, and that for no reason but that he lived in the Battery, near the harbour, where people were poor. There was D-Cup (Frankie) Jones who, the year before, at the School of St. Peter's Chains, came gamely down from the bleachers at an intra-mural basketball game to replace one of his classmates who'd been injured—whereupon some mischief-making ref declared that D-Cup's team must now go skins. D-Cup, so named for the size of his lobe-like drooping breasts, could have backed out but he didn't. He took off his blazer, shirt and tie, and shoes, and, in stocking feet and flannels, went up and down the court for half an hour, his breasts bouncing to a chorus of scorn from the bleachers.

These boys, except Joe English, Bag-Rot Pearse and Alice Skiffington, became my friends. Tommy Bates, Max Devine, Little Lawrence Englehart, Kiwi Williams, D-Cup Jones and I made up one of many groups that formed as the Grade 10 year progressed.

As the top class, Wise-Ones were given special treatment, which was sometimes good and sometimes bad. We got to go on field trips, to science labs and lumber mills, and the Arts and Culture Centre. Once a month, we went to the Friday Paramount Movie Classics, special matinées for school kids. We saw *Wuthering Heights* and Danny Kaye in *The Secret Life of Walter Mitty*, and a little-known comedy, *Cole Younger's Younger Brother Bill*.

On the other hand, it was ruled that, because we were smart, we did not need as much exercise as other boys. We had gym only once a week, and then only for half an hour. The gym teacher hated us. Deeming us hopeless at all sports requiring "strength, agility or bodily movement," he devised a game called Paddling Pansies, which we could play while sitting down. It was essentially a twenty-minute mimed canoe race. He would break us up into groups of five and six, and arrange us in rows side by side. When he blew his whistle, we would start paddling, and would not stop until he blew it again. Despite the fact that none of us budged from where we sat, he declared a winner every week. The winning row, he said, was that one which "best combined ferocious effort with at least some sense of style." This went on for about a month, until we complained to Brother Gilmore, after which we were allowed to play regular sports. The gym teacher got even, however, by lecturing us for twenty minutes every week on "basics," so that, almost invariably, gym period was over by the time we got our teams picked.

Our home-room teacher was Brother Bill Denny, a native Newfoundlander who had lived for a while in Montreal, and had played hockey with the Montreal Junior Canadiens. He was coach of the senior hockey team but, unlike the gym teacher, was not more abusive of Wise-Ones than of other boys. Brudder Bill, as we called him, was by no means alone among Brothers in endorsing a theory that boys, like horses, had need of breaking. One of the favourite games of the Brothers was Mock-Humiliation, the all-in-fun tearing down of a boy in front of his fellows. If you were singled out for Mock-Humiliation, your full co-operation was expected. Brudder Bill used MH the first day to find out if Tommy was broken:

"Stand up Bates."

"Yes Brudder."

"Are ye broken Bates?"

"Yes Brudder."

"Who broke ye Bates?"

"Me mudder Brudder."

"Yer mudder broke ye?"

"Yes Brudder."

"How'd she break ye Bates?"

"I can't remember Brudder."

"Ye can't remember Bates?"

"No Brudder."

"Were ye born broken Bates?"

"Yes Brudder."

"Born broken, were ye?"

"Yes Brudder."

"So why'd ye blame yer mudder?"

"I'm sorry Brudder."

"Sit down Bates."

"Yes Brudder."

There was also a procedure known as MMH, or Mini-Mock-Humiliation, which might happen to each of us two or three times a week. It went this way, with the whole class coming in on the last line:

"Yer a slime Bates."

"Yes Brudder."

"What are ye Bates?"

"A SLIME."

Brudder Bill would announce the MMH word first thing every morning. "Today's word," he would say, "is 'greener.' Everybody—GREENER."

"Yer a greener O'Malley."

"Yes Brudder."

"What are ye O'Malley?"

"A GREENER."

Brudder Bill's supply of MMH words was not unlimited. There were about twenty, I think; among them were "slime," "greener," "snot" and "fiend." Little Lawrence Englehart's mother wrote a letter to Brother Gilmore complaining about her son being "forced to profess himself a jockstrap."

Brudder Bill, the first week of school, went up and down the rows, and discovered to his mock surprise that not one of us was unbroken. He made us learn a rhyme which, when we misbehaved, he would have us say aloud. He had me say it once. He opened his eyes maniacally wide and put his face up close to mine. "Tell us O'Malley," he said, "how Brudder Bill breaks boys." I recited:

He takes the still-stout lads
Down to the furnace-room
He dresses 'm up in goalie-pads
And then KA-BOOM KA-BOOM
He shoots the puck
With any luck
The boys come back
All broken up.

No-one ever got kaboomed. We were too terrified to do anything really wrong.

I remember the warm days that fall when the girls from Heavy Heart came out and sat on the hill, looking down—rows of nyloned legs in the grass, their tunics black and blouses white in the sunlight. Kiwi was not the only weird one. I cut from a package of panty-hose a cardboard pair of legs, from an issue of *National Geographic* a pair of mud-caked thighs—also a torso and one bare breast. From my mother's magazines, I cut the heads of movie-stars. Pasted together, my eclectic lady had Caucasian calves and thighs from Ethiopia, a Nubian belly, a breast from Bora Bora and a head from *Homes and Gardens*. Actually, I tried on different heads, and sometimes replaced other parts, just to see what it would look like. I lent the eclectic lady to Kiwi in exchange for pages of lingerie ads from Eaton's catalogue. (My mother hid *our* catalogue away or, failing that, took scissors and cut out all the pictures.)

I did not, as D-Cup described Kiwi doing, "masturbate with melons," but confined myself to what Tommy Bates called "the basic right-hand jerk job." Tommy confessed himself a southpaw. Little Lawrence claimed to be ambidextrous. D-Cup told of having a sister who left her door unlocked. He watched her getting undressed, of course, but, even better, borrowed her bra when she was out and admired himself in the mirror. D-Cup assured us that, in a bra, he had "real cleavage." Max Devine said that, in his family, the nose was not the only over-sized bodily part. He claimed to be writing a book called *Masturbation and Marijuana (Jerking Off and Smoking Up): A Study of the Effects of Auto-Eroticism on the Cannabis Intake of Teenage Boys.*

Tommy owned a car, which his father had given him on his fifteenth birthday. His father had either confused his age, or had forgotten that you had to be sixteen to drive a car. In any case, Tommy liked the car so much, he wouldn't let his father take it back. After school some days, we took the bus to Tommy's house and drove up and down the driveway in the car. It was a big green, four-door Duster. Tommy jacked it up, and put Toronado tires on the back, and had gill slits cut on either side to make it look like a Barracuda. He installed a stereo and mind-blower speakers, covered the dash with black velour and the steering-wheel with leather. Some days, all six of us in the car, we parked, engine running, at the end of the driveway, hoping to impress any girls who came walking by. Tommy blew the horn whenever he saw some, and revved and waved, and we all laughed and secretly hoped that the girls wouldn't stop and make fools of us by asking to go for a ride. "Just wait till next year," Tommy would say, and put the pedal down, as if on time itself. There, in the car, we looked out at the street, and the girls who walked along it, a million miles away.

The fall was full of girls, and my mother began to worry about them. At that time, our maid was a girl only two or three years older than me. She came at four to cook supper and clean house, and left about six when my mother or father got home. She was beautiful. She had blond hair, and wore T-shirts so short you could see her belly. She had a habit of playing with her belly-button, rolling it like a wad of white gum between her fingers. Her name was Eleanor. When my mother found the eclectic lady under my bed, she got rid of Eleanor, and replaced her with a middle-aged woman named Mrs. Hiller. I made the best of it. After school, I hid under the back step. When Mrs. Hiller came out to shake the mop, I held my breath and, squinting through the dust, looked up her dress.

The first week of December, it was announced that there would be a Christmas dance in the gym. On the grounds that being totally kept from the company of the opposite sex might lead to a tremendous build-up of adolescent energy that could only find relief in rape or prostitution, or other, less wholesome, forms of deviance, Brother Gilmore and Sister Celestine Facundo, principal of Heavy Heart High, arranged a blind date between the student bodies of the two schools, an unprecednted *en masse* meeting of Heavy Hearts and Noonanites. Sister Celestine sent down 600 résumés for the boys of Brother Arthur to fill out. Name, age, grade, weight, height, hair colour, hobbies, vocational interests. Sister Celestine wanted to know everything about us. There was even a space on the résumés for something called General Self-Assessment (GSA), in which we were to rate ourselves on a scale of Fair to Excellent. (Brother Gilmore noted Sister Celestine's implied compliment—that it was impossible that a Barn boy be less than Fair.) Also, there was something called Your Basic Disposition (YBD). We were to choose which of the following best described our personalities: shy, quiet, mild, average, assertive, outgoing, aggressive.

The résumés were filled out and sent back to Sister Celestine. About a week later, each of us received a form letter, filled out by the girl with whom we'd been matched. It was not an invitation, but a request for an invitation. The only parts of the letter filled in by the girl herself were the opening and closing salutations, and the signature at the end. The standard part of the letter read like this: "your name was matched with mine and it has been suggested that you invite me to the first annual Brother Arthur Noonan/ Heavy Heart High School Christmas Dance. If you wish to do so, please inform Brother Gilmore as soon as possible."

As only the salutations were personalized, we read a lot into them. Little Lawrence, who on the GSA and YBD rated himself Excellent and Aggressive, and had lied about his height and weight, got a letter that opened "Hi there" and closed "Can't wait to see you," from someone called Suzi Benizi. Tommy Bates got "Well hello" and "Counting the minutes," from someone called Perpetua Blaise. I, who on the GSA and YBD rated myself Good and Mild and, fearing that Brother Gilmore would look at my résumé before sending it on, confessed I was bound for the priesthood, got "Greetings" and "Not Unanticipant," from M. Babb. Not Unanticipant M. Babb soon became known as Numb. I suppose it could have been worse. D-Cup, who, on his résumé, had been what Little Lawrence called "unnecessarily honest," got "Hello" and "Really, I'm not that bad," from Irene Boniface. Max Devine got "How do you do" and "Not signing because I hate my name—just show up I'll find you." Kiwi didn't do so bad. He got "Hi" and "Your name is nice," from Valery George. Joe English got "Here goes nothing" and "Honest to God I'm scared to death," from Clare Moore. One girl closed by saying "Boy this is really dumb," and signed herself Gorgonius. The identity of Gorgonius was discovered by the process of elimination and, for the boy who received her invitation, another date was found. This was possible because there were more girls than boys going to the dance—fifteen more to be exact. Those girls without dates were soon being referred to as "Gorgonius and the Fourteen Wallflowers."

We spent a day in the gym, making streamers, and setting up tables and chairs. We took down the stage curtain and replaced it with a huge sign that read:

THE BOYS OF BROTHER ARTHUR
WELCOME
THE GIRLS OF HEAVY HEART
OURS TO STOP THE RAGING STORM
OURS TO GO WHERE NO STORMS COME

As Heavy Heart was our sister school, its motto was complementary to ours.

A huge Christmas tree was erected to the right of the stage, and beneath it were placed 600 gift-wrapped copies of *The Ladies' Pocket Prayer Book*. Sister Celestine sent down as many copies of *A Young Man Prays: A Guide to Grace and Worship*. Six hundred cardboard hearts were suspended by string from the ceiling. It was Brother Gilmore's idea that, at the end of the dance, each boy would reach up and pluck a heart and give it to his date. Then, all together, we would say:

Take this heart
O Heavy Heart
Until we meet again
And if by chance
You hold a dance
Give it to me then.

The girls of Heavy Heart would answer:

On this night
O Noonanite
I take your heart away

Alas, alack
I give it back
To you another day.

The dance would start at eight and end at midnight. We were to gather in the gym and wait for the girls, who were to meet first in their own gym, and then march in the darkness down the hill, a good 200 yards in wind and cold, wearing nothing but what Sister Celestine, in a letter to Brother Gilmore, described as "pretty, dainty dresses." For us boys, she recommended "suits, but not tuxedos— and nothing sporty, mind. Perhaps it would be best if they simply wore their blazers." This letter did nothing to change the prevailing view of Sister Celestine as a too-long-reigning old crone, akin to Queen Victoria. She had been principal of Heavy Heart High since the Second World War and was said to write the Department of Education every September, requesting permission to resume bimonthly air-raid drills. But Brother Gilmore acceded to her requests. At the dance, he said, we would wear our school uniforms—white shirts, wine ties and matching blazers (crest gold on field of blue), flannel slacks, white socks and black shoes.

One of my favourite memories is of that night in the gym, before the dance: 600 of us, off to one side, waiting. It was dark in the gym, the only lights the lobby lights outside, toward which we looked when the singing started. It was a clear cold night, and we heard them far away, heard, as my father, who, having dropped me off, met them coming down the hill, said, "600 virgin voices raised in song." They came six abreast down Bonaventure, one hundred half-dozen, in tights and sunhats, holding hands. And singing:

Heavy Heart of Jesus hear us
Near us as we walk along
Heavy Heart of Jesus near us
Hear us as we sing your song

Nothing now can hold us back

Nothing take away our might
There is nothing that we lack
We are always in the right

Though we girls of Heavy Heart
Heavy Heart of Jesus High
Are not Jesus as Thou art
As Thou art Jesus need not sigh

(Clearly, the Heavy Heart poet had been influenced by Hedwig.)
Throughout the final verse, the volume of voices gradually declined until, close to the end, what little was left broke off abrupt-
ly:

Who would try to stop us now
Who would dare to block our way
We would raise a holy row
We would—

My father, who appears to have been the only eye-witness to what
happened, said the parade was coming quite nicely down Bonaventure when those half-dozen Heavy Hearts at the rear seemed, all at
once, to lose their footing on the icy hill and, falling backwards,
with arms linked like chorus girls, kicked the feet out from under
the half-dozen immediately in front—who, in turn going down,
took out the next half-dozen. And it went on like that, until all 600
had been mowed down, as if by some heel-high blade. A squeal, my
father said, a brief but high-pitched squeal, travelled from row to
row as they went down. And then, for a moment, they all sat silent,
motionless, still in formation, their dresses in the streetlight white
against the pavement. Then the rows began to rise in the exact
order in which they had fallen. And, because they were on a hill, it
must have seemed that all they had to do was sit up straight and,
raising their knees so that their feet went flat on the pavement, push
off with their hands. The last row did just that and, no sooner were
they on their feet, than once again they slipped; and their slipping

was perfectly timed with the rising of the row in front. The impulse to rise went down the hill, and was just as quickly undercut by the falling row behind it, so that, this time, there was not a mowing motion, but one more like a wave. Nothing, my father said, could have been choreographed more perfectly; nothing could have seemed more strangely appropriate than that vision of all those boy-bound girls caught up in some spell. In the end, the nuns who had been walking well ahead came back and, under their supervision, the girls resumed their march.

It must have been minutes later that the Brother we'd posted on Bonaventure came in to tell us they'd arrived. Looking out from the darkness of the gym, we saw Sister Celestine ascend the lobby stairs, like some visiting potentate, surrounded by a retinue of nuns —and then there came an army, a sea of sun-hats. The girls. Their outer chatter carried in and, too loud in the light, surprised them, and they looked at one another, and then looked back toward the cold and darkness, as if it was that all this was about, as if to get away from that they'd come inside. Sister Celestine stood in the doorway of the gym and, turning round, raised her arms for silence. The lights came up a little, as much as would be needed for the dance. Then Sister Celestine turned round again and led her nuns and girls into the gym. On cue, we started singing "Nay, Stay Brother Arthur," and continued singing as the girls of Heavy Heart lined up opposite. We sang two verses that Hedwig had written especially for the dance:

> Brother Arthur Noonan High
> Never graced by girls before
> You no doubt are wondering why
> There are 600 on the floor

> Brother Arthur Noonan High
> "Give me a boy," your namesake said
> He did not mean we should be shy
> We must have girls if we're to wed

Brother Gilmore went to the microphone at centre court and welcomed the nuns and girls of Heavy Heart. When he was finished, Sister Celestine explained the rules of the dance. There were twenty of what I can only describe as stalls on either side of the dance-floor —adjoining areas that were cordoned off with rope. Each stall was hung with a sign that gave its grade and tier number. Ours looked like this:

10—10
HRT Brother Bill Denny
Class pop 29

Boys and girls should find their stall and take a seat, Sister Celestine said. She pointed out that each Heavy Heart stall had a Brother or nun standing guard. Heavy Heart was also a ten-tier school, and there was to be none of what she called "intiermingling." 10-10 of Brother Arthur was directly opposite 10-10 of Heavy Heart, 10-9 opposite 10-9 and so on. All a boy had to do to ask his date to dance was go straight across the floor and give, to the Brother or nun who was standing guard, his dance pass, on which the name of his date was written. The guard would call the girl and give her a ticket as she left the stall. The girl would go with her date, dance, and then come back, returning the ticket to the guard. It was not permitted to dance two or more dances in a row. If, coming back after a dance, a girl returned a ticket of the wrong colour, she and her date would be sent home, The disc-jockey for the evening was a Brother from the School of St. Peter's Chains, who hid all night behind the WELCOME sign and, after each song, announced the colour of the next dance: "This is a green dance," he'd say, "repeat, a green dance," or "This is a blue dance, repeat, a blue dance."

Nor was it permitted to dance with someone else's date. Sister Celestine said that anyone caught stealing or trading dance passes would be expelled. Except to dance or go to the bathroom ("escorted by someone not a boy"), a girl was not to leave her stall. And, except to dance, go to the bathroom or get refreshments for himself and/or his date, a boy was not to leave *his* stall. Food and drink were confined to the stalls. "A boy may bring his date refreshments," Sister Celestine said, "but he must not loiter while she consumes them."

"Heavy Hearts remove your hats," she said. This was the signal to start the music. For a while, each side pretended not to notice the other, pretended to be caught up in some enormously interesting discussion, of which the dance itself was but the coincidental occasion. And even when the boys got up to ask the girls to dance, even on their way across the floor, they continued this discussion, shouting back to their friends and, only at the last moment, turned round to give their dance pass to the guard. While dancing, they affected the kind of preoccupation one sees at bus-stops, where what one is at is but a botherance to what one is really all about. The girls carried on in similar fashion. When their names were read, they got up and, like someone dragged away from conversation by a telephone call, kept talking, walking backwards, as if making sure to break at a point they could pick up easily afterwards.

Eventually, the dance got going—in every stall but ours. In 10-10, we were what my father, when I told him what happened, called "a horde of Hamlets." ("Nervousness," he said, "doth make morons of us all.") What bothered us most was not knowing which of the girls was our date until we asked them to dance. "If I just knew which one she was," we kept saying, over and over. We looked across the floor at them, wondering. We tried to match names and faces. Did the girl in the front row look like a Suzie Benizi, or more like a Perpetua Blaise?

"I wonder," I said, "which one's M. Babb."

"That's easy," Tommy said. "She's the numb one in the back."

Max was in a quandary. He didn't even know his date's name. He had a no-name date, he said, and repeated over and over her closing salutation: "Not signing because I hate my name—just show up I'll find you." "Find me," Max said, "she's not allowed to find me. I'm supposed to find her."

"So find her," Tommy said. "Just give the guard *your* name."

Max, who hated to be different in anything, must have seen that it was the only way. To everyone's surprise, he got up, then and there, and marched across the floor. "YEAH MAX," we said, applauding. We watched as he gave his pass to the nun and said something to her. She smiled and turned to face the girls. Max looked at the floor and, so, did not see what we saw—that, when the nun finished speaking, none of the girls got up, or gave any sign that they had even heard her. All they did was stare straight ahead. The nun gave Max his pass and, putting her hand on his shoulder, turned him gently around and sent him back toward our stall. It must have been the longest walk of Max's life. When it was over, he slumped in his chair, and we crowded round him, asking him what happened. He sat up straight and looked wide-eyed at his hands.

"The nun," he said, "ye know what the nun said. She said 'Mr. Max Devine has come to ask his date to dance.' Mister Max Devine. Jesus. No wonder no-one got up."

"But what happened then Max," Tommy said, "what happened when she said that?"

"Nothing," Max said. "The next thing I knew I was back here in this chair."

"Didn't the nun explain or anything?" Tommy said.

"No," Max said, "she just gave me back my pass and told me to beat it. 'Perhaps you'd better go back my boy,' she said. 'Perhaps you'd better go back my boy.' Oh God, I'll never forget it."

"Never mind," Tommy said, "maybe your date didn't show up."

"Yeah," Max said, "maybe. Or maybe, when she saw me, she said 'NO THANKS.'"

This last possibility terrified us. D-Cup began to imagine out loud the girls' point of view, to imagine what they'd think if they saw *him* coming across the floor. "They'd start praying, that's what," he said. "They'd say 'Oh God please, not him, please let it not be him.'"

"Shut up D-Cup," Tommy said.

Little Lawrence went next. Again we applauded and watched. It was between songs this time, so we could hear what the nun said. "Suzie Benizi," she said, "Suzie Benizi." Again all the girls stared straight ahead. Not one moved, let alone came forward to dance with Little Lawrence. Little Lawrence returned crestfallen. "It's a conspiracy," he said.

"Bullshit," Tommy said. He said it was Little Lawrence's own fault for telling lies on the résumé. "Ye shouldn't have said ye were six feet tall and 200 pounds. *She's* probably six feet tall and 200 pounds. No wonder she didn't dance with ye."

Tommy went next—and, a minute later, came back incredulous. "They just sat there," he said, "they didn't do anything. When I asked the nun what was going on, she made a funny face and said 'I guess the girls are shy.' Shy. Jesus, they're catatonic."

It went on like that, the lot of us successively repulsed. The girls, inasmuch as I remember them, hardly looked alive. They might have been some frieze of impassive resistance.

We decided to get the boys in Tier Nine to ask the girls who *were* dancing if they knew what was going on. The word came back in minutes. The girls in 10-10 were on strike, in protest over the treatment of Gorgonius, who was in their class, and who, when she demanded to be allowed to attend the dance wearing a name-tag identifying her as Gorgonius, was forbidden to attend at all. Gorgonius was said to have sent what Sister Celestine described as a "less than complimentary note" to Brother Ubaldus, telling him what she thought of him and his 600 boys, and she signed it "Semen Demon." Sister Celestine expelled Gorgonius, and the girls of 10-10 thought that, for what was, after all, only a practical joke, expulsion was an extreme punishment—and were staging a sit-down strike to prove their point. Apparently, the Wallflowers were in on it, too, for none of them had shown up. In that part of the gym set aside for them, there were fourteen empty chairs.

Tommy and I found Brudder Bill and told him what was going on. He in turn told Brother Gilmore, who said we should ignore the girls, and do our best to keep ourselves entertained for the evening. Minutes later, without announcement of any kind, 10-10 of Heavy Heart was led out of the gym by nuns. "There go our girls," D-Cup said.

"Wait a minute," Little Lawrence said, "everyone shout Suzie." We shouted "Suzie" as loud as we could and, as they were going through the door, all of 10-10 waved. It was contact of a kind, but, as Little Lawrence said, "I still don't know which one was Suzie."

Tour Hour was next. Class by class, the girls of Heavy Heart came by our stalls for what Sister Celestine called "an exchange of information." "Any questions girls?" she said, each time the Brothers finished telling them about us. There were no questions. The girls wore the dubious, uncomprehending look of tourists. Sometimes they stopped and stared blankly for a moment, then went on like window-shoppers. "Unexceptional," their faces seemed to say, "these boys are unexceptional." Our reaction to the girls was somewhat different. We were like official visitors to the country of some opposing ideology, always standing on tiptoe, wanting to linger, to give the impression that there was something going on behind the scenes that was being kept from us.

When the music started again, a bunch of us formed a circle with our chairs and began playing cards. Later, much later, when the dance was soon to end, Brother Gilmore, at the behest of Sister Celestine, sent us out on the floor as "spotters." Our job was to report to him instances of couples kissing, or otherwise getting "too familiar." We didn't want to do it, so we faked it, walking round the floor, looking vigilant.

The dance ended. The last song was played, and the Brother behind the WELCOME sign announced that even those Noonanites without dates should reach up and pluck a heart and recite the rhyme. We didn't want to do that either, but we did it, and felt like proper idiots. All of us from 10-10 reached up and grabbed a heart and, looking at the floor, recited with the others:

> Take this heart
> O Heavy Heart
> Until we meet again
> And if by chance
> You hold a dance
> Give it to me then.

It was even worse to have to listen to the girls:

> On this night

146

O Noonanite
I take your heart away
Alas, alack,
I give it back
To you another day.

Those boys who had no girls to whom to give their hearts, the
Brother said, should keep them as souvenirs. Twenty-nine Noonanites left the gym with a heart in their hands.

CHAPTER 7

A lot of things happened after Christmas. We moved again—for
the last time, my mother hoped. Two days after we left, the house
we had been living in burned down in the middle of the night. It
was empty, awaiting new tenants, and so no-one was hurt. But it
made us feel funny, as if we had just fled in time. My father talked
about a scorched-earth policy, about burning our days behind us.

Our new house was a bungalow, without even basement stairs,
so there was no question of bringing back the Teddy-Tank or the
Bob-Sled. Tommy and the others helped us move in. My father and
I went to town early one Saturday morning and picked them up.
"So," my father said, "you're all geniuses." He referred to D-Cup as
"the boy with the big boobs," to Max as "the boy with the big nose."

With all the boys and Rennie helping, it did not take us long to
move in. Ambrosia was there, too, but she didn't do much. She
stayed in the house and, every time my mother went inside, said
"Mrs. O'Malley, can I've some cake?" She developed a crush on
Tommy, and thought to endear him to her by sitting on things just
as he was lifting them.

"Just for a joke," as he put it, Tommy gave my mother a pamphlet called "Is Your Child on Drugs?" My mother was not amused.
Indeed, she spent the next month checking my body for needle

marks. She would look at the pupils of my eyes, dragging me from room to room to see what effect different light had on them. Sometimes, she got my father to help her stand me under a lightbulb and tilt my head back, so that she could stare into my eyes, searching for what the pamphlet called "the tell-tale crumbs of narcosis."

Our new house, Penny's, was near the school, though set back farther than it from the road; and it was all but adjacent to the graveyard which, from the north windows, was clearly visible, across an open field. Had we been closer to the road, we would have had next-door neighbours. As it was, we were pretty much alone. Until about ten years before, the house had been owned by the Church and let cheaply to anyone willing to look after the graveyard in their spare time. It was said to be haunted, a haunted halfway house, some people called it. They believed that, when someone died in Kellies, their spirit, because it could not be on its way until the body was buried, came to the house to wait until the wake was over. It was my father's theory that those three days of the wake were wretched ones for the spirit because, though soon to consist of "nothing but pure niceness," it suffered from a kind of accumulated hangover, the morning after the life before. It was during its stay at our house it "straightened up," maybe even went for a "hair-of-the-dog" visit with its family.

My father had time to become very interested in such things that winter because, in February, he was forced to resign as weatherman. As he would later outline them, the reasons for this were many. Foremost among them was the fact that he had taken too much time off to be with Harold's Mother. The situation had gotten ridiculous in January when, at forecast time every day, he was so badly prepared, the station manager accused him of making up the weather.

In the end, however, it was not forecasts that did my father in, but what he called a "hindcast," a summary of what the weather had been like the day before. It was one thing to make up what was going to happen, another altogether to make up what *had* happened. One day, my father asserted that "under sunny skies in Deer Lake they're digging out from yesterday's snowstorm." Soon, the switch-board was flooded with calls from Deer Lake, where they wanted him to know that the ground was green and they hadn't seen a snowflake in weeks.

The whole thing started when Harold's Mother told him she had decided to leave the province. She wanted to get away from her husband, she said; no matter where she went in Newfoundland, he would find her. She was taking the children to the mainland and would there start divorce proceedings. She asked my father to go with her. It must have been a bad time for him. I remember he was extra nice to my mother and me. I think he made up his mind to go and changed it at the last minute. I'm only guessing, of course, because, when all this was going on, I didn't know about it. All he ever said when he told me about it later was that, in the end, he decided not to go. I found him once, after dark, sitting, facing the window. It may have been the day she left, or it may have been a day when he still believed that *he* would go, and he was thinking about us. He was sitting with his feet up on the window, and the light was on, so he could not see out. On the way to my room, I paused in the doorway behind him, and he and I, and my mother at the table in the kitchen, were reflected in the glass. For a moment, my mother raised her eyes, and the three of us were caught looking at one another, caught in what we didn't know then was a line of love.

My father resigned on three quarters of his pension, and my mother, despite the loss of money, was happy. She talked about him having gone on to his "just rewards." "I'm not dead Agnes," my father said. "Of course you're not dear," my mother said, as if indulging a cherished illusion, "you're merely reaping what you've sown."

"I am not reaping Agnes," my father said.

"But dear," she said, "of course you are. The corn is high. The ears are full. I think I see the harvest moon. Reap, dear Teddy, reap." She became obsessed with the notion. She began to call home during the day to ask, "How goes the harvest?" "Reap," she'd say, "reap," if, on weekends, she found him lolling about the house. "The corn is high, the ears are full," became a refrain. My mother would start, "the corn is high," and my father would interrupt to say "the ears are full"; and then he and I, together, would say, "I think I see the harvest moon." My father, throughout, would pantomime. On "high" he raised his arms and went on tiptoe; on "full" he inflated his cheeks and bugged his eyes; and on "moon" he looked at the ceiling in mock wonder and, with his arms, made a wide, slow circle.

The first month, he tried to get his job back. We went to town one morning and, picking up the boys, drove back to Kellies and spent the day there, writing letters. Actually, my father wrote the letters, and we took turns making long-hand copies of them, so that there would be a nice variety of handwriting. These are the kinds of letters he wrote first:

Sir:

Re your decision to let O'Malley go. I beg you, reconsider. The weather without O'Malley? Impossible.

A Man Who Wants O'Malley Back
St. John's

Sir:

What? O'Malley gone? Why? For God's sake sir, bring back O'Malley. Such men as he are rarely found.

One of O'Malley's Many Female Fans
St. John's

To Those, I Trust, Who are Concerned:

"And now, to tell us today about tomorrow"—never again to hear those words? What, not see that face, that silver hair? Nay sirs, too cruel, too cruel by far. The people have spoken.

FANTOM
(Friends & Neighbours of Ted O'Malley)

Sir:

There are constants. The sun rises. The sun sets. Seasons come, seasons go. We die, give birth, pay taxes. O'Malley does the weather.

The list is short. Must it now be less by one? I beg you sir, say No.

Anxious

St. John's

"These all sound the same Mr. O'Malley," D-Cup said, when my father had finished twenty. My father agreed. "What should I do?" he said. "Be nasty," D-Cup said. "We've got enough nice ones. From now on, be nasty." "Nasty it is," my father said:

Sir:

Now that you have replaced O'Malley with that taseless tart from the CBC, I find I no longer have the slightest interest in any of your programs. Do not be surprised if I show up at your next licence-renewal hearing.

Disgusted

St. John's

Sir:

I am writing on the no-doubt naive assumption that someone at your station is literate and will be able to read you this letter. I should have known from your editorials that you'd do something like this. Give a pig a strawberry, my mother always said, and see what happens. She was right.

Contemptuous

St. John's

P.S. I refer, of course, to the firing of Ted O'Malley.

Dear Moron:

Just when I thought you had been as stupid as a human being could possibly be (viz. your 6 PM newscast, Jan 7) you go and do something worse. I am writing to ask that, if at all possible, you space out your imbecilities, the easier for us mere mortals to appreciate them.

Mad About O'Malley

St. John's

Dear Sir:

My mother is helping me write this letter because I am not allowed to use the 'F' word and you will know what I think of you. I think you smell and so does she. I think Mr. O'Malley was nice and so does she. You don't know my name, so you can't get me.

Six Years Old
St. John's

My father, when we finished writing the letters, sent them without return to the station. Nothing happened, except that, after a few weeks, his pension started coming, and he was informed that he was now eligible for unemployment insurance. He decided that, if he couldn't get his old job back, he'd find a new one. He applied, without success, to the radio and television stations for both weather and general-news positions. Then he tried to pass himself off as what he called a "freelance forecaster," but no-one was interested. Invoking his January weather reports, he tried to sell the newspapers on the idea of "fantasy forecasts." Never mind what the weather was really like, he said—the important thing was what the people wanted it to be like. He would give them heat-waves in February, and categorically deny the existence of fog and drizzle. He would tell them it was snowing in Barbadoes. He would take revenge on all the hot spots of the globe. People could vent their anger on certain parts of the country and the world by having him visit those places with meteorological disasters. He vowed that, as long as he was weatherman, the sun would never shine in Russia. He would rain down hail on Idi Amin. He would cause a cloud of sulfide smog to settle on Toronto, and would leave it there until all the Newfoundlanders got fed up and came home. He would be the first-ever cathartic weatherman. The possibilities were endless. But no-one was interested. The papers did him the courtesy of writing "no-thank-you" replies. My father wrote back, explaining in great detail how, every day from now on, "in the world of anti-weather," a twister was going to touch down and blow their buildings to pieces.

Every suppertime that winter, my father gave a forecast from the world of anti-weather. When he finished saying Grace, he would take out his forecast and read it, concluding with deadpan seriousness: "This is Ted O'Malley, reporting from the world of anti-weather." My mother would look at me during these forecasts and smile, as if inviting me to join in her absolute refusal to acknowledge what was happening. When he finished, she would say something like "Pass the pickles." And if, as often happened, I applauded, she would, while seemingly engrossed in something else—a forkful of food, perhaps—reach out with one hand and pull my hands apart. She seemed to believe that the world of anti-weather was a temporary, if offputting aberration which, if ignored, would go away.

It did go away, but my father had a lot of time on his hands and, when the world of anti-weather ended, he switched to the vacu-cycle.

Now that he was retired, we no longer had need of maids. As my mother told the SS, "Teddy does all the dusting now." The dusting included vacuuming the floors every day—and every room in the house, except the kitchen, was carpeted. Before long, my father got bored with it, and came up with a way of making it more interesting. He put his idea on paper first. Our vacuum-cleaner was the lawnmower kind, one that picked up dirt by driving over it. My father showed how the handle could be taken off and the vacuum car tied by rope to a tricycle, which would drag it backwards round the room. The driver of the tricycle would wear the vacu-bag on his back like an air-tank, anl it would be hooked by extension-hose to the vacuum car itself. He would need a crash-helmet, of course, and sneaker boots for better pedal grip.

My father and I went to town where, in store after store, he professed himself astounded that demand for adult-size tricycles was not such as to justify their existence. In the end, we simply bought the biggest tricycle we could find. And though my father, when driving it, often banged his knees on the handlebars, he was happy with it. It had a little bell so that he could warn my mother and me when he was coming around a corner. Soon, in hockey helmet, hunched over the handlebars, his eyes focused on the floor in search of dirt, he was tricycling around the house at all hours of the day and night. He looked, with the vacuum roaring behind him, the bag on his back, like some strange exterminator. He bumped into furniture, zigzagged in front of the TV while we were watching it. He went forwards, backwards, made sharp turns. If, when he came near you, your feet were on the floor, he would stop and, leaning out over the handlebars, stare at your feet, wordlessly waiting for you to lift them. When you did, he would ring the bell twice in appreciation and then be on his way. He would stop sometimes to attach what he called "vaccessories." These, the Nozzle, the Beak and the Brush, he kept in a pouch that he hung around his neck. "This corner requires the Nozzle," he'd say, and then look at my mother and me, his expression sagely quizzical, as if we, his fellow professionals, must be consulted. "No," I'd say, though my mother warned me not to encourage him, "the Beak, the Beak." My mother was most distressed by the vacu-cycle, even more than she was by the world of anti-weather. She begged my father not to drive it while the SS were in the house. He complied for the longest time, but, one night in March, the SS arrived early and trapped him in the kitchen, where he was about to begin the "eight-o'clock crumb patrol." The SS were in the hallway and, as he said afterwards, he figured his only chance was to leave the kitchen and go as fast as possible down the hallway, in the hope that they wouldn't see him. I remember the SS staring in disbelief as my father, with silent determination, confident of his invisibility, pedaled plainly into view and, making what he later called "a discreet left turn," suddenly accelerated down the hallway and disappeared into his room. It was me the SS looked at when my father disappeared, as if my being there rendered impossible the explanation that might have restored sanity to the world—namely, that what one of them called "the creature on the tricycle" had been me.

That incident with the SS was the next-to-last straw; the last straw came several nights later when, as we were sitting round the living-room, my father wondered how he could get my mother and me involved in the vacu-cycle. Perhaps, he said, he could buy two more tricycles, and we could have a train of them, joined by rope, and go for Sunday drives around the house. He imagined us going from room to room, the vacuum car following like some strange mechanical pet. But my mother said she was not about to sit on a tricycle, let alone wear a hockey helmet. And she forbade him to buy a tricycle for me, because it was too expensive. Fair enough, my father said, but he wondered if, from now on, I would like to walk in front of the vacu-cycle and search out dirt for him. He could get me a t-shirt that said Scum Scout or Dirt Detector. It was at this point my mother rose and, right in front of me, yelled at him. "Teddy," she said, "GROW UP OR GET OUT."

Downtown one day at lunchtime, I almost ran into my mother. She must have been walking ahead of me for some time, but it wasn't until she stopped to look into a window that I saw her. By then, I was almost upon her, and had to step to one side to avoid a collision. I stood behind her on the sidewalk, waiting for her to notice me, but she never did. I could see my face reflected, behind hers in the window. I followed her, intending at first to call out, or catch up with her. But something about the way she hurried down the sidewalk, so perfectly and vulnerably in character, changed my mind. Plowing straight ahead so that oncoming people had to step aside, she looked, in her high heels, like a novice skater trying desperately to stop. And though she no longer had a purse, she walked as if she had one, with her hands in front, tight against her body. For some reason, with her there on the sidewalk, not twenty feet in front of me, I had a feeling like remembrance, as if I was looking back from a time when she was gone. Sadness, a sweet hurt in my throat, came and went in half a second. And though the moment passed that quickly, I decided I would follow her. I did so for almost an hour, staying with her from store to store. I watched her buy a pie and take a drink of water from a fountain. From behind a pillar in Woolworth's, I watched her in Men's Underwear, buying briefs and socks with the kind of matter-of-fact confidence one sees in supermarkets. I suppose it was some clue to who she was that I wanted. I hoped that, when she thought no-one was looking, she would give herself away—pick her nose, or scratch her backside, or put a roll of candy in her pocket and walk out without paying. I grew so anticipant, my heart started pounding. A revelation seemed imminent—suddenly, while I was watching, a veil would pull away and there she'd be. But nothing happened. In the end I crossed the street and, exactly opposite one another, we waited for the light. I looked around at all the people who were unaware of the thread we were sustaining. But then, so was my mother unaware. Watching her like that was like touching someone who was fast asleep. When the light went green, I turned and headed back to school.

It was a grey wet winter. There were no more dances, but Tommy came of age and got his licence, and the six of us went driving almost every day, after school. We would park across the street from Heavy Heart and watch the girls as they came out. We even went to Gregg Academy once and watched the Gyro Girls. Often, we went to Rice's and sat around in our blazers, drinking Coke.

After school some days, Tommy drove me home and the others came along for the ride. On Sundays, they came to watch me serve mass, and gave me a going-over afterwards about wanting to be a priest. Tommy introduced me to his father as "Robert O'Malley, my spiritual advisor."

In April, Tommy got a letter from Perpetua Blaise that read:

Dear Tommy:
I think I know which one you were. If I'm right, you're cute. Why don't you ask me out?

Perpetua Blaise
P.S. You were the tall blond guy, right, with the blue eyes. If not, please disregard this letter.

We were all very excited about this, thinking that, through Perpetua, contact might be made with the other girls. It took Tommy about a week to get up the nerve to call her and, though he got her to talk to the other girls about the twelve of us going out on a date together, they said they weren't interested. Tommy told us that he and Perpetua were going to a movie, and then they were going to try to get into a bar. We got him so confused and excited beforehand, it's a wonder that first date wasn't his last. The ideas we had about sex—sex, for us, was a trick that girls, deep down, really wanted to have played on them. Sex was not the act itself, but all the subterfuge and two-facedness required to bring it off. Sex was something girls had that must be taken from them. And girls were the strangely attractive enemy, repositories of pleasure, ultimately concerned with entrapment, and ultimately successful. Hence, a boy must get all he can, get revenge in advance, be the hit-and-run hero, stealing sweets from dragons. "Dragons" we called them, to be on the make for girls was to be "hunting dragons."

The day after his date with Perpetua, Tommy admitted that he tried to talk her into skipping the movie and going parking on Signal Hill, whereupon Perpetua demanded to be taken home immediately. By D-Cup's reckoning, the date lasted seventeen minutes, and he said it would likely be as many years before she went out with him again. But, as it turned out, Tommy's conduct on that first date was exactly what Perpetua expected. When, a week later, he called her again, she agreed to go out with him. The second date, as Kiwi said, lasted "almost an hour." But as Tommy cooled down, the dates got longer, and he was soon urging the rest of us to ask girls out. Think of the fun we could have, he said, all going out together.

Often, after school, he came by in the car with Perpetua, and stopped to talk to us in the parking-lot. He introduced us to her, but neither he nor she got out of the car. And, of course, we never got in. Although I knew her for years, I cannot remember Perpetua except in the front seat of Tommy's Duster, looking out as on a world she was not likely to ever again have much interest in. There, in the car, in the parking-lot, Tommy would turn his face so that she couldn't see it and, looking at us, would motion back toward her with his head and grin, as if to say, "C'mon you guys, you gotta get one, too."

But the rest of us, that year, were content to ask him questions. By May, he claimed to be "getting some tit," which Kiwi, with his thumb and forefinger not very far apart, defined as "about this much breast." Tommy said that, when he went for more than tit, Perpetua (or Pettie, as he called her) went lifeless in his arms. Opening her eyes wide, she would stare off into space like a dead person, and would remain that way until he went back to tit or, better yet, left her alone. (Kiwi called this "the cadaver manoeuvre.") Perpetua was always on guard for what she called "moments of weakness." She made Tommy promise that, if she suffered a moment of weakness, he would be strong and stop what he was doing immediately. If, for instance, she let him touch both tits at once, he must recoil and head for home. Those nights when a moment of weakness seemed likely, but she still wanted to go parking, Perpetua sent Tommy to the back seat by himself, and they kissed between the head-rests. To avoid getting carried away, she would only mess around for as long as it took two sticks of Juicy Fruit gum to lose their flavour—a length of time that varied, depending on what Kiwi called the "chew-kiss ratio." The more they kissed, the less time she had to chew. D-Cup said Tommy should try to get her to switch to Double-Bubble, because it lasted longer than Juicy Fruit. "A couple of Double-Bubble," D-Cup said, " and she might go all the way."

We asked Tommy everything. What did a breast feel like? What did she do when he squeezed it? What was French-kissing like? Did the gum get in the way? Had she ever, as Max put it, "acknowledged" his hard-on? No, Tommy said, Perpetua did nothing except squirm and, on good nights, breathe heavily.

Near the end of June, when school was out, we started going places with them. Tommy would pick everyone up in town and then come through Kellies for me. D-Cup, Kiwi, Little Lawrence, Max and I had to squeeze into the back seat of the Duster, because Perpetua refused to share the front seat with anyone but Tommy. "I'm not gonna sit here with a bunch a boys crawlin' all over me," she said. She thought we were jerks, and said as much about ten times a day. She called us "groupies." On the way up the Shore to the park where we spent our days, lazing on the beach, she would slide across the seat and snuggle up to Tommy and, while licking his ear, look back at us now and then to make sure we were watching. Sometimes she looked at us all the while she was doing it, her face full of mock seductiveness as she lapped at Tommy's ear-lobe. Each of us reacted to this differently. Kiwi got an erection, and pressed himself flat against the door of the car to hide it. I was embarrassed, and looked at my shoes or out the window. D-Cup got mad because, with Perpetua snuggled up to Tommy like that, fully two thirds of the front seat was left unoccupied—and here were the five of us, crammed in the back. It seemed so unfair. "C'mon Tommy, let me get in front," D-Cup would say, but Perpetua, her tongue in Tommy's ear, would look at D-Cup and shake her head slowly and smile. Max would sit there, looking scared, unable to take his eyes away. One day, Kiwi told him that ear-licking was "aural sex," and Max, who had heard the words "oral sex," but had never seen them written, was easily convinced that what he was seeing, what Perpetua was doing to Tommy right in front of us, was the awful act itself. "Aural sex," Kiwi said, "blow-job, inflatio." Little Lawrence made fun of Perpetua. Closing his eyes half-way, the way she closed hers when nuzzling Tommy, and sticking out his tongue, he would roll his head around and make strange noises.

At the beach, the five of us would sit morosely and watch as she and Tommy went swimming. What with Perpetua's little blond body, and bikinis all around, we didn't trust ourselves to walk about in swim trunks. Kiwi, afflicted with what D-Cup called "the eternal bone," would sit all day in one place, in a half-crouch, with his legs crossed and arms folded, looking as if he had to pee. We sat on the benches usually, and Tommy and Perpetua lay on the sand in front of us. Perpetua would lie on her stomach, her head to one side and, at regular intervals, open her eyes to catch us looking at her. Then she would tell Tommy. "Tommy, they're lookin' at me," she'd say. "We're not lookin' at you," Little Lawrence would say, "you're lookin' at us." Then an argument would start. Perpetua would wonder why in the name of all that's holy she would want to look at Little Lawrence. "For thrills," Little Lawrence would say, "for thrills." When Tommy wasn't around, he called her "Pertitua."

Alternately ogled and persecuted, Perpetua hated us. And we were especially objectionable because we were what she called "under age." To Perpetua, someone was under age if they were less than sixteen. *She* was sixteen, Tommy almost seventeen. The rest of us were fourteen or fifteen. There was nothing a sixteen-year-old could do that a fourteen- or fifteen-year-old couldn't—except drive a car—but as far as she was concerned, we were under age. She seemed to believe that, by turning sixteen and getting Tommy, she had put hazard forever behind her. To be a child, or an otherwise unpaired person, was to be out in the cold, and she had had enough of it.

We felt foolish most of that summer. Here was Tommy well past tit, and we hadn't even started dating yet. Those not infrequent times when Tommy was off somewhere with Perpetua, I got a ride to town with my mother, and the five of us spent entire days roaming the city, looking for things to do that would prove we were not altogether being left behind. We did things on dares. "I dare you to buy a box of safes from the lady pharmacist." "I dare you to buy a copy of *Penthouse*." We didn't buy many safes, but we bought a lot of *Penthouse*, and took the bus to Bowring Park, where we would read them. We would tear the pictures out and make what Little Lawrence called "porno paper planes," and go up on the bridge and fly them down on unsuspecting young mothers and senior citizens. The park was a good place to watch girls, coming and going around the pool. We watched and waved, even whistled. We made proper fools of ourselves most of the time.

Some days we hung round Heavy Heart. Summer school was in session and Ambrosia was among those girls attending. Having failed Grade 9, she was trying to make it up before September. School got out at three, and she hung round afterwards and talked to us, and introduced us to some of her friends. She was disappointed that, most of the time, Tommy wasn't with us. In his absence, she turned her attentions on D-Cup. Before long, something like a romance was blooming. She was going through a phase of telling jokes. She intoned them, dispassionately, relentlessly, as if, though she didn't find them funny, she had heard somewhere that, if you told enough of them, something good would come of it. She would tell the same joke, over and over, her "I don't get it" expression becoming more pronounced with each telling. Instead of posing a riddle as a question, she posed it as a statement, followed by a question. "The man committed suicide when his dolphin died. Why? Because his life had no porpoise. You cross a penis with a potato. What do you get? A dictator. The second-biggest chicken of all time crossed the road. Why? Because the biggest chicken of all time was after him." The one who could be counted on not to laugh at any of these jokes was D-Cup, not because he didn't find them funny, but because he had heard them all before. Ambrosia, however, took his solemn expression to be the mark of a kindred soul. She began bringing him food from home. Every day after school, she would emerge, carrying a brown-paper bag and, word-lessly, give it to D-Cup. Sandwiches, chocolate bars, chips, buns, whole packages of cookies—clearly, she was raiding the cupboards. She would stand and watch from a distance while D-Cup ate, or otherwise disposed of the food, and then would come over and start telling jokes. As the summer wore on, the brown-paper bag got bigger, its contents more bizarre. Ambrosia gave D-Cup cereal, pancake-mix, baking-soda and, once, a five-pound bag of brown sugar. "The gift of groceries," my father said, "it must be love." It was from my father I found out what happened. Dola, early in the summer, alarmed at the rate at which treats were disappearing from the cupboards, stopped buying them altogether. There would, she said, be no more bars or chips or cookies. This left Ambrosia with the choice of bidding love goodbye, or falling back on staple goods. She chose the latter and D-Cup, embarrassed by her strange gifts, asked me to talk to her. And I did talk to her. I asked her one day what she imagined D-Cup was going to do with the quart of vinegar she had just given him. "He can give to his mudder, can't he?" she said. The next day, she gave him a package of pork chops, and that was the last of what had become known as "the love de-liveries," because Dola put locks on the cupboard and the fridge.

We tried to get D-Cup to ask Ambrosia out. As Kiwi said, "I think she's earned it." Little Lawrence said D-Cup might woo Am-brosia, not by whispering sweet nothings in her ear, but by putting "sweet somethings" in her mouth. But D-Cup, though not alto-gether unwilling to go out with her, was put off it by the prospect of a daytime date. It would have to be in the daytime because he had no car, and also so that Rennie, who was certain to think she was too young for dates, would not find out about it. They would have to meet at Heavy Heart. She would have to pip off classes, and they would have to be back to the parking-lot before Rennie came to pick her up at four. It was all too much for D-Cup, the risk-taking, and the embarrassment of setting forth on a date, and coming back from a date, under what would doubtless be the close and jeering scrutiny of friends. Summer-school ended, and although, that September, Ambrosia entered Grade 10 at Heavy Heart, their chance for romance was over.

CHAPTER 8

September came, the start of school, and we gathered in the gym and sang the school song:

> Brother Arthur Noonan High
> We six hundred fifty-four
> Soon will have to say goodbye
> We're in sight of that far shore.

What in Grade 10, on the part of the Brothers, had been a sense of urgency, became in Grade 11 pure panic. They would have us for ten months more, ten months in which to cram us with the wisdom that would have to last us all our lives. They might have been teaching us fire-drill in the face of some imminent conflagration. The intensity was exhausting. Young men with a mission, let loose on the world—that's what they wanted by June. Every moment, every incident, contained some lesson that must be got at, some kernel of moral that must be extracted. The world did not exist except as a teaching tool, a parable unfolding for our benefit. Children in Biafra starved that it might be brought home to us how awful is the starvation of children.

MHing was rare in Grade 11. The Brothers felt that, in Grade 10, our old selves had been leveled. Now, on the ruins of the old, new selves must be built, on our clean slates new characters written. What worried us most was that our being aware of what they were trying to do was no guarantee that they wouldn't succeed. There was the business of "the call" for instance, the call to the Brotherhood in this case. We believed that the call came independent of your will. It was like disease, something you caught by inhaling holy germs. And once you caught it, your chances of shaking it were not good. It was said that I had the priesthood strain of the call, and there was nothing to be done for me. Each Grade 11 class gathered once a month in the audio-visual room to see films on the life of the Christian Brother. I remember one in particular, taken at the seminary in Ontario, of a bunch of Brothers playing volleyball. These were what D-Cup called "Little Brothers," those not yet ordained. They were dressed like soccer referees, in black shirts and shorts, and were playing in what appeared to be a meadow in the middle of nowhere, with trees and bushes all around them. "At the seminary in Don Mills," the narrator said, "it's not all work by any means. Here, young men take time out from prayer and study to play volleyball. The Christian Brother understands the importance of recreation. In recreation, we recreate ourselves." After this, the word "RECREATION" came up on the screen, and the volleyball game went soundlessly on, as the young Brothers jumped in the air, and dove to the ground, solemnly recreating themselves. There were close-ups of boys who looked a lot like Archie, staring intently through the net, as if into their own future. The word "DEDICATION" appeared on the screen. Several Brothers went up in the air and, as they converged, reaching for the volleyball, the frame was frozen. The word "TOGETHERNESS" appeared. Several bad falls were shown, Brothers slamming into the ground, going head over heels. The word "TOUGHNESS" appeared. Little Lawrence said afterwards that, as he was too short to play volleyball, he'd certainly never make it as a Christian Brother.

In Grade 11, I went to as many masses and prayers at St. Stephen's as I could. And at the Barn, I was one of three boys who, every morning before school, swept the aisles of the chapel and polished the pewter candlesticks and the cruets of water and wine. We were not allowed to touch the tabernacle, and we had to genuflect when we crossed in front of it. I mention this because I remember mornings, the only light that of candles, and no sound except our slippers on the floor, feeling the pull of that dome like death. There was something strangely attractive about the kind of sadness and loneliness it excited. I even thought for a while about becoming a Brother, though I told no-one about it.

That fall, Kiwi got a girlfriend. They started dating in November. She was from Heavy Heart, of course, and had her driver's licence, and access to her father's car on weekends. After their first date, Kiwi told us about her. Her name was Brenda Ludlow. Most of the boys had known her for years. D-Cup described her as "neither gorgeous nor seriously deformed." Little Lawrence had her "an effete *petite* brunette with acne." She did have acne, enough to be referred to as Pimple Puss behind Kiwi's back. "Love is blind," Kiwi said. "And besides, I don't look at her that much." It became a regular thing for Tommy and Kiwi, after school, to go up to Heavy Heart in the Duster and take the girls driving. Sometimes, they came back to the Barn, and sat around in the parking-lot, talking. "Here comes Pertitua and Pimple Puss," Little Lawrence would say when he saw the Duster. Like Perpetua, Brenda would not get out of the car. She and Kiwi sat in the back, and she and Perpetua looked out the windows on one side of the car, while Tommy and Kiwi talked to us on the other. When Tommy and Kiwi were in the car, neither girl seemed to know the other existed. But when Tommy and Kiwi got out, they would begin to talk in earnest, heads confidentially close the second the car doors were closed. The girls were unsure of their success. They knew that, as long as four unattached boys were around, it was provisional at best. We were single, evil omens, competitors. On the other hand, we believed that girls were a fate which, though inevitable, must be resisted.

And Tommy and Kiwi, having fought the good fight, were taking their defeat like men. It was always with resignation and undertones of irony they left us and went back to the girls. They tacitly, and with that good-natured sense one has of one's own reprehensible weaknesses, acknowledged an attraction to that bit of bait girls held out in the darkness. The pleasures of giving in were such that boys could not be blamed. They were endearing heroes, sheepishly admitting that they were not quite capable of doing the impossible. It was the girl, enticer, temptress, who must be enjoyed and blamed at the same time.

It was just before Christmas my father started to write a book about our lives together, to be called *Our Memoirs: A Story from Family Memory*. He was sitting at home most days with nothing to do, he said, and writing would at least keep him busy. He tried not to seem too excited about it, probably thinking that, if my mother found out how much he was enjoying himself, she would get suspicious and refuse to co-operate. And her co-operation and mine, he said, were essential to the writing of *Our Memoirs*. He would write the story, but he would need us to help him remember what had happened. We would not see *Our Memoirs* until it was finished, but we would know what part he was at by the questions he was asking. My mother didn't like the idea. She kept saying "what's done is done Teddy, what's done is done." My father replied that this was a strange remark to come from someone who went to confession once a week. What was confession, he wondered, but a way of starting over, a way of disposing of the past—what was a priest but a kind of garbage-collector? My mother winced when he said this. She looked at me as if to assure me that I had not been called by God to collect garbage. "Writing *Our Memoirs* will be like cleaning out the basement," my father said. "Yes," my mother said, "you'll get rid of whatever you don't want." My father laughed and said she mustn't think his mind worked the way hers did.

It was a bad start for *Our Memoirs*, but after a while we settled down. By Christmas, we were meeting every night in the living-room. My father, with pen and paper in hand, would launch interrogations. What happened? When was that? Where? Were we sure? Sometimes, he disagreed with our answers, and arguments would ensue. At first, in front of me, they kept controversy at a distance, and did not so much remember things as recall details, settle minor differences. What was the colour of the rug at Duley's? Who was the tallest of the Fatal Four? What was the name of the man next door at Mortrey's? How long was I gone the day I ran away? When did my father start work at the station? My father reserved more sensitive questions until I had gone to bed. And after a while, they started sending me to bed early, just so they could argue. They hadn't talked in years, and they got worked up about all kinds of things. I lay awake and listened. *"I did not." "You did so." "That's a lie Agnes." "Teddy that's not fair and you know it." "God knows it wasn't me." "Oh no, of course not, no, never you."* Their voices would rise and fall as if, now and then, they remembered I might be listening.

Either because he felt he was losing these arguments, or because there were certain things he thought I should know, my father began, in front of me, to threaten my mother with revelations of old hurts and secrets. No longer waiting until I had gone to bed, he would, by tone of voice, imply there was something here that someone in the room would not want revealed. I learned a lot those nights in the living-room. My father, having scribbled for hours to get down every word, would suddenly put down his pen and blurt out something to make my mother mad—and then something else to make her madder until, finally, she would refuse to answer any more. Sometimes he asked questions that were revelations in themselves. "How did you feel when you opened the door that day?" *"Teddy, stop it."* I would sit there, frightened, trying to read between the lines. It seemed my father couldn't help himself. He got so worked up remembering even the most mundane details, he was certain, sooner or later, to touch on something dangerous. It was as if memory itself was setting him on. "That was in '55," he'd say. "My God, remember the rain. And that house on Cochrane Street. We had the top half. And the landlady lived downstairs. Remember Agnes. She asked me why, in all the time we lived up there, we never—" "TEDDY." My mother's voice would bring him back, and he would look as if he didn't know what he'd been saying. He seemed drunk, reckless. And if he persisted, and things came close to explicit discussion, my mother would leave the room.

It wasn't always bad, though. My mother, those times my father's questions were neutral or genuinely searching, would respond and seem to enjoy herself. "There were roses Teddy, remember," she said once, "roses all around the house. And a dogberry tree by the driveway. It was so red in the fall, and that walkway full of berries —Bobby used to mash them with his fingers. I'd come home after school, and there he'd be in the berries, making a mess of himself. Oh Teddy, I wonder where it goes." My father and mother, when they were getting on well together, kept coming back to what my father called "the night we made Bobby." I was amazed that she would let him say even that much about it. But though she blushed and hid her face, or looked at me and quickly looked away, there was something about that phrase, something that got her laughing. "The night we made Bobby." My father would slip it into the conversation and, soon, my mother was gone in gales of laughter— which was strange, because to say that to my mother was like reminding a pope that he'd been a banker once.

It was only afterwards when, in spite of rare good times, my mother decided she'd had enough of remembering and refused to sit with us unless we promised "that book" would not be mentioned; it was only when my father and I began meeting in his room after school, to continue work on *Our Memoirs* by ourselves, that I found out about the night they made me. For my father, telling the first part was easy. "A long time ago," he said, "your mother and I were making love and the door of our room was open." At the time, he said, they owned a dog, "a big, brown, dumb dog." The dog came into the room and, perceiving what appeared to be an assault upon my mother by my father, came to her rescue by biting my father's backside. It was, my father said, a case of "bite us, interrupt us—as if we hadn't been having enough problems." He spoke of my mother's "sperma frost," against which his "hydraulic drill kept breaking." Ever after, they called that night "the night we made Bobby."

It was when I asked him how they knew it was that night and not some other night I was conceived he started having difficulties. "There *were* no other nights," he said, and he said it as if, not knowing whether to laugh or cry, he had determined to do neither. Without so much as a smile or a tear, but in a voice becoming gradually more full of unburdened, blessed relief, he said the words he must have been waiting half his life to say. He told me that, because of my mother's "emotional problems," their marriage had not been consummated until "a good many years" after the wedding. Nor were there, he said, after the night they made me, "subsequent consummations." "We did it once." My mother's egg, my father said, was not "mauled by a million sperm," but approached in genteel fashion by a sperm ahead of his fellows, a cut above the average. "He wooed her. And what started out a single cell became, in nine months' time, a boy more various than all his unborn brothers and sisters."

It was their time together before the night they made me I thought most about, "the good many years" between the wedding and its consummation. I tried to imagine that part of my parents' lives. It must have had in it most of the hardest times, and yet it was lost to me, tossed off in three words as if it had never been All the waiting and worry and awful anxiety, and the loneliness that must have been there every day like a wall of skin-stripped flesh between them, too raw to touch or even talk about—all that was lost. The thought of a love that great, that relentlessly enduring, made me wonder where the love had gone. They broke the wall down once, and it went back up when I was born. Now it seemed they thought a person was nothing if not alone. How to live in that zone of pain that people close together share, they had no idea. Nor had I. It seemed an impossibility, in the absurdly unaccountable pursuit of which all the world was caught up. That one time, my father said, he felt my mother's fingers going up and down his back. At first, he thought it was her version of passion, fluttering fingers instead of endearments, tactile moans and groans. It was a while before he realized that it wasn't passion, but prayer. She was telling the knobs of his spine like beads. On her back in bed, with him on top, she was saying the rosary. "What a wonderful way to pray," he said. And he did seem full of wonder, and sadness, at the fact that such a saint should be his lot in life, that he had been part of that love-making miracle.

My father cried one night in his room, cried loud enough for my mother and me, downstairs, to hear. It went on for half an hour, and I remember how strange a sound it was, that irruption of despair into a voice that, until then, had been so tight against it. But it would have been as strange to hear hope come creeping in. Until that night, my father had managed to keep himself between hope and hopelessness. He found some neutral middle, some zero from within which he beat back both sides. I thought of going to him, but my mother told me not to. I don't say she took revenge for the times *she* cried alone, only that, in her rise, his fall, there seemed to her neat justice, from the full appreciation of which she would not be kept.

My father became interested in funerals. From the window of his bedroom, he could see the graveyard: in February, he bought himself a pair of binoculars so he could see it better. He found out from church announcements and the newspapers when funerals were taking place. They were mostly on weekdays, when my mother and I were out of the house. He would sit by the window in his room, with a bottle of beer and a bowl of popcorn, and watch the funeral through his binoculars. He had never realized, he said, how much dying was going on. People died every day. People were buried every day. It was a wonder, he said, there was anyone left alive. He began to keep count of who was dying, and to compile statistics about their age and sex and cause of death. Did we know, he wondered, that in Kellies men were dying faster than women, and children were hardly dying at all? Did we know that more people died of cancer than of old age? Did we know that the most popular colour for caskets was black, followed, surprisingly in his opinion, by grey? Did we know how hard it was to dig a grave in winter?

By March, he was giving out "The First Annual Funeral Awards."

Among these were awards for:
  Most Ostentatious Headstone
  Most Unbecoming Casket
  Most Florid Funeral
  Most Foibled Funeral
  Most Detached Mortician
  Most Meddlesome Mourner
  Most Cheerful Funeral
  Most Suspiciously Cheerful Funeral
  Most Depressing Funeral
  Most Visually Rousing Rendition of "Nearer my God to Thee"
  Most Stoic Spouse of Dear Departed
  Most Obviously Confused Pre-Schooler
  Most Unnecessarily Precocious Pre-Schooler
  Most Self-Conscious Pallbearer
  Best Display of Pseudo-Sadness by a Mourner Not a Relative
  Best Display of Grief in the Death-by-Natural-Causes Category
  Most Tasteless Display of Grief by a Mourner Only Distantly
  Related
  Most Convincing Graveside Swoon

By the end of March, my father was watching the graveyard almost all the time. On Saturdays, he locked his door and watched all afternoon. Soon, it was not just funerals he was interested in, but also graveside vigils and general graveyard comings and goings. He started to keep track of how often each grave was visited. In no time, he was handing out "The Ghost Who Must Have Been Most Awards." Based on number and duration of visits, my father determined the Ghost Who Must Have Been Most

  Liked
  Gregarious
  Lonely
  Boring
  Unkind
  Cruel

Indiscriminate in Choosing Friends
Reprehensible
Adulterous
Indifferent
Abhorred
Loved
Mocked
Neglectful
Profound
Confused
Devout
Tormented

There were special awards for the Ghost Who Must Have Been Most Popular, and for the Ghost Who Must Have Been Most Neglected. There were several winners of this last award, ghosts of graves that no-one ever visited. My father went to the graveyard once to see their stones close up. Wiped clean by wind and rain, they bore no inscriptions whatsoever.

The end of school seemed unreal, impossible, perhaps because the Brothers talked so much about it. They had made it, like death, something one believes in, but about which one does nothing. I believed that school would end, but that "the end of school," the final day, the apocalyptic fact of graduation, would somehow be avoided. Brother Gilmore said the final day was "a door between the antechamber of childhood and the great room of the rest of your lives." It suddenly seemed in April that that great room was below me. It was as if, like some cartoon character, I had been walking on air and did not realize it until I looked down and saw that door, not opening out of high school, but out of life itself—and immediately started to fall. I fell freely, not even grabbing at the hands my friends held out. All I could see was that door at the bottom, getting bigger, the seminary opening wider every day. The date had been set. On 27 June, I would leave by plane. Everyone at school believed I'd be a priest. In April, we had a Career Day in the gym, and people kept saying how lucky I was for having already made up my mind. Most of the boys had no idea what they wanted to be. D-Cup said he was thinking about becoming a Christian Brother, but Tommy said that was only because he couldn't get a girlfriend. Brudder Bill overheard this and asked Tommy if he imagined that was why *he* had become a Christian Brother. Tommy said no—he was sure Brudder Bill had lots of girlfriends. That was the kind of token resistance we put up in Grade 11. Our group was considered rebellious, though not seriously so. We were rebellious inasmuch as one could be rebellious at the Barn without being suspended or expelled. We rebelled not by actions but inactions. We volunteered for nothing, took part in nothing we didn't have to take part in. We showed no enthusiasm, and tried very hard to make it seem that we weren't trying at all. If we got MHed, we went along with it. If Brudder Bill asked us were we broken, we assured him that we were. When required, we sang the school song. We did what we were told. But all the while we looked bored, above it all. We smirked a lot, and smiled at things the Brothers said, as if, were we allowed to speak to them as equals, we could show them for the fools they were. And among ourselves, we made fun of everything.

On Career Day, Tommy told us that he was going to join his father's business and one day take it over. He had to get a degree in commerce first, he said, and added as an afterthought that he was thinking of getting engaged. We couldn't believe it, and neither, it seemed, could he. We walked about the gym, the six of us, shaking our heads, as if in wonder at the fact that we were really going somewhere, that despite the way we sneered at the world, the world was moving us right along. Until then, high school had been one long lampoon, as if we believed that, somehow, ours would be the first generation not to make the mistake of growing up. We did this, despite the fact that our lives were quite clearly headed the way of everyone else's. Career Day, wandering like window-shoppers from one display to another—Medicine, Law, Engineering—confronted with choices, alternatives, the fact of a future, a waiting world, our pose was all too evident. We felt, as D-Cup said, like a "great big bunch of bullshitters." Max said he was thinking about becoming an engineer, "an anti-establishment *avant-garde* engineer," he said. Little Lawrence rolled his eyes. Little Lawrence was going to be a "professor of something somewhere." He would get a Ph.D., he said, then tenure, "a nice bed in some asylum." Kiwi, helped on by the money his father made from the fruit store, was going to be a doctor—"a missionary doctor. Schweitzer, Bethune, Dooley, Kiwi Williams." We laughed.

"Priest, professor, doctor, Brother, engineer and businessman," D-Cup said. "Radicals all." We laughed again.

My father never said goodbye. Nor do I remember him doing or saying anything to indicate he knew his leaving would be for good. There was nothing into which, afterwards, we could read a double or deeper meaning. He went out that night as he had other nights since Harold's Mother left—whistling cheerfully, he might have been making fun of himself, mocking his own refusal to seem unhappy in front of us. It was the second Tuesday in April 1973. There had hardly been any snow that winter, nothing you'd call a storm. The ground was bare when he left, but an hour later, wet snow started falling. No-one knows where he went. It seems that, wherever it was, he went alone. No-one knows when he got back to the house, nor why, instead of coming in, he stayed outside in the car. I heard the car come into the driveway. It woke me, and I remember listening for the sound of him coming up the steps. After a while, I fell asleep. Otherwise, I would have gotten up to see what was keeping him. I slept lightly, and came to the lip of waking many times. I think that, all the while, I heard the engine running, but that the sound, the cry for help, was taken into my dream and there disguised. I dreamed that I was on a train, trying to sleep, and that the sound which, in the dream, was the rumble of distant wheels, was helping me. The sense of the dream was that, to sleep, I must listen to the wheels. I must listen, let them lull me, deeper. I must let them take me, as the train was taking me, to some place far away.

It was morning when I woke to the sound of my mother making breakfast. I could hear her in the kitchen and smell the bacon frying. I didn't know that, by then, it was twenty minutes since she had found my father dead outside; that, in another minute, Rennie and Dola would arrive and, after them, an ambulance. I got out of bed and put on my clothes. It was when I saw by the clock in the bathroom that it was after nine that I knew something was wrong. I headed for the kitchen, and was in the hall when Dola came bursting through the front door and threw her arms around me.

As nearly as I can reconstruct it, my mother's day began like this. She got up at seven, had breakfast and then decided that, rather than wake my father just to get him to move his car from behind hers in the driveway, she would go out and move it herself. He usually left his keys on the kitchen counter so, when she couldn't find them, she assumed he had left them in the car. Outside it was still snowing, and it occurred to her, crossing the lawn, that she might have to wake him up anyway to help her dig the cars out. All the windows of my father's car were so thickly covered with snow she couldn't see inside. She went round the car, trying all the doors. Unable to open any, she figured my father had locked the keys inside. She went round to the driver's window and pulled the snow apart as one might pull apart some drapes. The snow broke cleanly in half, and it was like letting light into a tomb. For there was my father at the wheel, still sitting up, like someone asleep. She knew he was dead. She didn't knock on the window or try to get inside. All she could think of was that no-one must see him. With her hands, she moved the snow back into place, and took some from the ground with which to fill the cracks. Only when she was certain that it was once again dark inside the car did she go back into the house, to call Rennie and Dola. And make my breakfast.

Not until long after did it occur to us to wonder why all the doors were locked, or why, instead of coming in, he stayed outside for hours. I imagined him there, in the car, looking at the house. The police said the battery was dead: the headlights had been turned off, but the car radio had not. When, after a few hours, the engine had stalled, the radio had gone on playing, running down the battery. By the fact of the radio being tuned in to a station that went off the air at two o'clock, they fixed what in their report they called "the lapse into unconsciousness" before that time. They said my father must have been too far gone by then to notice the sudden silence. The only other possibility, they said, was that the sound of the radio kept him, however barely, conscious, and that he "went out" the very moment the station went off the air. He could not have known, they said, that the snow that was coming down was heavy and wet enough to block an exhaust pipe.

I know my father didn't plan his death, but I can't help thinking he knew a good thing when he felt it coming on, and that he locked the doors because, to do that, seemed appropriate. He died in his sleep, they said. Maybe in the middle of a dream. I wondered if someone who died in a dream went on having it forever.

The first thing I heard my mother say that morning after Dola came into the house was a prayer. Dola had Rennie take me to the living-room, while she and my mother prayed in the kitchen. Rennie and I sat side by side on the couch, looking out the window, while Dola and my mother recited: "Grant that I may cheerfully take upon myself the mortification of the cross." They asked an indulgence for my father, a remission of punishment still due to him after sacraments. They asked for seven years. "Be not severe in Thy judgment, but let some drops of Thy precious blood fall on the burning flames."

The ambulance and the priest were arriving when, moments later, I was hustled past my father's car and out to the road where Rennie's truck was waiting. I had not even seen my mother, let alone spoken to her. We drove through the snow to Rennie's house. It had been decided that I would stay there until my father's body came back from the undertakers. The girls weren't at home. I found out later that they all came in from town by cab, and stayed at a friend's house for the day. Rennie was very upset, and I think if he'd had the house to himself he would have cried. He kept saying "Ted O'Malley was a good man. Yes sir, he was so," as if to defend my father against the charge of mortality that had been brought against him. From time to time, Dola called from our house, and Rennie, hiding his face, talked in whispers. He did not trust himself to sit with me. He said I should watch television. All day long, he came in from the kitchen with tea and soup. He ruffled my hair, and looked at me, as if trying to figure if, in his absence, I'd been crying.

Mostly, feeling cheated and bewildered, I looked out the window at the snow still coming down. I thought of the mound of white back home in the driveway, my father somewhere inside it. That my father could die while I was sleeping, his death take place unknown to me, that in the morning I could wake from sleep and not know he was gone—it hardly seemed possible. It seemed there were no links of love, or else how could one soul slip away and others not even notice? Then it occurred to me that there were people in Kellies who did not yet know that he was dead. Doubtless, word was spreading, but there were some who did not know. I ran to the window and put my hands and face against it. Out in the town, my father was dying. People were going from house to house, putting him out as one might put out candles. Something surged up in me, a feeling like waking from an unremembered dream. I started crying then, the only real tears I would cry.

I always imagined that grief could bring you outside yourself, that you could not be self-conscious about it. I thought someone bereaved let go, regardless of who they were, or who was watching. But what I felt more than anything else those three days was embarrassment. I didn't think of my father. I didn't pity him, or pray for him, or wonder what life would be like without him. Put on display, at all times closely watched, I thought only about getting through it. I decided I wouldn't give them anything to talk about. I said nothing and did nothing. Most of the time, even my mind was blank. I never went so far as to close my eyes but, from time to time, I let them lose their focus, and sat there, seeing nothing. At night, in bed, when the mourners were gone, I went instantly to sleep. I am still surprised how easy it was to get away like that, not only from the world but from myself. The word went out that I was numb with grief. "Just sits dere, he does, de poor little bugger. Never moves, never says a word." This was Dola, in the kitchen the second day, loud enough for all the house to hear. By my mother's request, no children were allowed at the wake, and that included Dola's four girls. Had there been other children, I wouldn't have gotten away with what the boys, when I told them about it later, called my "zombie act." Grownups, approaching the casket, saw me staring vacantly, and were willing to pass me over and go directly to my mother. My mother, from time to time, asked me if I was all right, and I replied, with just enough animation to keep her from getting either worried or suspicious, that I was.

I know, those days, I hated to see it getting dark or getting light. Early evening, just before the lights came on, there were hardly any mourners and, because of the sudden quiet, anyone who was there spoke in whispers, and tiptoed back and forth from room to room. It was then, at change of day, the sunlight fading from the room, we were reminded of the purpose for which we were gathered. And the house would fill with imminent sadness, everyone waiting, wishing the dark would hurry up and the people come back from supper. It was then my mother cried, soundlessly, with Dola's arms around her, cried carefully, with tissues, and apologies to people in the room.

The only time worse than early evening was early morning. Although every night I fell asleep, I woke before the sun came up, and watched the dark give way to day, the window turning blue above my bed. My mother, too, must have been awake and watching. The day on which my father was to be buried, she started in crying the moment of first light. I heard Dola running from my father's room to be with her, but she went on crying—not so that anyone would hear, but by herself, alone with it. A crying jag, Dola called it. It neither rose nor fell, nor gained nor lost intensity. It only went on endlessly, the sobbing broken by sharp intakes of breath, as if someone was sticking her with pins.

It was observed how much easier for my mother was this death, because she had a son who was almost a man and who would one day be a priest. The priest came by every day. He spoke with my mother and shook my hand. He smiled at everyone, and told us how much greater our love of God would be when this sad time was over. The nuns, one of whom was always there, took turns leading prayers. Sometimes, without warning, while all around them people were talking, they would get down on their knees and start the Our Father in such loud, censorious tones, everyone else was forced to join in. It was true, as Rennie said, that it was best, while near the casket, not to smile, because any sign that a good time was getting under way would provoke a rosary from the nuns.

I remember Dola and some of the SS in the kitchen, eating cake and drinking syrup, red-eyed, smiling bravely. Among the SS, it was generally acknowledged that, for reasons never made clear, my father was now "better off." They spoke as if he had died of some lingering disease. "It's over now," they said, and seemed to take some comfort from that fact.

"He didn't suffer, did he?" Mrs. Bailey said.

"No girl," Mrs. Smith said, "not a bit." No, their faces seemed to say, it was my mother who had suffered from having had to live with him so long.

"I keeps tinkin' he's not dead," Dola said. "I keeps tinkin' dat he's gonna get up an' say 'April Fool' or someting."

"Carbon monoxide," someone said.

"Imagine," Dola said, "ye never know, do ye?" They shook their heads.

"He looks so lovely," Mrs. Bailey said. "Not a mark on 'm."

"Invisible vapours," Dola said. "Dass what de police called it. Deadly invisible vapours."

Every night, Rennie and some other men gathered in the yard and passed a flask around. I went out one time on the step and stood in the dark where they couldn't see me. I listened to hear what they were saying, but I couldn't make it out. All I heard was the bottle going round, the liquor splashing when they tipped it up, the sound of swallowing and a kind of shrill sigh afterwards. And all of them stamping the snow to keep their feet warm. It was what Dola expected Rennie to do. It was what men did at wakes—stayed away from women, and pretended among themselves to be unfazed by death.

About six on the evening of the second day, Ambrosia phoned to tell Dola "Uncle Ted is on TV." Dola spoke to my mother, who agreed it would be nice to turn on the set and watch him. The TV was opposite the casket in the living-room, so everyone turned away from my father as Dola pushed the button. "And now," came the voice of the announcer, "to tell us today about tomorrow—Ted O'Malley." My father appeared, chalk in hand. It was strange to have him alive on one side of the room, and dead on the other. "Imagine," Dola said. But we didn't have to, he was there. My mother and Dola and some other people cried. "Brings it all back, doesn't it?" Dola said. A disclaimer came up on the screen. "This is not tomorrow's forecast. It is a videotape of the last forecast ever given by weatherman O'Malley, who passed away two days ago." I don't know who knelt first—it may have been my mother—nor why the kneeling started—it may have been those words, the fact of my father's death typed out on the screen, superimposed on a moving image of him, the words and the image contradicting one another. My father was there and not there, an animated relic. We all knelt down and watched and listened as my father gave us last year's weather. When it was over, the announcer said the station was going to give "Mr. O'Malley's widow, Agnes" a copy of the video-tape. My mother thought this was wonderful and, wiping her eyes and getting up off her knees, said she would cherish it forever.

Those who believed that it was at our house souls stayed until the body was buried must have wondered where my father's soul would stay. My mother had no doubts. She said the soul, at the moment of death, was so revolted by the body, it flew straight to heaven. That's where my father's soul was, up in heaven. She seemed to think of his soul as the man whom, if God had answered all her prayers, my father would have been, and of his body as the man he had been. Her eternal reward, then, would be marriage to a husband custom-made. This ideal vision of my father came up often those three days.

Warned by the undertaker that "we must not go unkempt into eternity," my mother decided that, in death, my father's hair-style should be different. Instead of being combed from side to side, it was parted down the middle and pinned behind his ears. His hands were folded on his chest, and a set of prayer-beads the colour of the Sacred Heart twined about his fingers. A lot of people touched him, his hands, his hair. One woman, accidentally I think, kissed his nose. Old people especially were affectionate. They would kiss him, and stand for minutes caressing his hands and looking about his body. My father, dead, was better liked than he had ever been alive. People sighed going by the casket, not sighs of sadness but relief, as if now that they had him standing still, they were able to figure him out. My father, by dying, had at last done something that people approved of. He was one of them after all. I had heard such things before, how dearly death is held, how by embracing it, people lose their fear of it. My mother said people liked to touch my father because it made them feel closer to God.

There with my mother beside the casket, I was acknowledged to be a brave young man. Someone said I was acting just the way my father would have wanted. It seemed, those three days, that all of Kellies came by. Annie and Little Annie, to whom none of us had spoken in years, were there, seeming full of fond remembrance. And people said things about my father that simply were not true. They sung praises he did not deserve. They stood there, throwing lies like flowers in the casket. But every time, my mother smiled, as if to say, "You saw him that way, too, did you?"

On the last day, just before the closing of the casket, my mother made me kiss my father. She stood behind me and held my waist as if to keep me from falling in. She said I had to kiss him on the lips, something I had never done before. And I suppose it was that, not having done it while he was alive, that made it seem so strange. That he was dead, cold and tasted faintly sour hardly mattered.

Later, at the graveyard after mass, as his casket was slowly lowered into the ground, I read his headstone:

IN MEMORY
OF A
LOVING HUSBAND

AND
FATHER
THEODORE O'MALLEY
MOURNED BY
WIFE AGNES
AND
SON ROBERT
R. I. P.
22 MAY, 1918–23 APRIL, 1974

My father, gone, was someone no-one knew.

Going back to school was not the worst part afterwards. Everyone knew instinctively that I did not want them to mention my father's death. D-Cup, Tommy, Max, Little Lawrence and Kiwi gathered round me the minute I got off the bus—they could not have known when I was coming back, so they must have been meeting in the parking-lot every morning just in case—and they pretended that, since I had last seen them, nothing out of the ordinary had happened. They gave me the news about Perpetua and Brenda and everything else they could think of. They didn't tell me what Brudder Bill told me later: that, aside from the wreath sent by the school, and the wreath from Tier 11-10, my father's death was acknowledged in another way. The day before he was buried, the student body gathered in the gym to sing the school song, including some special verses that Hedwig had written:

> Brother Arthur Noonan High
> We gather here in sorrow
> God saw fit for him to die
> They bury him tomorrow
>
> Brother Arthur Noonan High
> Bless Bobby and his mother
> It is for ourselves we cry
> When we can find no other

Brother Arthur Noonan High
That man's name they proudly bear
Will not ever really die
Just as long as they are here

No, it was not going back to school I minded, but the suddenly quiet, empty house, into which poured all the ghosts that, until then, had been kept out by the noise and company of mourners. We kept seeing my father around the house, and we heard him on the steps, late at night. Dola stayed with us for a couple of days after the funeral. My mother would have had her stay longer but, honestly trying to do what was best, Dola said that, sooner or later, we'd have to face "it" alone. It, as I discovered the afternoon she left, was the awful wrenching loneliness, the silence. My mother and I had hardly spoken since the morning my father died, and we dreaded what, until now, we had avoided—being alone with one another. Sitting in the living-room, we said nothing because we knew that our first word would be the final brutal word, an acknowledgement that he was gone, and that we were going on without him. After a while, my mother went to her room, and I went to mine. And we waited, each of us, for the sound of footsteps coming. In the end, she came to me. It was dark and I was in bed. She opened the door and said my name. "Bobby." She came in and stood by the bed, looking down at me, and I was sure we were going to hold each other. But she sat down too far away, near my feet, and patted my knee with her hand. "We'll have to make the best of it, won't we?" she said. I nodded. He was very much there between us, a distance we couldn't cross.

Though there was little life insurance, my father's pension would keep coming and, with my mother working, there would be no problem. My mother gave up the idea of ever owning a house. I would soon be going away, she said, and what was the use of owning a house if you had to live in it all by yourself? It was arranged that, when I was gone, she would move in with Dola and Rennie and the girls. She didn't mind, she said, giving up her dream for the sake of my vocation.

She decided to pack my father's things away. She had no intention, she said, of doing something silly like keeping his room just the way it was the day he died. In fact, she decided to pack all our things, excepting bare essentials. She was not moving until September, but she said it was best to do the packing now, while I was still there to help her and tell her what I wanted kept and what thrown away. Cleaning out my father's room, I found the notebook in which he'd been writing *Our Memoirs*. Most of the pages were torn out, and those that were left were blank. My first thought was that my mother must have done something with the missing pages, but on the back inside cover of the notebook, I found inscribed a table, of which the following is an excerpt:

DATE	PAGES FLUSHED
1 March	3
2 March	0
3 March	1
4 March	3
5 March	2
6 March	6
7 March	0
8 March	1
9 March	4

It continued, up to the day of his death in April. On that day, he "flushed" five pages. I might never have been sure just what he'd been doing if, upon searching his desk for clues, I hadn't found the single foolscap sheet upon which he'd made some notes. One side of the sheet looked like this:

Chapter One . . . . The Boy is Born
Chapter Two
Chapter Three
Chapter Four

Chapter **Five**
Chapter **Six**
Chapter **Seven**
Chapter **Eight** . . . . The Boy Gets his Wisdom Bum

There was no explanation as to why the chapters between One and Eight were unnamed. The other side of the sheet was, at first, even more mystifying. Pencilled in large letters across the top of the page was: *What is more final than flushing the toilet? Do this in memory of me.* Below this was scrawled the following: *The book is a pound of flesh on every page.*

It was soon clear to me why the notebook was blank. Each day, he'd taken what he'd written and flushed it down the toilet. *Do this in memory of me.* It seemed he would have my mother and me, perhaps on the anniversary of his death, kneel about the bowl and look longingly into the toilet. His headstone.

There was, my mother said, so much to do before 26 June. We wanted the time to pass quickly and, in some strange way, time obliged us. If we could help it, we were never alone together, and when we *were* together, we were always doing something. We went to supper almost every night at Dola's, and stayed there until late. We went to the grocery store, the post office, the drug-store. My mother liked us to be seen in public together so that everyone would know how marvellously we were coping, how by being, each of us, a rock of strength for the other, we were getting by. We went to the graveyard a lot. It must have been a common sight in that part of Kellies, the two of us heading up the hill behind the school, the grieving widow and loving son, hand in hand. We would kneel by the graveside, and my mother would say a prayer and then we'd go. There was never any lingering, never any words addressed directly to my father, only formal prayer and hasty retreat.

You could see my father's headstone from our house, which may have been another reason my mother didn't want to live there any more. The headstone was a column of white marble, the kind that never ages, but seems always to mark the grave of someone newly dead. It was to my father's room I would go and, with his binoculars look at his headstone. It was there, in his chair, looking out the window, I went into that closet I'd created at the funeral. I let my eyes lose their focus, and sat there, seeing nothing. It was hard, afterwards, coming back to life. And indeed, it got so that, in my father's room or out of it, I had to make a conscious effort to keep from letting go. My mother, who convinced herself that now, so nearly a priest, I was contemplating, going to my father's room to talk to God, did nothing to discourage me from being by myself. On the contrary, she said, "I guess you'd like to be alone," at every opportunity. I really didn't know why I was losing hold of myself. I didn't know what was happening to me. All I knew was that the day I got on the plane for Montreal, all the nonsense of my life would end. I would leave one world behind, and start out for a new one. It seemed to me that I was headed for great adventure, a life of negation and self-sacrifice. At school, I no longer tolerated snide remarks about the priesthood. I defended it fiercely when given half a chance. The boys did their best to go along with me, to encourage me toward something it seemed I wanted, but which none of them, even in their weakest moments, would have considered. (Even D-Cup, by the middle of May, abandoned all thought of becoming a Christian Brother. He said he was going to be a businessman like Tommy. He was going to get "even fatter," smoke cigars and generally enjoy himself.)

I served as many masses as I could, and I went to prayers every night. At school, I spent my lunchtime in the chapel. I thought about nothing but going away. I exhausted myself with it and, every night, on getting into bed, fell into dreamless sleep. And yet, through it all, I must, as my mother said afterwards, have known "deep down" what I was going to do. I think Ambrosia knew. There were things I had forgotten that Ambrosia could recall. "I know who you are," her expression seemed to say, "so you can stop pretending." When we went to her house for supper, and all the talk was about my leaving soon, she made it clear by her expression that she didn't believe a word of it. She knew the way things worked, and she was sure they included no provision that the little boy who, for fifteen years, had been the bane of her existence, would make her fondest wish come true by going away.

All I can say for sure is this: I didn't think about what I was doing that Saturday when my mother left the house. I opened up the boxes that our things were packed in and found the videotape the TV station had sent us. Then I went into my mother's room and took the box containing St. Joseph's beard from under the bed. Finally, I dug out a pair of scissors and a box of matches and went to the bathroom. Kneeling down beside the toilet, I pulled the tape out frame by frame and, with the scissors, snipped it off. My father's last forecast fell into the water, piling higher bit by bit. Soon, I couldn't see the water, only a mound of tape. On top of that I put my mother's hair. I cut St. Joseph's beard in tiny pieces and let them fall, and dropped the remaining hair in, strand by strand. Then I cut the box into pieces and threw those in, too. The toilet was almost full when I lit the match. The box caught first, then the hair, then the tape, until the bowl was blazing, as if hell itself was backing up inside the pipes. The bathroom filled with smoke. The flames grew higher and threatened to catch the curtain by the tub. On my knees, I had to keep my face back from the flame and reach around it with my arm to flush the toilet. Eyes burning from the smoke, my forehead hot, I somehow found the handle and pushed it down. As the water rushed in, the flames started going round and going out at the same time. The water ate in from the outer edge until only a core of flame was left, an island getting smaller, going round and round and down. Finally, there was just one central spark which, with the water at the bottom, seemed to turn inside out, then vanished. All the things that I'd thrown in, the tape, the hair, the box were gone. It was then I discovered to my horror that the toilet-bowl, inside and out, was black with soot. And when, on my way to get some cleanser, I opened the bathroom door, the house filled up with smoke.

It was into a smoky, smelly house that my mother came an hour later, and found me in the bathroom, scrubbing frantically. She went on for quite a while about the inadvisability of burning down the bathroom. It must have been five minutes before she thought to ask me why I set fire to the toilet. I made up some story about smoking cigarettes, about what happened when, sitting on a toilet filled with tissue, one dropped in what one thought was a fully extinguished match. My mother looked doubtful. "You didn't burn anything, did you?" she said and, when I said no, demanded that I give her all the cigarettes I had. I told her I'd only had the one, and that went down the toilet.

It might have been two months before she discovered the videotape missing, but that night, poking under her bed for something, she saw that the box of hair was gone, and I had to tell her what really happened. I told her that I burned the videotape and the hair, but that I didn't know why. She must have seen that there was, in my strange behaviour, something better left unravelled, because all she said was, "Never mind," and then went to bed.

I spent the next week, as D-Cup put it, "sort of fading out." At school, I couldn't pay attention, not even to what my friends were saying. My eyes kept going out of focus, and I had headaches. I didn't want to talk to anyone for fear that they would see there was something wrong with me. But no-one made too much of the way I was acting, because it was just six weeks since my father's death and they figured I was still getting over it. I stayed home two days from school, pretending to be sick. While my mother was at work, I sat in my father's chair, looking out the window. If there is a space between mind and world, I was in it.

Sunday was the day of the annual garden-party. My mother insisted that I go. I had been exempted from helping out, she said, so that I could go about the field and say goodbye to everyone. It was a chance I mustn't miss, everyone gathered together—all of Kellies would be there. My mother imagined fond farewells, a rousing send-off. She said everyone was counting on my being there. The priest was going to congratulate me. I might even be asked to say a few words. "Oh Bobby," she said, in the kitchen with tears in her eyes, "it's only three more weeks and you'll be gone." She kissed my forehead and, holding hands, we left the house together.

Amid sideshows and cash-wheels, we walked about, saying goodbye. My mother said goodbye as if she were going away too. "Good-bye Mrs. Clark. We're leaving in three weeks. Goodbye Mrs. Stack." We paused at the ice-cream tent so that the ladies there could shake my hand. They gave us each an ice-cream cone. We also got free fudge and cotton-candy and a glass of ginger ale. My mother was very happy and kept pointing to people I knew in the crowd. There were people from all the neighbourhoods we'd lived in, from Du-ley's, Mortrey's, Lawton's, Little Annie's—there on the field, the milling moments of a lifetime, taking no shape that I could see.

"I'm going home," I said.

"*What*," my mother said. "*But Bobby—*"

I pulled my hand from hers.

"I'm going home."

She let me go. She said if I wasn't feeling well, I *should* go home. She would explain to Father for me. "Go home and go to bed," she said. She would stay because she had to help out with suppers later.

I was glad of that. No sooner was I off the field than I decided I'd get drunk. In one of the closets at home, there was a bottle of rum my mother kept for visiting priests. I stopped at a store for a bottle of Coke, then ran all the way to the house. There, I mixed the rum and Coke so that both bottles were half and half. And then I went upstairs and, as Tommy would have it later, "started downing rum and Coke like crazy." Sitting up in bed, I chugged the better part of a bottle before I began to feel it. Then, knowing I didn't have much time, I started on the other. I don't remember blacking out, only that the darkness started going round, slowly at first, then faster, until all I could think was that I was on the end of a rope someone was swinging. And then it seemed that I was falling, falling from some hopeless height. I went round and down, faster and faster un-til it seemed that something had to give. It was my name that saved me. "BOBBY," someone said. And it might have been they touched me, for the spinning stopped. "BOBBY." And I was borne up by that sound as by some hand.

As Tommy told it later, I woke up with a start and, thinking to get out of bed, fell flat on my face on the floor. From there, he said, he and Kiwi carried me, legs and arms, into the bathroom, while D-Cup, Max and Little Lawrence laughed so hard, they fell together on the bed. They got me kneeling down and then, holding my arms to keep me from going head-first into the toilet, let me do the rest. All I remember is the sound of someone applauding every time I threw up—and a voice distinctly D-Cup's, saying, "Pissed, totally pissed." It's probably true that, as Little Lawrence said, I "paused between regurgitations to communicate a marked, if heretofore well hidden aversion to clerical life." According to Max, my exact words were, "I'M NOT GONNA BE NO PRIEST," and I said them so many times, D-Cup implored me to save some for my mother. They all agreed that, upon the word "mother," I jumped up and said, *Where is she?*"

It took them a while to get me back to bed, where I slept for a couple of hours. Upon waking, feeling empty, hungry, my head throbbing, I went out to the living-room, where the boys were watching television. They all grinned and, getting up, slapped me on the back and shook my hand. They were as happy as I was, all looking as if they'd won something. They said they'd gone to the garden-party, hoping to find me, and ran into my mother, who told them where I was. "She's not gonna like us much after today, is she?" D-Cup said. "No," I said. "She's not."

When my father left the south coast, he hitched a ride to Clarenville, then took the train into St. John's. There, though it was cold, he left his bags and went down by the harbour. This was in September. The sun was low, and wind was blowing through the narrows. And it was true, as he'd all his life suspected, that the sea 200 miles from home was different. The water was a different colour, and the wind looked different on it. It was then, he said, he knew he needed company.

He went to normal school, and there he met my mother. When I was nine, he told me how it happened: "She was walking down the hallway in this place we went to school together, twenty years ago. She had her nose up in the air, and I said: 'Don't look down.' Of course, she did look down and there I was." (My mother was eighteen, younger than I am now, and what I have heard her call the worst summer of her life was ending. Having agonized for three months about it, she had decided not to become a nun. Into the wake of that decision sailed my father—"a little red-faced fellow, with a brogue so thick I couldn't make out what he was saying—which, as I've since discovered, was just as well.")

My father gave up normal school and, when he and my mother were married, got a job writing copy with the island's first television station. In five years, he was weatherman. In five more, I was born.

A thing between two things can join them or keep them apart, can mediate or separate, depending. My father and mother had me between them. My father said they sent away for me, and they wondered for a while if they'd "wasted all those box-tops."

This story goes on past these pages. I can say that my mother and I are friendly the times I visit Kellies, but that is no ending—more like a beginning, I should think. As for the rest:

A year later, I went away to school. Most importantly, I went away. For often since, the pier at Port aux Basques receding, the land assuming shapes and lines, I've thought that only by leaving did I learn to live here.

I took the bus across the island, and got on board the ferry hours early. I was sixteen and starting out, for the first time in my life, across the Gulf. It was getting dark. We would cross by night and arrive in Sydney early in the morning. I was surprised to find that, like me, most of the people on the ferry had never been off the island before. Some people were going for good, and they were crying. Others had been home to visit, and they were crying, too. Those, like me, who were only going for a while, should have been able to help themselves. Whether it was leaving like that, at night, that did it, the sun just going down, I hardly know. But I swear that, there in the gathering dark, everyone was crying and waving to the people on the shore. I waved and cried, though there was no-one there I knew. It was true, as I heard one of the stewards say, long after the lights of home had disappeared, "The whole boat-load was bawlin' an' wavin' like lunatics." I suppose it doesn't matter if people part, as long as they say goodbye.